SAVED AT STEVENS STREET

Stevens Street Gym Book 1

By

Charlie Roberts

CHAPTER 1

Kenzie

This is the best erotic dream I have ever had. I feel something massive and rock hard nestled between my butt cheeks, very masculine hands caressing me in very intimate places. I don't think my nipples have ever responded like this to a man's touch ever before. His other hand is between my legs. What he's doing to me is incredible. I don't ever want to wake up. These kisses to the side of my face and neck feel so real. These sheets smell different though; the lilac scent of my detergent has faded. This bed, it feels harder than my mattress, and this pillow is too firm.

The mattress shifts and a body presses completely against me, shoulders to feet, all skin to all skin. We're both naked. *Oh, shit! I don't think this is a dream.* I let out a quiet moan. I hear a male moan in return and a stubbled cheek nuzzles mine. *Fuck!* I was out with my coworkers. How bad can this be? My boss, that would be the worst-case scenario. Not only because he is my boss, but also because he isn't someone I am even remotely sexually attracted to. No attraction at all, yuck, as a matter of fact. And he's my boss! Any of the software developers, sales guys, or technical support geeks, well, that could make my job harder, no pun intended.

Speaking of hard, the body pressed into me feels like a guy who knows his way around a gym. That eliminates all but a few of the guys I work with. The rest have spent more time lifting beers or video game controllers than barbells. Then there are the five guys who were laid-off yesterday. That would be the best-case scenario. I'd never have to see him again if it was one of them. The only one that has a halfway hard body is Jim, and he's married. *Oh, God, don't let me be in bed with Jim!* I crack open an eye and see a very muscled, tanned arm with blonde hair wrapped around my chest. It was his left arm and there was no wedding band on the hand that was groping my breast. It was morning. The sun was streaming into the room through half open curtains in a room that wasn't mine.

"Oh, crap," I moaned out loud, my hand coming to my forehead.

"Do you have a hangover, Kenzie?" An incredibly smooth voice asked. It was like one of the Three Tenors was speaking to me, but with no Italian accent.

"I think so," I squeaked out. He knew my name, that was a good start, and I didn't recognize the voice, definitely not my boss or any of my coworkers, either. Okay, this might not be the worst thing that could ever have happened.

I felt the mattress heave and the warmth of his body left me. I heard him leave the room. Looking around, from the laying position, because yes, my head did not feel so good, I could see a male bedroom, nothing frilly or feminine in sight. I didn't recognize this room.

Shots, my group did shots last night, five, one for each of the guys laid off. It was starting to come back.

Holy mother of God! He walked back in carrying a can of what I don't care, but that body, oh my God! His cock was huge, swinging between his legs when he walked, a pendulum hypnotizing me and trapping my attention. How he could even walk with that thing was beyond me. I finally pulled my eyes up his body as he reached the bed. He had perfectly formed muscles, everywhere. Abs that defined what washboard meant. Chest, shoulders, and arms that I've only seen on the covers of romance novels, with the perfect splattering of tattoos. His face was incredibly handsome, with short blonde hair and bright green eyes. If a man could be described as beautiful, he was beautiful.

"Here, drink this. I guarantee you a can of this, another hour of sleep, and you'll be as good as new," he said with a smile. Had I not been completely naked, it was a smile that would have had me removing my panties at a fast pace.

I took the can from him as he settled back in the bed beside me. His leg grazed mine. Just that slight touch got my attention. Now, I normally wouldn't just drink something given to me from a guy I didn't know, but at this point, I figured what could it hurt? I was obviously in his bedroom, naked, and I was sure we had had sex, unprotected sex at that.

God! Why couldn't I remember any part of who he was or how I had ended up here? And that incredible cock! How could I not remember what it had felt like to have that inside me? He was watching me expectantly. I downed the drink, which tasted like some sort of thick, weird, coconut water, and then he took the can from me and sat it on his night stand. He surrounded me with his arms, snuggled close and pulled me into his frame. His breathing evened out, and I knew that he was asleep.

I tried desperately to remember him, to remember anything, but I couldn't. The last thing I remembered was saying goodbye to my coworkers and going towards the bathroom at the bar as they all left. Wait, no, I also remembered suddenly feeling drunk as I left the bathroom, more-so than when I went in, more-so than I should have been. I was near the exit and could feel the fresh, warm, night air blowing into my face, with just a hint of the cigarette smoke from the smokers clustered around the entrance way closer than the legally required distance of fifteen feet.

That was it. Nothing more. A blank slate replaced whatever came after. Listening to his even breathing and feeling the warmth from his body behind me, I relaxed and drifted, hoping if I stopped thinking so hard, maybe it would come back. I certainly didn't think I could go back to sleep.

"Kenzie," a smooth voice pulled me from the dream, that wonderfully erotic dream.

My eyes opened, expecting to see my beige bedroom walls. Fuck, not even close! They were gray. I was still in this strange bedroom with this unknown, sexy man. He leaned in and kissed me, right on the lips, slow, sensual kisses. He added the right amount of tongue, groping hands, and an erection poking into my side. I should have pulled away. I should have confessed I didn't remember him or how I got here. But why compound one mistake with another? So, what did I do? Of course, I kissed him back because the way he kissed was so incredible, so sensual, so consuming.

He kissed his way down my body, giving special attention to my breasts, and he went down further, licking a trail down my stomach and sliding his tongue over my clit and as deep inside of me as it could go. I gasped out, the sensation mind-numbing. After a few minutes of pure heaven, I was on the edge, but he denied me a release and nibbled his way back up my abdomen, his gorgeous green eyes locked onto mine. As he came completely on top of me, his powerful legs spread mine. He then slowly began to penetrate me. I should have stopped it and confessed. I should have stopped it long before now. Again, I did not. I was too busy moaning from the pleasure he gave me, and I was reveling in the sound of his moans, as well.

The sex we had was nothing short of amazing. This man sure knew what to do to female anatomy to give the maximum pleasure. If this was what it had felt like last night, I was even more disappointed that I didn't remember anything.

Clinging to his body I suddenly felt very self-conscious. This man had zero percent body fat and model quality muscles. I thought about the jiggle in my tummy and the love handles on my hips. His hand on my butt reminded me that it was way too flabby. I ran my hand over his butt. It was solid and sculpted like the rest of him. What was he thinking about me? Did he have any memory of picking me up? Or worse, any regrets?

He was running his fingers through my short black hair, tousling it. I gazed up into his face. He had the cutest smile as he watched his own hand rearrange and spike my curls.

"I didn't even ask. Does your head feel better?"

I laughed nervously. "Yeah, it does." I tried to get up, but his hands stopped me. "I should get going."

"Let's shower before I bring you back to your car," he suggested, but he didn't let go of me or try to get up.

That settled one mystery. I hadn't driven here. That was good. "I can order an Uber, you don't need to," I said sweetly as if I was trying not to impose.

His lips frowned. "You are not going to call an Uber. I brought you here, and I promised I would bring you back to your car." His eyes narrowed on me. "You're not regretting coming home with me, are you?"

3

"No, no, not at all," I said forcing a smile. How could I regret something I didn't remember? He was staring at me, looking for more. I wasn't sure what to say. "I'm um, really glad I met you," I told him somewhat honestly. Met him, yeah, no memory. Had sex with him just now, yeah, really glad about that.

"Good, because, remember, I don't do one-night stands. I do relationships. Trina deserves that. We're still on for tonight, right?"

Remember? Hah! Not a blasted thing. What was tonight and who is Trina? My smile was nervous and forced. I decided that this was a situation playing it coy could resolve. "Remind me."

He grabbed his cell phone from the nightstand. He stuck it in my face while hitting play on a video. There he and I were in living color, in that bar with beers in front of us. "I Mackenzie Collins hereby acknowledge that Andy Stevens doesn't do one-night stands," Video-me proclaimed. We were both smiling at each other and laughing.

"All of it, and use my legal name, Andrew, this is official," Video-guy advised me, still laughing.

"Okay, Andrew Stevens doesn't do one-night stands. He's looking for a relationship and in going home with him tonight I'm acknowledging that I'm open to a relationship, as well." Video-me overplayed it, hamming it up.

"And you'll go out to dinner with me tomorrow night, a real date," Video-guy pressed.

"Absolutely," drunken Video-me replied.

Well, that solved another mystery. His name was Andy or Andrew Stevens. Evidently, I had already agreed to go out to dinner with him tonight too. I gazed back at his face. He looked very pleased with himself. "How about you text me that video, in case I need to be reminded again?" My voice was flirty, but I desperately wanted that video, needed that video.

He hit a few buttons on his phone. "Done."

So, he already had my phone number too. Speaking of which, where was my phone? Where was my purse?

He got up and pulled me from the bed a little while later. We enjoyed a leisurely shower with a lot of caressing and kissing. He washed me thoroughly from head to toe. It was one of the most erotic things I had ever experienced and would forever redefine the description of what a good shower is in my book. I found my dress and underclothing on the floor of his bedroom but as I gathered them up, he handed me a pair of black shorts and a gray tank top.

"Here, wear these. That was fine on the bike last night but will totally look like the morning after. Besides, it's nearly eighty out."

Bike? Eighty degrees? I glanced at the clock. It was already eleven. I slid the shorts on with no panties and held the top up. It had the words 'Stevens Street Gym' around a barbell across the front of the top. It was quite form-fitting and hugged my braless breasts tightly. He handed me a small plastic grocery bag, and I stuffed my clothes and shoes into it. I looked around but didn't see my purse.

"My purse?" I asked him.

"It's on the kitchen table," he said pointing towards the door. A hallway lay beyond.

Thank God! I hoped my phone was in it. I followed him into the hallway. Within the first door to the left was, what could only be a little girl's bedroom. The frilly, white lace curtains on the windows were open, the light streaming in bounced off the bubblegum pink and violet purple walls. I couldn't help but stand there and gaze in. The room was decorated with ponies and rainbows. The furniture was white and there were dolls and books scattered all around.

I followed him past several other doors, a bathroom on the right, another bedroom to the left. The hall opened into a kitchen to the right, a closed door to the left and a large family room at the far end. Picture frames filled with family lined the hallway walls. The whole space was nicely decorated in neutral colors but had several toy boxes and shelves overflowing with toys situated throughout. On the kitchen table sat my purse. I went to it and found my phone inside. Relief!

"Kenzie?" Andy called from my right. He was at the refrigerator holding up a bottle of water.

"Yes, thank you," I replied.

He handed it to me as I took in the little kid drawn pictures held to the refrigerator by magnets. The largest had all upper case writing on it, Trina. The picture drawn in crayon was what I made out to be a little girl with long black hair and green eyes in the center surrounded by a blonde man with very short hair and green eyes, Andy, a blonde woman with blue eyes, another man with longer blonde hair and blue eyes, and a second woman with short blond hair and green eyes. The drawing was, of course, rough, but I assumed the two stick figures wearing dresses to be women, the two figures with pants to be men. Her family with two sets of parents?

I followed Andy into the living room, towards a door on the far wall. He grabbed his keys from the table next to the door. I lifted the picture frame up from the table and gazed at the little girl cuddled in Andy's arms. This must be Trina. She had shoulder-length black hair, his vibrant green eyes, and a sweet cherub face. I couldn't help but smile. My eyes met his. "She's adorable."

"She's my life," he said with a smile bursting with pride. "That was taken last month at her fourth birthday party. I can't believe my baby is four. It's true what people say, that they grow up so fast."

5

I smiled and nodded. I wondered about her mother. Were they divorced? Or ever married? How often did he get to see his little girl? The house sure looked like she lived here twenty-four-seven. I wondered where she was.

I followed him out the door onto a raised wood deck, the sun momentarily blinding me. I dug around in my purse to find my sunglasses. The wood decking was hot beneath my bare feet. The deck was maybe fifteen feet long by ten feet wide. Four chairs sat around a square table in the middle of the deck. A second identical door lay a few feet away to the right, with a grill at the far end. To the left, a wood staircase led down to a small parking lot area that two cars were parked in. A detached garage set back and across the parking lot. It was surrounded by flowering bushes. We descended the staircase, and he led me to his motorcycle, parked beneath the deck in front of a windowless door that led into the building. It was closed.

"Just keep your feet up on these pegs and they'll be fine." He opened the saddlebags and placed my purse and the bag containing my clothes and shoes inside. Then he straddled the bike. I couldn't help but watch him. I was captivated by how he moved with such strength and confidence. He looked at me with expectancy. I climbed on the bike behind him, pulling myself in close, my arms wrapped around him, my hands clutching his tight, defined abs. The Harley came to life with a throaty roar.

He made a left out of the driveway which ran behind a parking lot. Another left and we drove past Stevens Street Gym, a storefront in an old downtown area of brick buildings with commercial property on the first floor and two to three stories of mixed residential and commercial above. He drove cautiously, obeying the posted speed limit signs. After a few turns, I relaxed my grip a little, feeling confident that he was a safe driver. I'd only been on the back of a bike a few times, so I was not an expert by any means, but he put me at ease quite quickly.

Fifteen minutes and several turns later we arrived in the parking lot of the bar I had been in the previous evening and there sat my car where I had left it. Several other cars sat scattered around the lot, belonging, no doubt to those who had gotten either too drunk to drive home, or had gotten picked up, like I had been. I didn't feel too good about that realization.

We reached my car. Andy turned me, so my back was against my car, and he leaned into me. My core tightened, and my pulse raced. He held his hand out to me. I just looked at him questioning what he wanted.

"Your car keys," he said. I fished them out of my purse and handed them to him. "So, I'll pick you up at six," he said as he unlocked my car door.

I nodded agreeing to the time. He didn't ask my address. He must already know that too. He gave me another long incredibly passionate kiss. Whew! This man certainly knew how to kiss. He didn't seem in any hurry to say goodbye, and I didn't mind. I smiled at him, knowing it was one of those flirty, shy smiles that would make him kiss me again, even more deeply, and he did. Then he pulled away and he stepped back and motioned me into my car.

"If we keep that up I'm going to take you back to my place and make love to you again," his sexy voice growled. He placed my keys in my hand, his fingers wrapping around mine.

Yes, please. "You say that like it would be a bad thing," I squeaked out.

He chuckled out a sexy laugh. "I wish I could, but I do need to stop by my mom's and see Trina. I already sent a text to my mom asking her to keep her today and all night again, so I won't see her till tomorrow morning if I don't stop by. And I want to get my truck. I can't take you out for a nice dinner on my bike."

So, his mother was babysitting. Was this his weekend for visitation and he was with me instead? Now, that just wasn't right. I slid into my seat and he closed the car door. After I had started the car, I lowered the window. "Have a good day, Andy," I said.

"You too, and I'll see you at six." He leaned in the window and gave me another kiss and then he got back on his bike and turned it over. He watched me pull out and leave before he did as well.

CHAPTER 2

Kenzie

I followed the GPS on my phone as I had no clue how to get home from there. I'd never been in this part of town before last night. Now that I was away from him and the wild hormones that had surged through me in his presence, I tried to figure out how I could have gotten that drunk from what I had ingested the night before. It seemed impossible that I had.

I dialed a stored number on my phone at the next stoplight. She answered on the third ring, the sound of her voice bringing me something, maybe not the calm I had been hoping for, but something I needed. "Margot," my tight voice greeted. "It's Kenzie."

"Yeah, I know. What's the matter?"

That was no-nonsense Margot. "Sorry, yeah. Are you working today?"

"Kenzie, you're worrying me. What's wrong?"

I moaned and breathed out a heavy breath. She knew me so well. "Yeah, I need to see you. Can you stop by my place sometime today?"

"You're driving, I can hear the traffic. Where are you?"

I looked around. I still wasn't one hundred percent sure, but I wasn't going to tell her that. "I'm heading home. I should be there in about a half hour."

"Kenz, what's the matter?"

I knew I was frustrating her. "In person, Margot, okay?"

"I'll meet you there."

Margot disconnected, and I imagined her making a U-turn where ever she was to go to my place if she was on-duty or not. I was sure she would be sitting in my driveway when I got there.

***

As expected, Margot was waiting for me when I arrived home. Her dark colored, force-issued plain sedan was in my driveway. I guess she was on duty. I pulled past it and into my garage. She was beside my door before I had even put the car in park. She scanned me up and down, studying the logo on the tank top I wore, taking in the shorts and bare feet as I pulled myself from the driver's seat. A disapproving scowl was etched across her face.

"Don't even," I warned her.

Her eyebrows raised, and she pinned me with an accusatory stare with her dark brown eyes. She didn't need to say a word. I knew what she was thinking. Her eyes then focused on my chest. I assumed she was silently questioning me as to why I was wearing a Stevens Street Gym advertisement and not checking out my breasts, which were clearly on display. The tank top was a tad too tight and my bra was in the grocery bag with the rest of my clothes. The cold garage floor had instantly hardened my nipples.

"I know that place; it's that Meathead gym across town. They offer discounted memberships to cops and firefighters, EMTs and military. I personally would never work out there, but I know more than a few guys from the department that do."

I shot her a scowl, grabbed my purse and the shopping bag with my clothes and led her through the door into the house.

"I'm going to assume you don't work out there either, so this is a morning-after walk of shame I'm seeing here," Margot said.

"You've known me how long? When was the last time I hooked up with some random guy and had sex?"

Margot barked out a laugh. "Junior year. So, what's this?" She did a Vanna White wave over my chest.

"Exactly! Look, I'm trying to piece this together but it's not adding up right." I grabbed my bottle of liquid vitamins from the shelf in the refrigerator I kept it on and downed a tablespoon.

"What do you mean? I'm not following."

I held a bottle of orange juice up, offering Margot a glass. She shook her head no, but she nodded yes when I held up a bottle of water. "So, as you know we all left work at 3:30 yesterday after the meeting notifying us of who got cut."

"Yeah, I remember. You called to cancel our dinner date."

I shot her a glare. She knew it had not been a date. "From four till eight I had exactly two beers, five shots of tequila and several plates of appetizers. At eight o'clock everyone was leaving." I paused as I took a gulp of the OJ.

"You're not making much sense here, Kenz."

I ignored her. "That's where it gets fuzzy. I went to the bathroom and I remember suddenly feeling really drunk. As in too drunk. I remember leaving that bathroom and I was near the door to the parking lot and that's it until I woke up this morning in some guy's bed."

"Wait a minute, from the time you were near the exit until you woke up this morning, you remember nothing?"

"Not a damn thing, blank slate," I confirmed. "I know I can drink a lot more than that. Jeez! There were times I drank a hell of a lot more than I did last night and

I've never forgotten a night, and Lord knows there have been some I've wanted to forget."

I saw in Margot's face the cop switch turned on. She grabbed a notebook out of her coat pocket. "Tell me about this guy. You think you were roofied, right?"

"I don't think he did it. I think it was someone in my work group," I said starting to shake at the thought of it. "But I evidently spent several hours with him at that bar, then went home with him, had sex and fell asleep. Can you do all that if you've been roofied? When you're slipped a date-rape drug, don't you pretty much pass out?"

"You're taking his word you did those things."

I pulled my phone out of my purse and played her the video. I cringed as I heard it, watching her face as it played. "How can I not remember that? Look at me! I looked a little drunk but was fully functioning. Can you do that if you've been drugged?"

"It depends on what you were drugged with," Margot replied, pulling her phone from its case on her belt.

"I'm not making an official report yet," I told her.

Her gaze held mine, silently reprimanding me. "I'm calling a friend to come take some blood to test to see what you were drugged with."

I moaned and prostrated myself across my kitchen table.

"At least tell me you think he used a condom during the sex."

I pulled myself off the table and looked into her eyes. "Sure, I'll tell you that."

"Oh, Kenz, Jesus!" She motioned to her own private parts, knowing I knew that had not been the case. "You're sure?"

"Yeah, no condom. But at least I'm still on the pill." Which reminded me I had to take it yet today. I rose and plucked the pack from the counter near my coffee pot and pushed today's pill through the foil. "Look, he really seems like a nice guy and let me tell you, the sex with him was incredible."

"What do you mean the sex was incredible? You said you don't remember anything from last night?"

"The sex this morning, not last night," I explained.

"What, you had consensual sex with him this morning?" Margot demanded.

"Well, yeah. You should have seen him, and damn did he know how to kiss. And it was obvious that we already had unprotected sex, so not having it this morning would have been like hooking up the fire hose after the building had already gone up in flames."

Margot groaned and ran her hand over her face and through her hair. She wanted me to go to the hospital to have a rape kit done. I declined. Her friend arrived and drew my blood. I gave Margot all the information on Andy that I had as well as provided her the list of names of my coworkers who went out after work. Two hours after I had arrived home, Margot had all she needed, and she gave me a hug by the door.

"Are you okay Kenzie?" She asked before stepping out. She knew me so well and could tell I had gotten more rattled over the past two hours.

"Yeah. Man, when I fuck up I really do it good, don't I?" I said laughing at myself. It was better than crying, which was my other option.

She hugged me again. "I'll be in touch soon." And then she left.

CHAPTER 3

Kenzie

I forced myself to yank open the front door but stopped dead at the information counter. Gazing at the pretty young thing behind it, I wondered what I was doing here. She filled out the Stevens Street Gym tank top a lot better than I had. Her physique boasted sculpted, sexy arms, perky C-cups, an unnaturally narrow waist, no love handles, a flat stomach, and what looked like toned legs beneath the knee-length tight-fitting pants she wore. In the mirror behind her, her perfectly sized and shaped ass stared back at me. And of course, she glowed with a flawless tan, sprayed-on no doubt. Her blonde hair was piled atop her head in a messy bun that looked perfect except for the dark roots. The only natural thing about her was her blue eyes under the incredibly thick eyelashes that hadn't grown there on their own, and those really could have been that blue due to contact lenses.

"Welcome to Stevens Street Gym. Can I help you?" She ran her eyes up and down me as she spoke. Her smile was as fake as her C's.

I forced a smile. "Yes, is Andy around, um, Andrew Stevens?"

"Is he expecting you?" She flipped through a scheduling book on the counter.

"No, not exactly, but I need to see him if he isn't in the middle of something important," I said.

An expression of annoyance flitted across the young woman's face. "He is busy, as a matter of fact. Andy usually only sees people by appointment."

"Ash, don't be a bitch. He's just lifting," a blonde, muscled man who was ducking behind the counter, volunteered. He flashed a white smile of straight teeth at me while concentrating his blue eyes on me. To his credit, his eyes stayed on mine. He too wore a tank top with the gym's name on it, which he filled out nicely. He was perfectly muscled, tanned, and had incredibly good looks. Not as good-looking as Andy, but I was sure he didn't lack female attention. The young thing behind the counter protested his words, but he ignored her.

I returned his smile nervously. For a split second, I had been relieved that Andy wasn't available. I was losing my nerve, but I knew talking with him and confessing was the right thing to do. "Thank you," I said, my eyes on him, also ignoring Miss Fake-body.

He ducked back under the counter and came up to me. "Come on, I'll take you back. I'm Logan," he said as he began to lead me towards the back of the gym. "And don't let Ashley's attitude color your opinion about the gym. We're all friendlier than that around here. It's a good place to work out. She's just got her panties in a bunch about something today."

He led me through all the cardio and weighted machines. The clientele was predominantly muscled men. I saw only a few women, mostly on the cardio equipment. He led me through a doorway at the back that led into another room with free weights, barbells, and weight racks. This room was filled with serious lifters, guys with weight belts, wrist wraps and a lot of bulging muscles. I didn't belong in this room!

Logan led me to the right and I could feel eyes on me. It was unnerving. I didn't like it. What was with men thinking they could openly gawk at a woman like this? We stopped in front of a group of men and my heart stopped as I saw Andy, with a barbell and I don't know how many hundreds of pounds. He lifted it from the ground with a deep grunt, his muscles straining and bulging, and damn-it but did he look amazing. That's what all those muscles were for and that's how he got in the spectacular shape he was in. Wow! He looked even sexier doing that then he did naked in bed this morning.

His eyes flashed recognition. He breathed out and dropped the heavy barbell back to the floor. It bounced, and a loud bang rang out. At first, I thought he was upset to see me. His surprised expression quickly changed to a smile that reached all the way to his brilliant green eyes.

"Kenzie," he greeted me, quickly closing the distance between us. The other men who had been near him busied themselves, but I could tell they were watching us.

"You're Kenzie?" Logan asked. He'd obviously been told about me. He seemed surprised.

Andy's large hand gently grasped my shoulder and gave me a little squeeze. "Kenzie, this is my friend, Logan," he introduced.

"It's nice to meet you, Logan," I said. I didn't reach to initiate a handshake and thankfully, neither did he. My palms were sweaty. I just wanted to get this over with.

"I didn't expect to see you for a few hours," Andy said.

"I'm sorry, I know. I need to talk to you," I said in a whisper. "Is there someplace private?"

This time, his eyes flashed confusion. "Sure," he said. He motioned me to a door across the room. We stepped through and were outside, beneath the raised deck and the stairs we had used to leave his apartment earlier. His bike sat in front of us. He crossed his arms over his wide chest and leaned back against the wall. "What's up?"

Oh, God. Talk about making it hard on me. His voice was cold and guarded as though he was bracing for the worst. I could understand his wariness though. I could only imagine what he thought this was about several hours before our agreed upon date. I sucked in a breath as if the air was a shot of tequila and it would give me courage.

"I am not canceling our date tonight, but if you want to cancel after I tell you this, I'll understand. I value honesty and always try to conduct myself with the utmost integrity but I'm ashamed to admit that I didn't do that this morning." His eyes flared in surprise. "I could have waited to talk with you about this until tonight, but I knew that wasn't the right thing to do. You seem like a great guy and you deserve the truth. The truth is Andy when I woke up with you this morning, I couldn't remember where I was or who you were. I was mortified! I haven't drunk too much and not remembered any part of a night since college. I haven't gotten picked up in a bar and had sex with a stranger since then either." My voice cracked, and I felt my lip quiver. My stomach was doing flip-flops. "I don't remember anything since I came out of the bathroom in that bar after saying goodnight to all of my coworkers." Andy's face showed complete surprise. "I was too embarrassed to tell you and felt completely disgusted with myself."

Andy blew out a breath, glanced at the underside of the little porch, examining each board of it and the staircase above him. He ran his fingers through his hair. Then his hard stare refocused on me. "But we made love this morning?"

"Yeah," I said drawing the word out. "I was going to stop it as it started, should have stopped it as it started," I rephrased it, "but it felt really amazing and the way you kissed me was probably the best kiss I've ever had. And everything else you did to me, well, let's just say I'm really disappointed I don't remember what we did last night." I paused and couldn't help but laugh at myself. "Probably the best sex of my life and I don't remember it." I felt the heat rising, a blush spreading over my cheeks. "This morning was pretty damn incredible though."

A smile tugged up the corners of Andy's mouth. I could tell he was trying not to smile. "Yeah, it was," he agreed.

"But in thinking about it, and trying to piece everything together, I don't think I drank too much. Before my coworkers left, I only had a couple of beers and five shots of tequila and that was over a four-hour period of time. Plus, I ate a lot too. I've drunk that much and more and have never blacked out. I do not think you had anything to do with it, but I think I was roofied or something."

"What?" He questioned, outraged.

"I do not think you had anything to do with it. I really don't," I repeated. "If anything, I think meeting you and staying inside that bar, and then coming home with you saved me from whoever did do it. I think it was one of my coworkers and he was probably waiting outside that bar. When we all said goodnight, I was the only one who went to the bathroom. Everyone else left and would have been long gone from the parking lot by the time I left, had I walked out right away after using the bathroom."

"You're serious?" He questioned.

I shook my head yes. "I talked to a friend of mine who's a cop. I didn't file an official report or anything, but I did talk to her about it, and she agrees that it's very possible something was slipped in my drink. I never left my drink alone, but I did leave it with someone from my group watching it several times. We all did. That's why I think it was one of them." I pulled my sleeve up and showed him the Band-Aid that covered where my blood had been taken. I pulled it and the folded-up gauze pad off, surely the bleeding had stopped. I showed him the needle mark. "My friend had a lab tech take some blood to run to see if any drugs are in my system."

"I think you should file an official report if you really think someone drugged you," Andy said after a few long moments of dead quiet between us.

"Would it be okay if she came by to talk with you, unofficially? Maybe you saw something in the parking lot as you came in that could be helpful."

He nodded yes and blew out a frustrated breath. "Sure, whatever you need."

The silence stretched for another uncomfortable minute. "I'm sorry, Andy. I am really glad I met you and I really wish I remembered last night." I fought back the tears I felt filling my eyes. "I think you're a really great guy and I can't believe this happened on the night I met you. And if you don't want to see me again because of this, as I said I understand, but you can believe if I find out who did this, if it was someone in my group, I'm going to kill the bastard for costing me a chance with someone like you." I couldn't look him in the eye. I looked down at his feet, hoping the tears weren't too obvious in my eyes.

He stepped forward and wrapped me in his arms. I felt his fingers run through my hair. It felt good, so good. I dropped my head against his hard chest. His shirt was damp, and I smelled sweaty man, but I didn't mind. He actually smelled kind of good. Even if he canceled our date because I had been dishonest this morning at least I had this moment, which was exactly what I needed. I felt a kiss press on my forehead and then he pulled away.

"Kenzie," he said tilting my chin, so I was forced to look into his eyes. "Tell me two things, honestly." I nodded. "Had you been yourself, would you have come home with me?"

"I'm sorry, no. I never do this. I would have made plans to see you, but," my voice trailed off. I felt like I was being so cruel to him. He didn't deserve any of this.

He smiled a small, sad grin. "You told me last night that you're looking for your forever man, that you want to get married and have kids. Is that true?"

"Oh, my God, I did?" I couldn't suck in a breath. I felt like I was dying. If you looked up mortified in the dictionary, it would show a picture of me on the page right at this very minute. He nodded. His eyes were probing mine. I bit my lower lip.

15

"I have never said that to a guy before and certainly would never the first night I met him." His smile dropped into a frown. "But yeah, that's the truth," I admitted. What the hell? After everything that happened, I wasn't going to lie to him about anything. A nervous laugh came out of me, from I don't know where. "Call me a romantic sap, but I believe in happily ever after and believe it's out there for me. And kids, yeah, I've always wanted to have kids. I'm thirty-two and," again my voice faltered. This was a train wreck. He would run as fast as he could away from me, and who would blame him.

The smile spread over his handsome face. He started to chuckle. "You are telling me the truth, aren't you?" I shook my head yes. "Where are you parked? I'll walk you to your car."

My heart sank. That was it. He was done with me. I'd said I would understand, but that didn't mean I wouldn't be tremendously disappointed, or wouldn't be hurt by it. "Around front," I said. I knew my voice cracked, and I was on the verge of tears. "And you don't have to walk me," I forced out, my chest burning.

I moved away, my eyes on the ground. He caught my arm and turned me to look him in the eye again. He saw the tears. I felt ridiculous. All I could think about was getting out of there, getting to my car and driving away.

"Hey, are you okay?" He asked.

I nodded yes as the tears slipped down my cheek. "I'm fine," I said trying to step away.

He wrapped his arms around me and pulled me into his solid form again. He held me, and I leaned into him. "You're not fine. Take a few deep breaths." I felt a few kisses to the top of my head. One of his hands was stroking over my back. It felt soothing. "I'm sure this is very upsetting. For the record, if you figure out who did this, I'll kill the bastard before you get the chance to. What kind of fucking scumbag drugs a woman with the hopes of getting laid? I'm sorry someone did this to you, Kenzie." His voice was angry.

"Thanks."

"So tonight will truly be a first date for you." He laughed. "You remember nothing?"

His words filled me, like a stocking on Christmas morning with all my favorite things. The smile that came to my lips, did so on its own. "I'm sorry, Andy, before I woke up, I don't remember a thing. Margot said that if I was drugged, in time a few things may come to me, glimpses of the night, images that by themselves won't mean anything."

"Margot?"

"My friend, Detective Margot Malone."

He guided me around the building, his arm around me the entire way. "I'll be here all afternoon. Send her over whenever she's free."

We reached my car. Andy turned me, so my back was against my car, just as he had earlier. He leaned into me. My body reacted to his. God! What this man did to me! He held his hand out to me. I knew he wanted my keys. I took them out of my pocket and dropped them into his awaiting hand. After he unlocked my door, he opened it and handed them back, this time kissing the back of my hand he had wrapped around them. Then his hands clutched either side of my face. When his lips met mine, every part of me responded. My lips returned his kisses, just as passionately. Where his body pressed against me, my nerve endings fired, wanting more contact, naked contact.

"Do me a favor tonight, will you?" I asked.

"Anything."

"Can we have the normal first date getting to know each other conversation without you telling me what you already know, what I told you last night when I tell you again tonight? Let me have the pleasure of asking you about yourself and engaging in normal conversation like two people would, who just met."

He chuckled. "Two people just meeting who have already had amazing sex."

"Yeah, a normal first date scenario." I smiled wide and then chuckled a nervous release.

He laughed too. "Yeah, we can do that, but I want you to do one thing for me, no panties." His eyes sparkled as he spoke. He pressed a soft kiss to my lips and then stepped back, motioning to the door. "See you in a few hours."

I wasn't sure what to say about his request, so I said the only thing that came to my mind, "Yep. See you then."

Andy

Logan was hovering just outside of the office as Detective Margot Malone and I talked. He was a good friend and protective, much the same as I imagined this cop was of Kenzie. I left the door open on purpose, wanting Logan to hear what we discussed, in case I needed a witness. I knew Kenzie had not filed an official report, but I wanted to be helpful in case she'd legitimately been roofied or something. I was still trying to decide if I believed that or not. I hoped she had been, if not she was a drama queen or worse, a crazy, and I didn't want or need either in my life.

"Mr. Stevens," Margot Malone began, but I interrupted her.

"Please, it's Andy," I said.

She nodded her head and forced a pleasant expression. "Andy, you know Kenzie believes she was drugged because she can't remember anything from last night after using the bathroom when her work get-together broke up, prior to meeting you."

"Is there a question in there?" I asked.

She seemed annoyed. "Was there anyone that you noticed hanging around and watching her?"

I shrugged my shoulders. "I honestly noticed only her. After we met and sat down to have a beer together, I saw no one and nothing else. Your friend is really something special."

"Yeah, she is," Margot agreed. She eyed me hard. "How about before you went into the bar? Anyone hanging around the parking lot?"

"I'm sorry, I didn't notice. After I parked my bike, I was looking at my phone to see if Logan texted back to see if he was still inside or not."

"But he hadn't until after you were already sitting with Kenzie, is that correct?"

"Yeah." I reached into my pocket and took out my phone. I pulled up the ongoing text conversation with Logan. "Here, see for yourself."

The detective scrolled through reading all of it. I could see she was making note of the times. "Is this common, that your friend asks you to meet him at a bar, but leaves without telling you before you get there?"

I couldn't help but laugh. Yeah, pretty much so. Logan is quite the player and doesn't always think of anything but his cock and where he is going to put it, but I wasn't going to tell her that. "It's happened before, so it wasn't a huge surprise."

The detective closed her little notebook. "One more thing, I know you just met Kenzie last night but was she acting unusual at all?"

I felt the smile on my face spread. "She was more open and honest than any other woman I've ever known. She was uninhibited and fun, and one of the nicest people I think I've ever met. That came through loud and clear. In retrospect, I guess you could consider that unusual. She actually told me that she is looking for her Mr. Forever to marry and have kids with. A lot of people would call that pretty fucking unusual."

Margot Malone did not seem to appreciate my humor. She scowled. She handed me her card. "If you remember anything else, and Andy, I will get to the bottom of this. Kenz is my friend and I won't let anyone hurt her." It was a warning. She stood a little taller as she said it and her face was beaming determination.

"If she was roofied or something, I hope you do figure it out and arrest the scumbag that did it," I agreed meeting and matching her stare.

"I'll be in touch if I have any further questions," she said.

"You know where to find me," I said with a nod.

I watched her leave the office and then pass through the doors and out of my gym. She didn't look back once. Logan came and hung on the door frame after we both watched her drive away. "She so thinks I had something to do with it."

"Stupid dike," Logan replied. "Is this Kenzie-chick worth all this crap?"

"Logan," I began, my voice tight.

"No, man, listen, getting you mixed up with the cops, I don't want to see you dragged through any crap again. Look what happened last time?"

"Yeah, I got my daughter." I stared him down. I was pissed. There was no comparison between Kenzie and Trina's mother. I didn't like him lumping them in the same category.

Logan raised his hands in a surrendering gesture. "I didn't mean it that way, man, you know that. It's just," he paused spearing his fingers through his hair and exhaling heavily. "I don't want you to have to go through any shit. You didn't deserve it then and you sure as hell don't deserve it now. I'm just trying to have your back here, that's all."

I clapped him on the shoulder. He always did have my back. "I know," I said and then sighed. "And yeah, Kenzie's worth it."

I saw the gears turning in Logan's head. "If she wasn't roofied," he began, but paused, probably reconsidering his words.

I laughed. "Yeah, she's either bat-shit crazy or a drama queen I will have to purge from my life. None of that shit is getting anywhere near Trina."

"Good man," he said and then moved back into the gym.

CHAPTER 4

Andy

Kenzie opened the door dressed in a fitted royal blue dress that accentuated every curve on her incredible body. The neckline was sexy, revealing enough skin to get my attention. The tapered skirt hugged her legs, the hem falling a few inches above her knees. She had on strappy black sandals with three-inch heels leveling her height off even with mine. I saw the tips of her blue polished toes peeking out of them. I already knew how incredible her legs were, but this dress showed them off spectacularly.

"Wow," I said when my eyes met hers. Yeah, I had been a typical horn-dog in how I had let my eyes sweep over her body. "You look fantastic."

Her full red lips smiled that great smile of hers, somewhat shy mixed with flattered. She had more makeup on this evening than last night when I met her. She made an effort for me, which I appreciated, though it was hardly necessary. I thought she was a knockout last night, this morning when we woke and even after our shower when she didn't have a trace of makeup on.

"Thank you," she said. Her big brown eyes were sparkling, surrounded by a smoky and smudged look to her eye makeup that was beyond sexy. "You clean up real nice, yourself," she added.

I appreciated how her eyes swept over my body. The smile on her lips told me she liked what she saw. I leaned in and kissed her lips but fought the urge to take her face between my palms or to pull her body completely against mine. Her lips were soft, and I couldn't get enough of them. Her smell was intoxicating. I wanted to take her to bed now.

She had a small black purse clutched in her hand and had not stepped back to invite me into her home. I hoped that would not be the case after dinner. Not only did I want to be invited in, I wanted to stay all night. "Are you ready?" I asked, taking a step back and motioning for her to come out onto the porch.

She locked her door, pushing against it to test the seal the door made, and I guided her to the driveway, my hand resting on the small of her back. My eyes couldn't help but notice how the dress hugged her perfect pear-shaped ass or how it swayed as she walked. I wanted to slide my hand down and knead those voluptuous cheeks. Knowing that she didn't have any panties on, made me want to bend her over and bury my cock inside of her. Speaking of which, it was getting hard just thinking about having her. This was going to be a long-ass dinner. I couldn't get enough of this woman.

Kenzie

We rounded the garage, and I got my first look at his truck. I don't know what I was expecting, but what sat there reflecting the early evening sun was the most gorgeous cobalt blue and gleaming chrome vehicle I'd ever seen. She was in pristine shape. Her lines were classic. They didn't make them like this anymore.

"Wow, beautiful truck!" I said.

"Yeah, she's a beauty, isn't she?"

"What year is it?"

"She's a 1945 Ford F-1," Andy said proudly.

"It's in amazing condition. Did you restore it?"

"Me and a buddy that has a shop. It took two years. You should have seen her when I got her. She was a wreck." Andy opened the passenger door and helped me in. Then he secured the seatbelt around me. No man had ever done that. It was an act that was steeped in old-fashioned gentlemanly manners that made me smile. I could see my dad doing that for my mom back in the day.

When I had told Andy he cleaned up well, what an understatement that was! How could this man be single? He was a God! He wore a dark blue long-sleeved button-down shirt that was fitted so well to his form, it had to be tailor-made. It had a slight shimmer to the fabric, and I couldn't wait to touch it to see if it was as silky as it appeared. It was tucked into perfectly fitting dark blue jeans that hugged his body making my mind think about what was underneath them. And he smelled masculine and spicy.

Andy

Peeking back in the window at her I couldn't help but smile. She looked great in my truck. She looked great on the back of my bike. She looked great in my bed. I knew I had it bad for her. "So, I made reservations at The Toad and the Hoot Owl. I hope that's okay with you." I turned the truck over and shifted into reverse. I saw the smile that came to her lips. I was undoubtedly trying too hard. That was a pretty expensive place, and it was probably obvious I was trying to impress her.

"It is, great choice," she said. "My friend Madeline owns it and is the head chef. We go way back to when she was just Maddie with pigtails and braces." Kenzie laughed. It was a sound that was relaxed and sexy, and I wanted to hear more of.

"She was one of the few girls I grew up with whose dad wasn't in the Corps. We military brats tended to stick together."

"Marine Corps?" I asked somewhat surprised.

"Yeah, my dad was a career Marine, twenty-four years, retired a Gunnery Sergeant."

"So, did you move all over as a child?" This conversation was new to me. This hadn't come up the night before. I was glad. I wanted to learn more about her.

"No, by the time my sister and I were in school he managed to bounce between Twenty-Nine Palms, Camp Pendleton, and duty as a DI in San Diego. We lived in Oceanside and stayed there until I graduated and went off to college."

A Marine Corps Drill Instructor. He would so not like the fact that his daughter was seeing a former Army-man, I was sure. "Lucky," I said. "Not many children of military parents get to stay in one place for very long. I did ten years in the Army," I volunteered.

"I thought you had served," she said gazing at me with that smile I loved. "I recognized the tat on your shoulder as some type of military insignia."

"Yeah, my unit. A few of the others are for buddies we lost over there." I regretted bringing that up immediately.

"I'm sorry," she said, her face taking on a sad expression.

"No need. It was another life, and we all knew what we were signing up for. Anyway, where did you go to school then, somewhere near home? And how did you end up here in Lexington of all places?"

That giggle slipped out of her again. I loved that sound. "Yeah, I went to school there, at San Diego State University and I ended up here because of my first job. I got transferred from San Diego for a great opportunity within the organization, but that company went belly-up only a year after I transferred. I was here and got the job with Any-Time Systems, where I've been for the past six years."

"What kind of degree did you get to be a project manager?" I chuckled. "Sorry, I already broke the rule of knowing what you do for living from our conversation last night." This was going to be harder than I thought it would be.

She laughed. "That's okay. I know you own a gym, it's kind of the same thing. I actually got a marketing degree. I was hired to do marketing for my organization but got sucked into the project management end almost right away. It's not really what I wanted to do, but it was what they needed, and it turns out I'm good at it. And I've been able to do some marketing for them. It's paid well so I have no regrets. Someday I may want to actually work in marketing again, but for as long as I have this job, it's good."

"Is your company in trouble? You said five people got let go yesterday?" I asked.

She nodded. "There is a lot of competition in the industry and most firms that utilize our type of service are moving from hosted to SaaS," she said. Upon seeing my confusion, she clarified. "Software as a Service. It's a different way of delivering the service to them. My organization was slow to move to the SaaS model. A few other companies deliver it better and for less, so we're struggling to define our role in the industry."

I still didn't understand what that meant, but for now, it didn't matter. The general gist was that she got a marketing degree, was working as a project manager, but someday would like to work in marketing again. Her organization had just let five people go as they were in trouble, having problems competing. Thankfully I pulled into the parking lot. I didn't want to have to admit my ignorance in anything tech or computer related.

"Is your job in jeopardy, or do you think it will be at some point?" I asked as I put the truck in park.

"I think I'm safe for a while. I wear three hats there. If another round of job cuts come, I'll be okay," she said. "And hopefully by then, we'll figure our new business model out."

She was something! She was knowledgeable and professional. I imagined she was very good at her job. I was impressed. She was different from the waitress bimbo types that frequented the gym, groupies there to drool over the muscles. I wanted a woman with her own career, with a brain, and self-confidence. "Good, I'm glad," I said as I got out of the truck.

As we walked into The Toad and the Hoot Owl, I was impressed by the simple décor of the restaurant. Soft cream tones with black accents were everywhere. I felt like I was walking into someone's patio. Lanterns of many sizes were placed strategically on the floor and glowed a warm yellow. The decorator of this restaurant should be commended on the comfort and warmth that was reflected everywhere.

Kenzie

The hostess seated us at a small table tucked into a corner at the back of the restaurant. It was so small our knees touched under the tablecloth. Andy immediately glanced over the wine menu. "Do you like wine?" He asked.

"Yes, red. I've been here a couple of times. They have a really good House Cab if you like Cabernets." I knew the wine list was expensive. The House Cab was decently priced. I smiled at him as my eyes wandered over him. He had strikingly attractive facial features. His green eyes were vibrant, and I couldn't help but stare at them when they looked at me. I couldn't imagine this man in fatigues on the battlefield. He was too gentle and gentlemanly.

He put the menu down. "Sounds good, we'll get a bottle." He reached across the table and took hold of my hand. I got tingles just from the contact.

The waiter came and introduced himself, rattling off the evening's specials as he filled our water glasses. He took the wine order and was preparing to scurry away, but I stopped him. "If you get the chance, would you please tell Chef Madeline that her friend Kenzie Collins is here?"

"Certainly, Miss Collins," the waiter replied. "I'll get your bottle of wine while you make your dinner selections."

When I looked back at Andy, he was staring at me with a smile that I couldn't help but return. "What?" I asked. He looked as though he wanted to say something.

He shook his head, his smile morphing into a smirk. "It's just that you are so beautiful, and I am happy to be here with you." His voice was low and sexy. "And I was wondering if you honored my request, just the thought you did is sexy, and you have no idea how much it turns me on."

I felt embarrassed. Yes, I had honored his request. I was sans panties. It wasn't something I normally did. I did feel sexy and naughty though because of it. I felt the heat rise up my cheeks and knew I was blushing. "I did," I confirmed.

Andy

She was actually blushing. It was cute. It proved to me that she normally didn't do this kind of thing. For some reason that made me feel special that she would go panty-less for me. I wondered what else she would do for me. "You are you know?" I said.

"Are what?"

"Beautiful," I said.

Her eyes dropped, and she smiled wider, the blush spreading over her cheeks. "Thank you," she replied shyly.

"You don't normally do this kind of thing, do you?" I finally asked.

She giggled again, ending in a deep suck-in of air, her eyes to the ceiling. Her smile that settled back on me was impish and inviting. "I decided before I came to see you this afternoon to tell you the truth that I was going to be one-hundred percent open and honest with you and just be me. No censoring what I said or what I did," she paused and shook her head, "and that was before I knew I told you I was looking for my Forever-guy to get married and have kids." Now she laughed freely. "So, no. I normally wouldn't go panty-less at the request of a guy I just met, but I have to admit, it's fun and it makes me feel sexy and naughty."

I knew there was a whole lot of other naughty I could introduce her to and I was sure I could sway her into letting her hair down to enjoy. "We'll have to see what other sexy-naughty-fun we can get into," I said with a wink, my voice low.

She looked surprised but didn't say no, and she was smiling. I took that as her agreement. At that moment, the waiter returned with our wine and an appetizer which he informed us came with compliments from Chef Madeline. He poured the wine and gave it to me to taste. I honestly didn't know that much about wine. I've seen others sniff it, swirl it and sip it before giving their approval, so I did the same, feeling ridiculous. I didn't know what I was doing.

A petite woman with dark hair piled messily atop her head approached the table. She was in her early thirties and wore no makeup. She was a natural beauty with big brown eyes that had beautiful glints of gold in them. She was dressed in chefs clothing.

"Maddie!" Kenzie exclaimed and came to her feet. The two women embraced. "Thank you for the appetizer, it looks wonderful." Kenzie's eyes led her to me. The smile on Kenzie's face warmed my heart. "Chef Madeline Shaw please meet Andy Stevens. Andy, my very good friend Madeline."

I came to my feet and shook her small but surprisingly strong hand. "It's nice to meet you," I greeted.

After our handshake, she pulled me into a hug. "It's nice to meet you too." She pulled away and looked up into my face. "I'm a hugger." She shrugged. "Please sit," she said pointing to our table. "Enjoy the appetizer. The lamb special is exceptional tonight. I highly recommend it. I have to get back to the kitchen, but I wanted to come say hi." She took a sip of Kenzie's wine and gave us both a wink. "I hope you enjoy dinner. Kenz, don't be a stranger. Let's get together for coffee next week, okay?"

Kenzie agreed and then Madeline moved away from our table, the waiter assuming her place immediately. We both ordered the lamb, taking her recommendation as gospel. Kenzie sipped her wine, her eyes never leaving me. That sexy little smile tugged the corners of her lips up.

"She's not what I expected," I said.

"What were you expecting?" Kenzie asked.

"I don't know," I confessed. "I didn't expect the owner and head chef to be so down to Earth."

Kenzie laughed freely. "Yeah, well she is one of my best friends. Did you really think she'd be stuck up or all hoity-toity?"

Now I laughed. No, I couldn't envision Kenzie being good friends with anyone not friendly and down to Earth. "So, tell me about your cop friend. She's a tough one."

Kenzie smiled fondly. "Yeah, she is. I'm sure she came on like gangbusters when she talked with you. I'm sorry if she treated you like a suspect. She's a good friend and was only looking out for me."

"How'd you meet her?" I asked.

"We went to college together, were roommates in the dorm."

"You roomed with a lesbian?" I asked.

Kenzie laughed. "Yeah, that was interesting, to say the least."

"How'd she end up here too?"

"When her dad retired, he was Navy, her parents moved here. He got sick about five years ago. Her mom needed her help, and she was lucky enough to get on with the police department here."

Kenzie

"So, tell me about Trina," I said.

The smile broadened over his face. "Well, as you know she's my life."

"And she's adorable. She's got your green eyes," I said. "You said she just turned four?"

"Yeah, last month. She's a great kid. She's happy, and that's what matters most to me. She's really close with my mom, who has helped me with her since she was born and there are a few moms of kids in her preschool class that help me out with her as well, getting her to and from school. I have her enrolled at Zion Lutheran, a few blocks over from the gym. I give them free gym memberships and personal training sessions to compensate them for helping me. Logan and Ashley both live in apartments over the gym and they help me out quite a bit with her too. Even with Logan and Ashley helping at the gym I put in an average of sixty hours a week there. There are some things that I can't delegate. I own the place, so it's on me. I couldn't do it all without the help I get from everyone," Andy said.

I was confused. "What about her mother?" I asked cautiously.

"Trina's biological mother chose to be out of our lives since the day she was born," Andy replied.

"Oh, my God," left my mouth with little thought. "How? Why?" That came out of me with little tact, I knew, as soon as I had spoken it.

Andy's lips turned downward in a deep frown. "Trina's mother was looking for a quick buck. A healthy white baby with specific traits can go for a lot of money in an illegal adoption arrangement."

I was shocked and horrified. What kind of person would do that? I knew I couldn't ask any questions without sounding insensitive. And not knowing what his prior relationship had been with Trina's mother I didn't want to say the wrong thing. "God, that's shocking," I finally decided on.

"Yeah, it was for me at the time, too. It was a really rough time for me. I ended up getting arrested, had to legally force a paternity test, and sue for custody. That was all a few weeks before Trina was born. I wasn't allowed to be in the room when she was born, but I got to hold her a half hour later. The judge in the case was great, a little Jewish man in his sixties. He was impressed that after all that shit with Trina's mother that I would still welcome her in our lives. I wanted to do the right thing and believed I could. She signed her rights away before she left the hospital and I haven't heard from her since, which probably has been the best thing for Trina."

"God, Andy, I am so sorry," I said truly shocked. "You've raised her all by yourself. That's amazing."

"Not really, women do it all the time. And I have had a lot of help. My family really has been great. And I know my parents were proud of me for stepping up and doing the right thing. That little girl has been the center of our lives for the last four years." He paused and laughed. "My dad even told me how proud he was of me when he bailed me out. More importantly, I can look myself in the mirror and know I did the best I could for her, am doing the best I can for her every day. She's my baby, and she deserves nothing less," he said with such conviction I was in awe. "So, that's why I don't do one-night-stands, wouldn't even introduce her to anyone I'm not serious about. I don't want a parade of women in and out of her life. That wouldn't be fair to her and would confuse her."

I nodded, impressed with his beliefs. "Well, I think that is incredible. I'm sure you're a great dad. Does she ever ask about her mother?"

"Sometimes, but I've made sure all the adults in her life are on the same page. I don't ever want her to know what her mother was. Luckily, several of her good friends are being raised by single moms and she just accepts that some kids live with either their mom or their dad, some see both, some don't. Right now, she just accepts it, but I know I will have to keep having age appropriate discussions with her as she grows up and has questions."

"Yeah," I agreed. "Sounds like you'll have it under control though."

"So, I hope you will understand that I may want to see you more often, but there will be limitations on my availability," Andy said plainly.

"Not only do I understand that I respect it too," I replied. "I travel usually three days a week every other week, sometimes more. I go onsite for installs and bringing clients up, to conduct training, or to troubleshoot problems."

We were still holding hands across the table. Andy leaned in and drew my hand to his lips, softly kissing the back of my knuckles. It was erotic to watch. "Good, because I really like you Kenzie. I want to see you, as often as possible, but Trina can't be shorted the time she needs."

"I understand, and I wouldn't want you to." I laughed a little. "I honestly was wondering when I was at your place this morning if this was your weekend for visitation with her and she was with your mom instead. I thought that just wasn't right if that was the case."

Andy laughed. It was a sexy sound, a rumble that had all my lady parts coming alive. "I like that. Thank you." I felt his hand brush my knee. He leaned forward a bit more over the table and I felt his fingers lightly draw circles up my inner thigh. I sucked in a surprised gasp becoming wet instantly. "So, I know you normally wouldn't have sex with a man you had just met in a bar, but how about after a second date, a dinner at a nice restaurant?"

Jesus! How long was his arm? His fingers were damn near to my pussy. "I'm uninhibited with you, remember?" I teased, the desire rising faster than his fingers were. "They have a great fudge brownie here. We should get it to go and have dessert at my house. I have some vanilla bean ice cream in my, freezer," I gasped, the word freezer coming out an octave higher and a little louder as his fingers penetrated me.

Andy's sexy rumble softly washed over the table. "Now you're talking. God, you're wet," he whispered. I felt his fingers press against the uppermost portion of my thighs. "Spread them and give me more room."

I gasped a second time. "Not here," I squeaked.

"No one can see under this tablecloth and as long as you don't scream as you come, no one will know."

"Andy, I'm not that uninhib, oh," I gasped again. His fingers were doing something to my clit that it had never felt. "Oh, my God," I whispered. He didn't stop, and the crest was rising so quickly. Before I knew it, my entire body quaked, and an orgasm exploded inside me, drenching me and Andy's hand, I was sure.

"Guess I didn't need more room after all," he said quietly with a very satisfied expression on his face. I watched as he withdrew his arm from under the table, used his napkin to wipe his hand but he slid one wet finger into his mouth. His eyes rolled back in his head. "Heaven, I can't wait to have more after we get to your place."

I nervously glanced around the restaurant. Not a single person paid us any attention. The only eye I caught was our waiter. He hurried tableside. "Could we get a fudge brownie to go, please," I asked.

"And the check, please," Andy added.

Andy

Damn had Kenzie been wet, and she was so fucking responsive, orgasming so quickly. My dick was uncomfortable in my jeans. That check couldn't come fast enough. I escorted her out quickly, knowing the front of my pants left nothing to anyone's imagination. Thankfully the place was kind of dark and I followed closely behind her. At my truck, I pressed her against it, my cock straining to reach her through the fabric. She felt it right away and reached between us to stroke me.

"Oh, fuck," I moaned at the contact. I devoured her mouth. My hand slipped behind her and I kneaded that perfect ass.

"Get me home," she breathed into my ear, "or I'll take it out of your pants right here." And then her tongue and teeth went to work on my ear, and I wanted her to. I think I doubled in size.

I fumbled with my keys and got her door open. "If we weren't in a parking lot, I'd take you across my seat right now," I said, wanting to do it.

"We'll have to add that to our naughty list, in the truck, but not in a busy parking lot," she said as she got in.

I helped her up, my hand sliding between her legs again. This time, she spread her thighs wide for me. Fuck! This woman was undoing me. I looked around, considering it, but just then an older couple came out of the restaurant and were heading straight for us. "You're lucky," I growled at Kenzie, shut her door and went to the driver's side. "Good evening, folks," I greeted the couple as they came up to the car parked beside by truck.

The older man smiled knowingly at me. Oh, yeah. He knew what he was interrupting, and he was jealous. "Good evening," he said.

Kenzie was biting her lower lip as I got in. after I drove away, my hand returned to where it had been, and so did hers. She had my shirt untucked and my jeans undone before we reached her house. I had to stop her before she made me wreck the truck, so I made her come again. She followed my command to hike her dress up and spread those incredible thighs wide. She was practically doing the splits on my seat. This time she was not quiet. She gasped aloud, moaned and cursed, her hands gripping my dashboard as though her life depended on it.

"Oh, fuck," she cursed again when she had caught her breath.

"As soon as we get in your front door," I said, pulling into her driveway.

CHAPTER 5

Kenzie

Andy was out of his truck and around to my side before I even had my seatbelt off. He opened the door and helped me down, my body sliding against his as I dropped to my feet. Every part of me tingled at the contact. He kissed me again, my desire rising even higher. I'd already had two orgasms and knew we would get naked quickly after getting inside. I had never felt a hunger like this for any other man I had been with. I couldn't wait to get in my house.

We hurried up the sidewalk to my front door. Andy took my keys and unlocked my front door. He took me into his arms and gently kicked the door to close it. It closed with a slam, something that only happened when the back door was open. Immediately we heard a small crash coming from the hallway that led to the kitchen. Both of our heads swung in that direction.

I gasped, my chest tight, my heart pounding. "Someone's in there, Andy," I said, my voice sounding strained, even to my own ears.

"Stay here," he ordered as he bolted into the dark hallway.

I ran after him, reaching the kitchen as Andy reached the open back door. "Andy, don't!" I screamed as Andy ran out the door.

He stopped and looked back at me. His eyes looked behind me and I turned to see what he was looking at. There was nothing and no one there. He rushed back to me, took me into his arms and quickly guided me back towards the front door. We stood by his truck. I was in shock. Someone had been in my house. I suddenly realized Andy was on his phone. He had dialed 9-1-1 as soon as we had exited my house. I pulled my phone out and my shaking hands dialed Margot.

The dark night was lit up by the many flashing red and blue lights on the several police cruisers that parked in my driveway and in front of my house. Andy and I waited by his truck as several uniformed police officers went through my house, my eyes fixed on the one uniformed cop that stood with us, his hand on his gun belt. Once it was declared all clear, Andy, and I went back inside just as Margot arrived. She joined us in the kitchen seconds later. We relayed the events of the night to her and the uniformed cops who stood in my kitchen. Andy had seen a figure running across my yard in the brief second that he was in my back yard.

"Why did you break off the chase and come back into the house?" Margot asked Andy.

"Kenzie yelled to me to stop, and I realized I had no way of knowing if someone else was inside. I couldn't leave her in here alone."

"Are you sure the door was closed when you left, Kenzie?" Margot asked pointing to my back door.

I rolled my eyes at her. "Of course, I'm sure. I always lock up. You know that Margot."

Margot's eyes slid to Andy. "Were you in the house before you left for dinner?"

Even I understood the accusation that was coming through in her question. Andy remained calm, calmer than I would have. "No. Kenzie greeted me at the front door, and we left right away. I never entered until we got back after dinner."

Margot's stare at Andy was hard. "And the front door was still locked when you got home?" Both Andy and I nodded. "Are you sure it was closed tightly when you left?"

"Kenzie pushed against it after she locked it. Yes, it was secure," Andy volunteered.

"Is anything missing Kenz?" Margot asked.

"I haven't looked closely yet, but not that I can tell," I said. My laptop still sat on the kitchen table where I had left it. "But," I said, noticing the kitchen towel I had hung from the refrigerator door handle on the floor. "That was hanging from the handle of the fridge."

Margot opened the refrigerator with her gloved hand. "Kenz," she summoned me over.

My vitamins were knocked over, laying on their side, the top loose, the liquid slowly seeping out. "That lid was on tight. Margot, you saw me take them and reseal the cap earlier. You saw me sit the bottle on the shelf. It was upright!" I felt panicked and afraid. Someone had been in my house. My vitamins were laying on their side and leaking. I felt hands grip my upper arms. Andy was behind me, gazing into the refrigerator as well. I leaned into him.

Margot took out her phone and took several pictures. Then she sat the vitamin bottle upright. She turned to the officers. "I want the back door, as well as the refrigerator, dusted for prints. Bag this bottle and recover as much of this fluid as you can from the shelf. Get it to the lab." Then Margot turned to me. "You shouldn't sleep here tonight."

I stared into Andy's eyes. "She'll stay with me tonight," he said. I nodded.

"That's not a good idea," Margot argued. "You can stay at my house tonight, Kenz."

"No, that's okay Margot. I'll stay with Andy." I said. She started to debate it. "Margot!" I snapped. I knew she didn't like or trust Andy. But I did. "Thank you, but I prefer to stay at Andy's tonight."

"Kenzie, you really need to have a security system. I've got a friend who installs them. I can have him over here tomorrow as soon as the police have released the crime scene," Andy volunteered.

"I'm not sure I can afford that," I said.

"Don't worry about the cost," Andy said. "You need a security system. He'll give you a good price and I'll give him some personal training to help defray the costs to you."

"I agree a security system would be a good idea, but I don't think you should have a friend of his do it. There are a lot of companies out there, Kenzie," Margot said.

"Just let me know when we can get back in my house and I'll deal with a security system then," I bit out. I couldn't make any decisions right now. I just wanted to curl up in Andy's arms and not have to deal with any of this.

"Can Kenzie go now?" Andy asked. His hands were gently caressing my arms.

Margot nodded, but it was obvious she didn't like it. "Yeah, we'll go through the house carefully tomorrow to see if anything is missing. We can add to the report if need be later."

"Can I get some of my things from my bedroom? I'll want a change of clothes for tomorrow," I asked.

"Yeah, that's fine," Margot said.

I glanced back at her as I led Andy from the room. Her face wore a disapproving scowl. I knew she wasn't happy about this, but I knew Andy had nothing to do with it. Whether she liked it or not, I felt safe with Andy. I led him up the stairs. All the lights were on, probably from the search the officers conducted of the whole house. I wondered if I could turn them off. I wasn't going to ask permission. I flipped each light switch off as I came to each of the three small bedrooms and the hall bathroom. Then I led him into my bedroom. We would have been in here over an hour ago, had this not happened. I felt anger boiling up inside of me with this realization.

Andy sat on the bed and watched me fill my backpack with clothes and toiletries. I heard him laugh as I folded my spaghetti strap nightie and place it inside. "You know that won't be on your body tonight." His voice was flirty. I sat the backpack next to him. He took hold of both of my hands and pulled me to his lap. "Are you okay?"

"Yes, no, I don't know," I replied nervously. He embraced me. It felt good, safe.

Andy

"Breathe, babe," I whispered in her ear. "It's okay. Let's get you to my place and into bed."

Kenzie rose and went back into her closet. She came out carrying a pair of jeans and a tank top. She turned her back to me. "Can you help with the zipper?"

I came up behind her and wrapped my arms around her, my cheek nuzzling hers. "Please don't change. I've been fantasizing all night of taking this dress off you, but not like this and certainly not for you to put anything else on." Kenzie's head nodded.

"Uh-hum," I heard from the doorway. Margot stood there; her disapproving glare fixed on me. "Kenz, I'll lock up. I'll call you tomorrow when you can get back in and I'll meet you here to go through and look for anything missing."

Kenzie pulled away from me. She dropped the clothes in her hand onto the bed, went over to, and hugged Margot. "Thanks. I appreciate you and all you've done. I won't come back until I hear from you."

"You're sure you want to go to his place?" I heard Margot say. My anger rose hearing her trying to persuade Kenzie.

"Don't," Kenzie warned her.

"If you need anything at all, anytime, call me," Margot said. Her eyes were boring through me.

I picked up Kenzie's backpack and drew her away from Margot, and into my arms, my eyes silently challenging Margot to speak up against my action. She remained quiet, but her face showed concern and anger.

"Thank you," I voiced. "We'll see you tomorrow."

The half hour drive back to my place was very different from the drive from the restaurant to Kenzie's house. "Your house is nice," I said to cut the quiet tension in the truck.

"Thanks," she replied quietly. "Why is this happening?" She asked just as softly. "I can't believe this!" She exclaimed louder. She was getting anxious.

I took hold of her hand and gave it a gentle squeeze. "It's okay, Kenzie."

"I'm sorry how Margot treated you."

"She doesn't know me, doesn't trust me," I said. "She's protective of you. Logan's like that where I'm concerned. They're just being good friends."

"I trust you," Kenzie said, her hand squeezing mine. I saw honesty and vulnerability in her eyes.

I brought her hand to my lips and placed a gentle kiss to her knuckles. "Thank you," I whispered. "I'm going to take care of you. Nothing and no one is going to hurt you, you got that?" I said. I could tell she needed to hear that she would be okay, that everything would be okay.

When we got to my place, I led her up the back stairs as I had the previous evening. She stood awkwardly by my kitchen table. I took her by the hand and drew her towards the bedroom. Within, I unzipped her dress and slid it off her shoulders and down her perfect form. As I pushed it from her hips, freeing her smooth flesh from the covering, the beauty of her flawlessly formed ass stared at me and I couldn't help but drop to my knees, knead her cheeks, and press kisses to each cheek. My hands then snaked around to the front of her thighs. I caressed her, my fingers inching up slowly.

Kenzie

I thought I was going to orgasm just from Andy's touch. His wet tongue drew a line straight up the middle of my back. I moaned aloud from the sensation. He made fast work of taking my bra off too, and before I knew it, I was standing naked beside his bed. When he turned me, so I faced him, I melted into him. The kiss he gave me was unlike any kiss I had ever had. It was soft and consuming, sensual and passionate. I knew from his kisses he would take care of me. Nothing and no one would ever harm me, just like he said.

Before I realized it, I had removed his shirt and my hands were fumbling with the button on his jeans. Seconds later we were both naked, and he pressed me to his bed. My hands couldn't get enough of him. The events of the evening slipped away and all I could think about was the incredible sensation of his touch as his hands caressed over my tingling body. The love we made was even more intense than what we had done to each other that morning.

CHAPTER 6

Kenzie

The warmth of Andy and the smell of him filled me before I even opened my eyes. I moaned and snuggled closer. I heard his sexy chuckle. My hand stroked over his sculpted muscles. The bright sunlight streaming through the windows assaulted my eyes when I opened them.

"What time is it?" I muttered.

"Nearly ten," his smooth voice replied. He held his cell phone. "My buddy that installs the alarm systems can meet us at your place as soon as Margot releases your house."

I sat upright. "My phone."

He reached to the nightstand and held it up. "Margot hasn't contacted you yet."

I laid back down and snuggled close to him again. He had everything handled. There was no way he could know how much I appreciated him. "How much will your friend charge me?"

"Don't worry about that," Andy said. "I'm sure we can come to a price you can afford. I'll give him as much personal training services or boot camp classes to make up the difference."

"I won't let you do that. It's not fair to you," I protested.

Andy laughed. "You won't let me, huh?"

I rose to gaze into his eyes, into those beautiful, bright-green eyes. They were sparkling at me, a flirty grin lifting the corners of his lips. Seriously? How was this man single? And what was he doing with me? He was reclined, his head on his pillow, the sheet pulled up to just below his navel. God, was he sexy! He was so comfortable in his own skin, unlike me. I tucked the sheet under my armpits to hold in in place.

My phone rang. Margot! Andy handed me my phone. It was the ringtone I had set for her and her picture was displayed on my screen. "Margot," I greeted. "Can we get back into my house now?"

"Good morning to you too, Kenzie," she said. Her voice had a sarcastic edge.

"Sorry, good morning," I said.

"The house will be released in about an hour. I'll meet you there," she said.

"Thanks, Margot. I appreciate it." I hit end and sat up, my eyes on Andy. "I really need a shower, and I would kill for a cup of coffee."

"No coffee in the house. I don't drink it. Get in the shower. I'll get you an energy drink." He pulled himself from the bed and walked naked from the room. I watched his toned ass and muscled back retreat down the hall. Wow! That had been quite a sight.

He joined me in the shower, presenting a plastic shaker bottle filled with a neon yellow liquid. It didn't taste bad, but it wasn't coffee. By the time we were both dressed and ready to go, I was buzzing around the room like I had drunk six cups of coffee.

"What was in that energy drink?" I asked.

Andy laughed. "Yeah, better than coffee, isn't it? It's just vitamins and minerals. No caffeine or sugar at all. All natural."

I was impressed. He had convinced me. I'd have to find out where to buy it. He grabbed two granola-like bars and handed me one as we passed through the kitchen. It was a brand I was not familiar with. As he pulled out of the driveway, I read the nutritional values. Twenty-four grams of protein, twenty-four grams of carbs, eight grams of fiber, and two hundred forty calories. Andy had finished his before I even tore mine open. It had a good taste and filled me up, much to my surprise. A healthier diet wouldn't hurt me, I decided.

An odd feeling washed over me as Andy pulled the truck into my driveway. Margot's force-issued sedan sat in front of my house. This all felt surreal. First being roofied. Then a break-in at my house? How could any of this be happening?

"Kenzie?" Andy's concerned voice pulled me from my thoughts. He stood beside me; the truck door already open.

"Yeah, sorry," I apologized.

I held his hand as he led me up my walk. Margot opened my door as we reached it. She didn't look thrilled to see Andy with me. Like I'd come alone? Wait until Andy's friend arrived to install the security system. She'd be even more pissed about that.

He waited by the door for his friend. Margot and I started on the second floor looking to see if anything was disturbed or missing. By the time we descended the stairs back to the first floor, Andy's security system friend was there. He and Andy were talking in the kitchen, near the door that led out to my garage.

"Kenzie, this is Brian Porter," Andy introduced.

Brian Porter flashed a white smile at me that was surrounded by a neatly trimmed, black mustache and beard. His black hair was cropped short beneath the ballcap on his head. His eyes were a light brown, and they fixed on mine. He took my hand. I noticed his muscled biceps swelling out of his short-sleeved t-shirt.

"It's nice to meet you Kenzie." His voice was warm and friendly. He had a manner that immediately set me at ease. "Andy told me what happened. We're reviewing what points need monitoring. I'm thinking sensors on all first-floor doors and windows and cameras covering all common areas and entry doors as well as up in the hallway outside of your bedroom. The system can be accessed and viewed on your phone, the same as the system I put in the gym for Andy. I think you should have a system that auto-notifies manned monitoring while this is going on."

Margot stepped forward and presented her badge, identifying herself. "What manned monitoring will it tie into?"

"Any you would like. We can even have it autodial 9-1-1 if you want," Brian replied.

Margot nodded. She turned to me. "I agree with his plan and assessment." She turned back to Brian and Andy. "Make it 9-1-1, for now."

While the men worked, Margot and I continued to go over my house. Nothing else was disturbed and nothing was missing. Margot informed me that the test results on my blood, on the vitamins, and running the fingerprints should be in the next day. She was rushing everything through.

"My vitamins, Margot?" I asked. "Someone would have to know how regimented I am in taking them."

She hugged me. "Does Andy know about your vitamins?"

"No!" I protested. "I just met him Friday night. He wasn't in my house until we got back from dinner. I never mentioned my vitamins. Why would I?"

"You have no idea what you told him or didn't tell him Friday night," she reminded me.

My anger spiked. She was right, but I wouldn't admit it. I don't know why I felt so much trust for Andy, I just did. "Margot, please, don't be so eager to pin all this on Andy that you don't check out all other possibilities."

She hugged me again. "I won't, I promise." She pulled away and pinned me with her eyes. "What do you know about him, though? Seriously, Kenz, why are you so adamant he had nothing to do with any of this? Why do you trust him?"

I ran my fingers through my hair and rubbed my stiff neck. "I can't explain it. I just do. The way he is with me, it just makes me trust him. And seriously, why would he? Look at him and look at me. He's a freaking God and I'm, well I'm me."

"Don't say that. You're beautiful Kenzie. Anyone would be lucky to be with you." I knew she was being honest, about how she felt about me.

"Oh Margot," I said. I hugged her again. "That's sweet. Thank you. It's true though. Do you have any idea what it's like laying naked with him and his zero percent body fat?"

"No Kenz, I'd have no idea what it would be like laying naked with him or any other man," Margot said. Her voice was saying duh Kenzie.

I giggled. "My point is, he doesn't have to drug a woman to get her into bed. I can't imagine he would have any problems in that area. And look at how much he has to lose, his business, his daughter."

"He's been arrested Kenz. For stalking and unlawful restraint."

"Was that five years ago?"

"Yes," Margot replied, confused that I knew.

"He told me. That was his daughter, Trina's mother. She was trying to sell her in an illegal adoption scheme without acknowledging him as the legitimate father. He loves his daughter more than anything else. He seems to be a great father, has raised her by himself," I was proud to tell her. "Look into the whole case. He was granted full custody."

"I will," Margot said.

"You do that." She knew I was annoyed with her.

"I'll be in touch when I get any of the test results back. Your house is clear. Keep that alarm system on and armed. And call me if you need anything at all. Stay vigilant, Kenz."

I promised her I would. I was almost afraid to be alone. It was a few hours later when Brian and Andy finished installing the system which included changing all my exterior door locks. The system had electronic door locks as well as keys. They had continued working through lunch, eating the sandwiches I made them as they worked.

I tried to get some work done on my laptop at the kitchen table but had a hard time concentrating. Brian downloaded the app to my phone and laptop and showed me how to use it and the master control panels at the door to the garage within my kitchen and in my bedroom. He seemed to be a good guy, had a great sense of humor, was friendly, and thorough in the job he did. He and Andy worked very well together too. There was obviously a close relationship there. He was leaving when I realized he hadn't given me a bill.

"Brian, wait," I called as he was going out my front door. "My bill?"

His eyes went to Andy. They exchanged looks that told me something was up. "I'll bill you next month. Use the system and be safe." He turned and left.

I turned to Andy. "How much is this costing me?" I demanded.

Andy

I laughed. "When your neighbor's house is on fire, you don't negotiate a price to let them use your hose. You put the fire out and worry about the rest later." I wrapped my arms around Kenzie and kissed her to silence her protest.

Yeah, she wouldn't be getting a bill from Brian. I had already settled it with him. He had also hooked me up to monitor Kenzie's house on my phone, laptop and iPad, giving me full access to all feeds and alerts. I knew she would be pissed if she found out, but I had to keep tabs on things. I cared about her far too much to not be able to see for myself that she was safe. I'd just have to be sure she didn't find out.

It was midafternoon. I figured I could spend a few more hours with her before I had to go pick Trina up from my mom's. It was Sunday. It was my last day with Kenzie until next weekend. I knew how I wanted to spend this precious time. I watched her arm the system as Brian's dark-blue, panel van pulled away and then I lifted her into my arms and carried her up the stairs. I placed her on her bed and covered her body with mine. She had a surprised smile on her face. I took her face between my palms and kissed her, feeling my arousal flare. I was hard in seconds. I wasn't sure how I would go all week without making love to her. There was something about her that made me want to spend every second with her, preferably with my cock buried deep inside of her.

I made love to her, reveling in the sensation of our bodies entwined. After, as we lay together, I held her and memorized every curve on her amazing body as my hands skimmed over her. She was just as content as I was to lay silently. It was comfortable. I knew I would miss her this next week. Maybe I could get her to come to the gym one night and workout with me. I wanted to do whatever I could to draw her into my world. Several nights a week, Ashley or Logan would stay in my apartment with Trina while I worked or worked out. If Kenzie would come during that time, I could spend time with her and not impact Trina.

Kenzie

Shadows crept across the bedroom wall. I knew it was late afternoon. I knew Andy had to go soon. I tamped down my trepidation at the prospect of being alone in my house, put on a brave face, and angled up to gaze into his eyes.

"I know you have to go soon. Please don't worry about me. Thanks to you, I have the security system and will be safe." I kissed him passionately.

"Yeah, I do," he said when our lips parted. "I'm sorry, Kenzie. I'd stay if I could, but I have to," he began.

I interrupted him mid-sentence. "You have to get your daughter. Don't apologize for that." I forced a smile. I wanted to put him at ease.

"What are your plans the rest of the day?" He asked.

"I have about an hour or two of work to do. I have a proposal that needs to be done to email to a potential client first thing in the morning. I'll sit at the kitchen table and work on it while I have dinner."

"Can I call you later, after Trina is in bed?"

I felt the smile spread across my face. "I'd like that."

"I usually put her to bed by eight, eight-thirty at the latest."

"I'll be done by then, I'm sure," I said.

He kissed me again and held me tightly. I took it in, memorizing how good it felt so I could call the memory up later when I was alone. I knew I would miss him so much this next week. It was surprising how accustomed to his presence in my life I had gotten in two short days.

"Can we take a shower before I go?" Andy asked, breaking in on my thoughts.

"Yeah, of course," I replied. I tried to pull away and get up, but he stopped me.

"What does your week look like? Any chance you could come workout with me at the gym one night this week?"

I knew I was smiling like a fool. I loved that he wanted to see me before next weekend. I was nodding yes without thinking about it. "Wednesday would work best for me," I said.

Andy

It was hard to pull myself away and walk out her door. I wanted to stay with her all night again. Once I was down the block, I pulled over and checked my phone. She armed the system. *Good girl!* I drove directly to my mom's house.

Trina threw herself at me the second I entered the house. "Daddy!"

"How's my girl?" I asked as I scooped her up in my arms and gave her a bear hug. I kissed her cheek. "Love you, baby."

"Love you, Daddy."

Mom had her hair in two high ponytails on either side of her head. My little girl was looking older every day. I held her tightly wanting to stop time. I felt my mom's hand on my shoulder. I gave her a hug too.

"Thanks for keeping Trina all weekend, Mom."

"You'll stay for dinner, won't you?" She asked with a smile.

I was hoping she'd ask. Something smelled fantastic, and she was a great cook. We stepped out the back door. I sent Trina to the sandbox. Mom and I sat at the table on the patio. The sun was low in the sky, but the temperature was still in the mid-seventies. It was a beautiful day.

"She missed you," Mom said.

"I missed her too, you know that," I defended. Mom's green eyes sparkled at me. She wasn't reprimanding me. She was looking for information. "Her name is Mackenzie. I met her Friday night. She's," I paused as I smiled at my mom. Her face held a knowing gaze. "Yeah, she's really something."

"I figured she must be. Nothing and no one has kept you away from Trina for an entire weekend."

"I can't let her meet Trina just yet. You know how I feel about that."

Mom laid her hand on mine. "Andy, you have always done right by that child. If this Mackenzie is meant to stay in your life, a few weeks of keeping her from Trina won't make a difference. Trust your instincts. They're good and have always served you well."

"So, you'll keep Trina all next weekend for me too?" I asked with a smile and a wink.

Mom laughed.

"Only if I get to meet her shortly after you introduce her to Trina."

"Deal."

CHAPTER 7

Andy

I checked the security system feed on my phone repeatedly through dinner and after Trina and I returned home. Kenzie sat at her kitchen table on her laptop the entire time. I should feel bad for watching her this way, but I didn't. I needed to watch and know she was safe. She had the cutest habit of pulling at one of her curls when she was deep in thought as she worked. I hadn't noticed her doing that at any point the previous two days.

Logan stopped by right as I put Trina in the tub. He pulled a kitchen chair up in the hallway and sat just outside the open bathroom door. I sat on the closed toilet seat while I bathed her. He filled me in on the aspects of the gym I needed to know. He had handled everything for me Saturday night and all day today.

I had text messaged him and told him about the break-in at Kenzie's the night before. He knew Kenzie had spent the night here with me last night and that I was at her house all day. He was a good friend, and he held back asking anything about it until after Trina's bath and after story time. I knew I'd get the third degree as soon as Trina's bedroom door was closed. After we both tucked her in he pulled two beers from the refrigerator and plopped himself down at my kitchen table. He didn't say a word but pinned me with his laser-focused blue eyes.

"Yes, she's worth it," I said.

"Drama or crazy?" Logan asked.

"Targeted. She's the farthest from a drama queen that I've ever met." I knew a smile spread across my face just thinking about her. "There was someone in her house when we got back there last night. I chased him out the back door."

"You can run faster than anyone I know, and that's humping an eighty-pound pack. How'd you not get him?"

"I broke off, had no idea if someone else was inside. I couldn't leave her standing there unprotected."

Logan shook his hair back as he took a long pull from his beer. "So how does this play out, Andy?"

I wish I knew. I wanted her here with me, period. I wanted her in my bed and in my life. Mom was right though. If this was meant to be, a few weeks wouldn't make a difference. I couldn't break my rule and let Trina meet her, yet. "She's going to

SAVED AT STEVENS STREET

come workout with me Wednesday night. Trina will be up here with Ashley. Mom will keep Trina all next weekend again, so I can spend it with Kenzie." I saw the glare Logan was giving me. "Trina loves being with my mom."

"I will admit I was surprised when I met her. She's not your normal type."

I laughed. "I didn't know I had a type."

His eyes considered me with a hard stare. "She has a professional job, owns her own house, short hair, soft bod, natural tits."

I laughed loudly. "Jesus, are you describing the opposite of your normal type? Oh, wait! You don't have a type per se, you fuck anything with a vagina."

"Fuck you, man," Logan said then laughed. He grabbed two more beers. "Seriously, what is it about her?"

How could I explain what it was? I didn't completely know myself. I know I had a dumb grin on my face as I considered it. "She's it, man. I don't know how I know, I just do."

"Seriously, after forty-eight hours you know she's it?"

I finished my first beer. Logan's second was already half gone. I cracked open my second and took a big swallow. "Yeah, I'm sure. Being with her is just so right."

"You need to slow this shit down," Logan warned. "I'm not going to let you short Trina." He pointed to his own chest. "God-father prerogative."

"I'm not going to short Trina and I'm not going to let Trina meet her until it's appropriate. But fuck, man. I deserve this." I wasn't sure where that had come from. "Trina deserves this. Kenzie believes in happily ever after, wants to get married and have kids. I can see how good she'd be with Trina. I think she'll make a hell of a mom to her."

"Fuck, you really need to slow this down." Logan's eyes were boring through me. "What the hell do you mean you deserve this?"

I shook my head and moaned. "Dude, my life is all about Trina and the gym; has been for the last four years. The last forty-eight hours it's been about nothing but being a man and being with this incredible woman. Being with her has been, fuck, it's been like it was before, like I'm just a man with nothing to think about but getting to know this amazing person who I just can't get enough of."

"It's about sex?" Logan asked.

"No, not entirely. It's about her. Getting to know her and relating to her in a way I haven't related to anyone in a really long time, even when we're not in bed. It's comfortable but still exciting." Logan was regarding me with a disbelieving smirk. "And yeah, it's about great sex. I can't explain it. It's not just the sex. She's so open, unlike anyone I've ever been with. She's fun and uninhibited, but not a slut. She blushes, man. I hear her laugh and want to do everything I can to hear it again. When I lay with her I," I paused seeing Logan's face. You'd think I had three heads the way he was looking at me.

"Damn, you got it bad for her."

"Yeah. She's special," I admitted.

Logan's stare was unwavering. We sat in silence for several minutes. Logan finished his beer and then came to his feet. "I'll take care of Trina whenever you need. I was wrong. You don't need to slow this shit down. You need to spend every waking second with this chick, bang her brains out, and get her the fuck out of your system."

I laughed. "And if it doesn't get her out of my system?" I was sure it wouldn't.

"Then you need to get a ring on her finger as fast as you can and settle this." He patted me on the shoulder and was out the door into the upper hallway. I heard his apartment door close.

I checked my phone. It was nearly nine. I pulled up the system info on Kenzie's alarm system. No alerts and it was armed. I checked the camera feeds. She no longer sat at her kitchen table. She wasn't in any of the camera feeds. Her bedroom door was closed. I sat in my recliner, so I could see down the hallway in case Trina got up, though she rarely did after she was put to bed. I dialed Kenzie.

She answered on the first ring. "Hi, I was wondering if you were still going to call."

"Sorry," I said. "Logan stopped by to touch bases on the gym. He was in charge the last day and a half."

"No apology needed. I was just disappointed that I may not get to say good night to you."

I smiled wide at her statement. "Did you get your work done?"

"Yeah about an hour ago. I came up to my room and was going to take a bath, but I, um," she stopped herself from saying more.

"I get it. You were nervous because of the break-in."

"Yeah, stupid, I know. I would never have thought twice about it before."

"Kenzie, it's going to take time. Don't be hard on yourself. Your house, your fortress was violated. It's going to take time to feel safe." She was quiet for a few long seconds. I could hear her breathing, so I knew she was still there. "Kenz," I said.

"Yeah, I know." She paused. I gave her a minute. "You hear about people feeling violated and think jeez, it was just a break in, get over it. But it's not that easy. I have a security system now. My doors are all locked. Jesus, even my bedroom door is locked, something I never have done, and I feel," she paused again.

After a few quiet moments, I finished her sentence. "Afraid."

"Yeah, and I told myself I wasn't going to."

"I'm sorry I'm not there with you."

Kenzie

I wanted to say me too. I wanted to ask him to come back over. But I wouldn't lay a guilt trip on him. I wiped the tears that were streaming down my face. "I know you can't be. And I can't refuse to be alone in my own house." I paused again and breathed out hard. "I'm thinking about getting a gun."

"Do you know how to shoot one?" He asked.

"My dad was a Marine, remember. He taught me how to handle a gun, though it's been several years since I've fired one."

"Let me know if you get one. I'll take you to the range for a refresher."

My lips smiled despite my tears. "Thanks. I know this is just going to take time, and it'll be okay." I know I was trying to convince myself. "Anyway, how was Trina when you got to your mom's?"

"She was good. We stayed for dinner. My mom is a fantastic cook," he said. "She's already agreed to keep Trina all next weekend. I wasn't sure what your availability was, but I wanted to be able to spend as much time with you as I could."

I felt my smile spread wider. "I like that. I'm pretty open next weekend, have no plans at all." Like any plans could be more important than spending time with him? "I know we haven't really talked about it, but Andy, I don't sleep with someone I'm not committed to. I have no interest in seeing anyone else." I breathed out nervously. I hadn't planned to put that out there. I didn't want to send him running with talk about commitment, but it just kind of came out.

I heard his sexy chuckle. "I'm glad to hear that," he said. "I honestly think I'd go ballistic if some other guy was holding you, kissing you, making love to you. I have no intention of seeing anyone else either, Kenzie. I think you're pretty special and want to see where this can go."

I felt downright giddy. My smile was so big it was hurting my face. How crazy it was to feel this good after crying just minutes before. "I think you're pretty special too, and I am so glad I met you."

"What are you wearing right now?" He asked.

I felt a blush creep up my cheeks. "That little purple nightie, you know, the one I didn't wear at your place."

I heard that sexy rumble through the phone again. I swear it made me wet. "I'd sure like to take that off you next weekend," he said.

I glanced at the empty spot in the bed he had laid in earlier. I wished he was reclined there right now. "I think that can be arranged," I flirted.

We said good night but sent flirty text messages for another hour. I'd typed out *I miss you* several times but deleted it each time. At ten-thirty he said he had to be up at five and though he hated to, he had to say goodnight. We promised we would talk and text tomorrow.

CHAPTER 8

Kenzie

I'd slept poorly, my ears homing in on every sound. The alarm system would tell me if there was an intruder and would auto dial the police. I knew I was being foolish, but I couldn't stop feeling afraid. I downed a couple cups of coffee as I got ready for work and filled my tanker to take with. I had to find out where Andy had gotten the energy drink. And I had to get another bottle of vitamins, too.

I arrived at the office on time and went straight into my boss's office. Dale Miller's face showed surprise when I shut the door. Rarely did anyone's doors get closed there. I relayed the events of the weekend to him, well the suspected roofiing with no details of waking up in a stranger's bed. I did tell him about the break-in with the tampering of my vitamins without mentioning the date with Andy. I told him a detective wanted to interview everyone from work who had been at the bar. He reluctantly agreed. At our regular Monday morning staff meeting he told all my coworkers, advising them that it was his wish that everyone made themselves available when the detective arrived.

Several of my coworkers approached me after and asked me a lot of questions. Everyone seemed supportive and shocked that something like this could happen. No one acted oddly, something Margot had told me to watch for. But still, it was uncomfortable for me.

She arrived around eleven and we set her up in the conference room, so she could conduct interviews with each of the twenty people who had been at the bar Friday night. She began with my boss.

After he had finished with Margot, he came over to my desk and leaned in close. "You made it sound like there was proof positive you were slipped something. The detective said the blood tests aren't back yet."

"Both the detective and I am sure it will come back positive."

"I'm not sure I would have granted the interview requests of all our employees had I known it was not proven yet," he said, much to my surprise.

"Why not? Dale, I know I was slipped something. If anyone saw anything suspicious, it could help. I'm not accusing any of our coworkers," I said.

Dale pointed to the conference room. "That detective sure seems to think it was one of us."

"She's just being thorough," I said. I didn't tell him she was a good friend of mine, nor did I mention that I was quite sure it was one of my co-workers.

I walked Margot out after she had spoken with everyone. Besides diagnosing several of my coworkers as falling somewhere on the Autism spectrum or exhibiting antisocial behaviors, she didn't have any suspicions of anyone. She felt everyone had tried to be cooperative, but no one had seen anything helpful. She didn't have any test results back yet, but she did have a match on some of the prints that were found on the outside of my sliding glass door.

"Do you know a Kevin York?" She asked.

"Not ringing any bells," I said. She showed me a mugshot picture on her phone. "I recognize him. He lives down the block. I don't really know him though."

"He's a registered sex offender, Kenz and his prints were all over your back sliding-glass door."

"Holy shit," I said. I clasped my hands together to keep them from shaking.

"It doesn't prove he was in your house Saturday night, but he didn't belong there so I'm going to go talk with him now. I'll go see your five co-workers who were let go after."

"You'll call me after?"

"Don't worry. I will. Stay vigilant and keep that alarm system on when your home, okay?" Margot's voice was tight.

I went back to my desk and my shaking fingers sent a text message to Andy telling him everything. I knew I wasn't mentally into work, but I didn't want to go home yet either. I could have taken a sick day, but what would I do at home besides jump at every noise? Andy messaged me back several minutes later asking if he could call. I stepped outside and sat on the smoker's picnic table. No one else was around. I called Andy.

"Are you okay, babe?" His concerned voice asked. He had not called me babe before. I liked it.

"Just a little shaken. A registered sex offender, oh my God!"

"You're not going back there alone if he isn't locked up tonight. I can get someone to stay with Trina," he said.

"Let's not get ahead of ourselves. Let's see what Margot comes up with. I was so sure it was one of my coworkers and Margot's talked to all of them, so if it was, maybe he will back off knowing the police are involved," I said.

"You say the word and I'll be there tonight," he said.

I appreciated it more than he knew. I wanted to say yes on the spot, but I couldn't take advantage of him like that. I had to be alone at my house sometime. "Thanks, Andy, I'll let you know," I said. "How's your day going?"

He laughed. "Better than yours."

I laughed as well. "Yeah, well, it wouldn't take much to top mine." Two of the smokers came out and lit up near the table. "I have to go. I'll talk to you later, okay?"

"Sure, call me when you know anything.?"

I assured him I would, and I disconnected.

Lindy Hall, one of the sales associates I knew quite well was staring at me, puffing on her cigarette. "That cop thinks it was one of the guys who work here," she said.

"She was just being thorough," I said. "This is all just surreal. This kind of stuff happens to other people."

"I've never known anyone who was roofied or who's house was broken into," she said.

"Me either," Todd Johnson, one of the Network guys chimed in. "How did you get home Friday night?" He asked.

Dread hit me, and I froze. I hadn't thought out what I'd tell anyone who asked something I wasn't going to tell the truth about. I certainly was not going to tell any of my coworkers I ended up naked in a strange man's bed.

"Your car was still in the lot at the bar when I came to get mine Saturday morning," Todd added.

"Why was your car in the lot?" I asked.

He looked kind of embarrassed. "I took an Uber home; knew I had drunk too much and I can't get another DUI."

I didn't know he had a previous DUI. He had admitted to it so casually. "That was smart," I said. "Did you really drink that much Friday night?" I asked, hoping to divert the conversation.

"Yeah, I felt really buzzed. I guess I did."

"But you don't actually remember drinking that much?" I asked. My curiosity was peaked. Could he have been roofied too? That would certainly change things.

He looked confused. "Maybe it was the mixing of the beer and the shots. I haven't done shots in a long time. I don't know how you can drink that Blue Moon shit. I chugged nearly half my pint after I accidentally took a drink of your beer. So yeah, I'm sure shot-gunning that glass helped to bring the buzz on faster, too."

"You drank some of my beer?" I asked horrified. "When was that, Todd, when in the night?"

He seemed to get what I was thinking. It hit him with an ah-ha moment, and I could damn-near see the lightbulb go on over his head. "Shit, you think it was in your beer and I drank some?"

"Think really hard about this, please, when exactly did you drink out of my glass and do you think you felt more buzzed than you should have?" I pressed. I knew my voice was pleading.

"Oh jeez, Kenzie, I don't know. It was after we ate, and the waitress took our plates away. The happy hour appetizers were out from four till six, so it was after that."

"We all went out for a smoke after they took the appetizers away," Lindy spoke up. "You came out with us that time, Kenzie."

"I went out every time." Even though I didn't smoke I tended to go out with them to be social. "Who stayed with our drinks from our group?"

Both Lindy and Todd did a palms-up and shrugged. Yeah, I couldn't remember either. "Was it after we went back inside you accidentally drank from my glass, Todd?" He shrugged again.

"It had to be," Lindy piped up. "After the last smoke break around seven-thirty, you were on the other side of the table hitting on Christie."

"I was not hitting on Christie," Todd argued.

Lindy laughed. "Oh, you were so hitting on her. I couldn't believe you were trying to get her into bed."

That wasn't like Todd. I was convinced he had drunk from my glass after the drug was added. "Todd, this is really important. How much did you drink? Think!"

"Sorry, Kenzie, I don't remember. I know I did the five shots, just like everyone else. I remember ordering at least three beers. It could have been more."

"Can I have the detective talk to you both again about this? This could be important. If we can narrow down the timeframe of when the drug was slipped into my drink, we might be able to figure out who. And I don't know if anything would still be in your system, but I'm wondering if we should have your blood tested too."

"Fuck," Todd swore. "No blood, Kenz. It's going to show drugs. I went out partying with some friends Saturday night."

"Oh, okay," I said, surprised. He'd done recreational drugs Saturday night and just admitted it. Who did that?

"But I'll talk to the detective again. She took my phone number. Tell her to call anytime after nine and I'll talk to her then. I've got bowling tonight."

I didn't know he was on a bowling league. I guess I didn't know much about him at all. I thanked him. Lindy was available to chat with Margot any time after six. I went back to my desk and tried to get some work done.

"How are you holding up?" Marcus Holland's familiar voice asked, pulling my eyes up from my laptop. He stood near my desk, which wasn't unusual.

"Hi Marcus," I said with a smile. "I'm okay."

"You really think you were roofied or something?" He asked quietly.

I knew Marcus pretty well. We had gone on more than a dozen on-sites and as far as the geek-guys went, he was more normal than most of them. I breathed out heavily, almost sorry I had brought all this into the office. "Yeah, I do. I'm really sorry Detective Malone made it sound like she suspected someone from the office. She's just looking out for me."

"I hope you don't suspect me, Kenzie. I thought we were friends," he said even quieter.

"Oh, Marcus, no. I don't actively suspect anyone. She was really just looking to see if anyone saw someone else, not in our group, hanging around or watching me. Or if anyone else approached our table at any point," I said, trying to deflect my suspicion of everyone in our group.

"Well, if you need anyone to walk you to your car at night, or need anything at all, just let me know," he offered.

"That's so nice of you Marcus, thank you," I said.

"I mean it, just let me know, anything you need," he said again. He smiled and moved away from my desk.

Margot sent me a text message right before I was getting ready to leave asking me when I'd be home. She'd meet me there. I felt anxious as I turned onto my street until I saw her force-issued sedan sitting in front of my house. She met me inside my garage again.

I grabbed us both a beer from the refrigerator. She declined. She was still on duty. I popped mine open anyway and took a swig for courage. I still hadn't told her about my conversation with Todd and Lindy.

"Kevin York copped to peeping at you and every other woman on the block but is adamant he didn't roofie you or break-in Saturday night," Margot said. My eyes went to my sliding glass door. "You really need to get some curtains for it."

"Yeah, I've been meaning to," I said. I chugged my beer.

"It's enough to keep him locked up until he is arraigned tomorrow. With his record, it might be enough to put him back inside," Margot said in her most efficient cop voice.

Jail? He'd be locked up tonight and maybe go back to prison. I felt a sense of relief. I finished my beer while telling Margot about the conversation with Lindy and Todd. Then she told me about her dialogs with the five men who had lost their jobs. She didn't get any bad vibes from four of them, but one, she wanted to take a closer look at.

"That Randy Halverson, he's defensive and pissed."

"What's he pissed about?"

"Being let go. He said ATS owes him a lot more than the package he got, claims some of his intellectual property was ripped off by ATS. He's got some real anger issues. I'd steer clear of him if I was you."

"Given he no longer works there, that won't be a problem," I said. I hadn't known Randy well. He worked in the Geek-room where they kept the technical nerds and he was never assigned to any of my projects. He worked mostly alone doing the coding for conversions.

"I got the sense he was being dishonest about something. I'm going to stay on him."

Margot promised she would reach back out to both Lindy and Todd. "By the way, I had to open this as an official investigation. You've filed an official report now," she informed me. "I should have the test results back tomorrow. I'll call you as soon as I get them."

I thanked her, walked her out, and then locked up and armed the alarm system. Knowing that sex-offender was locked up for the night, I felt relieved even though I didn't think he had roofied me. I was convinced it was someone from my job. I called Andy and told him everything. We talked for over an hour. He promised he'd call me again after he had Trina in bed. I ate dinner and saw my birth control pill pack on the counter as I stacked my dishwasher. I had skipped Sunday's pill, so I took both, chastising myself for forgetting it. I had to get my head back on straight. I settled in bed by eight to watch some television and relax. I was exhausted.

Andy

"I won't need you to stay with Trina tonight," I told Logan who stood in the office with me. I had stepped outside to talk with Kenzie but returned inside the gym when we ended the call. "They have that fucking pervert locked up for the night."

"Fuck, man, a registered sex offender in her neighborhood. Did she know what he was?"

"I don't think so."

"There's supposedly a website you can go on and look up registered sex offenders in your neighborhood. We should probably check into that. We don't want any of that shit near Trina," Logan said.

"Fuck, I don't want it in this gym. Is it legal to check out my members and cancel their memberships if they're registered?" I plopped down in my desk chair. I felt so relieved that guy was locked up. He was damn lucky I didn't catch him if that was him fleeing Kenzie's house Saturday night. "I'll keep it away from Trina, obviously, but I wanted you to know I took a gun out of the safe this afternoon. I think till this shit going on with Kenzie is resolved I should keep it easily accessible."

Logan pinned me with his eyes. They were icy. "You going to tell Ashley?"

I slowly shook my head. She didn't need to know about anything deadly. "She's not one of us, wouldn't understand."

Logan understood my meaning. "Good call. She's come a long way, but she's not there yet."

I had a late session scheduled with a client for personal training. He walked in and greeted both of us. I pulled myself up and put on my game face. A one-hour, one-on-one session and then I'd be up in my apartment with Trina for the night, on the phone with Kenzie after Trina was in bed. I hadn't gotten in my workout as planned as I had been on the phone with Kenzie. I'd have to make sure to squeeze a long one in tomorrow.

After Trina was in bed, I laid on my bed and called Kenzie. My hand found its way to my cock in anticipation of hearing her voice. I wanted to get naughty on the phone with her tonight, maybe send each other some risqué pics. Her phone rang six times before her very sleepy voice answered.

"Babe, I'm sorry, did I wake you?"

"It's okay," she mumbled. "I came up and laid down with the TV on to wait for your call. I didn't think I'd fall asleep. I was pretty tired though, didn't sleep well last night."

"I'm sorry," I said. "Maybe you will sleep better if you leave the TV on, some background noise."

"Yeah, maybe," she agreed.

"Look, I'm going to let you go so you can get back to sleep. We'll talk tomorrow morning sometime, okay?"

"And I'll see you tomorrow night. Just don't kill me with the workout," she said with a little laugh.

I was happy she had remembered and still planned to come to the gym tomorrow night. Unable to will my erection down, I took a shower and jacked off, my thoughts going over every luscious curve on her body. I loved her soft natural breast and the fullness of her kneadable ass. Too many women had ass cheeks harder than mine. Might get some guys off, but not me. I liked my women soft and curvy with no implants falsifying who they were.

I settled into bed early and thought about how I could get in a quickie with Kenzie while she was here tomorrow night. I thought about bending her over a weight bench, her legs wrapped around my waist as she dangled from a barbell resting high on a rack, and even thought about how hot she'd look naked in the middle of the sparring ring down in the MMA training area in the basement. I drifted off at some point but woke with a raging hard-on. I clearly woke with the same thoughts I had fallen asleep with.

Kenzie

I was nervous waiting for Margot. It was just after nine a.m. and I had only been at work for an hour when she called to find out where I was. She had some of the test results and wanted to come see me. She wouldn't tell me over the phone. That spoke volumes to me. My phone vibrated. She was in the parking lot. My heart was pounding as my steps brought me to the passenger side door of her car. I opened it and dread really settled over me when I saw her face. I'd never seen her look so serious.

"What is it?" My voice was a whisper, all I could manage.

"Your blood test results, and your vitamins show the same drug." When I got dizzy, I realized I wasn't breathing. She gave me the scientific name as well as the street name for the hallucinogen I'd been given. I'd never heard of it. "The good news is it's not addictive," she added. "You're not breathing Kenz."

I sucked in a breath. "I can't believe this," I said. "Now what?"

"I plan on talking with Andy Stevens again, maybe bring him in."

Her words hit me like a splash of ice-cold water to the face. "Margot, no. I just know Andy had nothing to do with this."

"He was with you either when it happened or shortly afterward. I can't ignore his arrest record, Kenzie. And you know he's a Vet who saw combat. Some of those guys just aren't right in the head any longer."

"Jesus, Margot! Nothing like jumping to conclusions and being prejudice." I stared at her in disbelief. "What about Saturday night? Someone was in my house when we got back, messing with my vitamins."

"I'm going to look real hard at that friend of his, John Logan. That guy has an arrest record too. Mostly drunk and disorderly's, bar fights, and a resisting arrest. Neither of these guys are altar boys, Kenz."

"You promised me you wouldn't focus on only him, that you'd still look at my coworkers. Margot, that drug hit me when I was in the bathroom. My glass hadn't been alone and I'm sure someone from my group would have noticed someone like Andy if he had come up to our table."

"I'm just going to dot some I's and cross some T's with him, okay? If Andy is innocent, he has nothing to worry about."

I covered my eyes with my hand. This could not be happening. Andy would run as fast as he could away from me. To have Margot barge in there and accuse him, or actually bring him in, was something he just didn't deserve. If I were him, I would never forgive me.

"Damn it, Margot! Please, for me. Don't do it this way. Give him a chance, will you? I really like this guy," I admitted.

"When he took you home with him Saturday night, the smug look on his face made me want to arrest him on the spot for something, anything. You don't know how hard it was for me to let you go out the door with him."

"I'm not gay, Margot! I just can't feel for you, the way you feel about me. You're clearly jealous of him."

Margot laughed and rolled her eyes at the ceiling. "That isn't what this is about. I accepted a long time ago that you and I are and will always just be friends. I made my peace with it and prefer to have you as a friend than not in my life. I'm not carrying a torch for you. One day, I hope to stand up for you at your wedding to some lucky guy."

"And that just may be Andy," I told her. "Please, go easier on him. Talk to him and ask him about his record. He is amazingly open and honest. He'll tell you anything you want to know, I'm sure."

"Interrogations don't work that way, Kenz."

"But conversations do. Please, try it my way and if you're not satisfied, then you can go hard on him, for me," I begged.

She agreed. Her car wasn't even out of the parking lot when I dialed Andy. I cut off his pleasant greeting. "Andy, I'm sorry. You have to listen to me. She'll be there soon, and you have to know."

"You're not making sense, babe," he said.

"Margot. She got the test results back. Both my blood and my vitamins showed an illegal street drug. She's coming there to you now. I'm sorry, Andy."

"What? She still thinks I had something to do with it?" I could hear the anger in his voice.

"I don't and that's all that matters. It's your record, the arrest when you went after Trina's mom. You need to tell her the whole story. Andy, I know if you talk to her and just be yourself, she'll drop this and like you." I had to stop myself from saying that she'd love him.

"She has feelings for you, you know that, don't you?"

"Once she sees you're legit and that you really care for me, she will be okay. She just doesn't want me to get hurt."

"That wasn't what I meant," he said.

"I know." There was a pause. I knew he was looking for more. "Please, keep your cool with her and just be honest. I don't want her to find a reason to bring you in. Do it for me, please," I pleaded.

"Anything for you, babe."

"Call me after she leaves?" I asked.

Andy

Gazing out the front window I saw Margot pull up. "I will. She's here now," I said and then I disconnected.

Margot's walk showed determination. Her eyes flitted to my phone, her face showing annoyance. "Andy Stevens," she said in an official voice.

"Welcome, Detective. Kenzie said you would be coming by." Out of the corner of my eye, I saw Logan approaching. "Logan, can you please watch the shop?" I turned to Margot. "I thought we'd talk up in my apartment this time."

She nodded stiffly. I led her through the gym, and up the stairs. I entered in my lock code on the door that separated the gym and the three apartments and then again on the lock to my apartment. We entered my apartment. She looked around taking in every detail. Her eyes focused longer on the many toys scattered all around and on Trina's drawings on the fridge. Good, exactly my intention.

I pointed to my living room area and then the kitchen table. "Where would you like to talk?" She looked over the many family photos I proudly displayed on the wall across from the kitchen that ran down the hallway. I could see she stared at the picture of Trina and me at the zoo from earlier in the spring. I held her in my arms to lift her high enough to see over a railing. It was one of my favorites. "That's my daughter, Trina, my life. She's at preschool right now. I have her enrolled at Zion Lutheran in their four-day, full-day program."

Margot wandered back to my kitchen table and sat. I offered her a bottle of water. She declined, but I got one for myself. "Kenzie couldn't remember the name of the drug you found. How bad is the shit?"

"It could have been worse," Margot admitted.

"Margot, I promise you, I had nothing to do with it, any of it. Ask me anything you want, give me a lie detector test, whatever you need to do to stop looking at me, and get to work finding the scumbag who did this to her."

"You'd voluntarily take a lie detector test?" She questioned.

"If that's what you need. We'll go do it now. Margot, I think Kenzie is special. I really like her a lot. I want to see where this can go with her. I don't play games with women. I'm looking to settle down with the right someone. I've got Trina to think about. I want her to have a stepmother who is special, who wants to get married and have kids, herself. In her drugged-state Friday night, Kenzie told me she does want to get married and have kids. And I can tell she'd be an amazing mother. So yeah, I want this issue resolved as soon as possible so we can see where it can go."

"Trina's mother is out of your lives," she said it as though she knew, knew the whole story.

"She gave up all rights the day Trina was born. She'd never planned on being a mother, was going to sell her in a private adoption scam. She tried to buy me off with $100-K when the paternity test proved I was the father. I was still willing to try, hoping she'd change her mind when Trina was born. How could you hold your child in your arms and not want them? In retrospect, it was the best thing for Trina. She's a happy, well-adjusted four-year-old, not sure that would be the case if her mother had stayed in her life in any way. If you haven't read the whole file, the long and short of it was that I did stalk and unlawfully restrain her, and I was arrested.

She was trying to get away and disappear before the paternity test results came in. There was enough money involved in the adoption, she very well could have disappeared. I wouldn't let that happen. I just knew it was my baby, and my baby wasn't going to get sold to the highest bidder." I knew I sounded angry. I still couldn't get past it. I shook with fear every time I thought about my little angel never being a part of my life. "The judge in the case awarded me full custody and told me he was proud of my dedication to my daughter and to doing the right thing. I did everything the court asked of me. The judge took a chance on me when he saw how badly I wanted to make it work, raising Trina on my own."

"Your friend John Logan, he has a record too," she said.

"Yeah, Logan had a hard time adjusting after our time in the Army was up. We both served ten years, most of it in the same unit over in the sandbox. We saw some shit over there, shit no one should have to see. It's hard to come home for some after that and adjust to life where Facebook statuses, keeping up with Kardashians, and all the other trivial shit so many people focus on is important. He got counseling and came through the other side. I wouldn't have let him anywhere near Trina if he hadn't." I chuckled a little. "It was actually Trina that helped bring him out of it. He loves that little girl as much as I do. He's her godfather, and he takes the role very seriously."

Margot seemed to consider what I was telling her carefully. She went back over to the family picture wall. There were several with Logan and Ashley in them, as well as my mom, dad, and four siblings. I hoped the pictures portrayed that Trina was the center of our lives and we had created a good life for her. I hoped that Margot would know that for me to do that, it would make it impossible for me to do any harm to Kenzie, to anyone.

"She's a cute little girl. Looks very happy in all these pictures."

"She's the center of all our lives. I will only let the right woman be in her life. I'm not desperate for a mother for her. She has plenty of good female role models. I have a strict policy of not letting her meet anyone I'm seeing if I'm not very serious about her. I don't want to confuse her or hurt her. She's only met one woman I've seen." I shrugged. "Being a single dad, I honestly don't date much. Trina and running my business takes up most my time. And I'm very choosy about who I spend time with. So yeah, Kenzie is very special."

"If you're BS-ing me, I'll find something to arrest you for," Margot warned. I could tell it was for show though. I had gotten through to her.

"I'm not. Everything I've told you is the truth. Did you want to go do that lie detector test now?" I asked.

"No, but I reserve the right to call you on it anytime."

"Fair enough."

I walked her back down to the gym where Logan stood nervously near the front windows, near the door. He noticeably relaxed when he saw I wasn't in cuffs.

"Detective," he said with a nod.

"Mr. Logan," she replied. Her eyes shot a warning to him.

Kenzie

I was nervous as I pushed through the door into Andy's gym. I had changed at work into a pair of those skin-tight crop pants like Ashley, the young woman who had been behind the counter Saturday afternoon, wore. I had gone out at lunch and bought them. I had a loose-fitting short sleeved t-shirt on that hung low to below my hips. I couldn't bring myself to wear a tight tank top like Ashley and many of the other women I had seen in the gym wear. Unlike Ashley, I didn't have the body for it.

Andy's friend Logan stood near the door. I had text messaged Andy when I arrived. He was initially nowhere in sight.

"Hey, Kenzie," Logan greeted me with a smile. "How are you doing?" He closed the distance between us and shook my hand.

"Good, thanks. You?"

Then his hand settled on my shoulder. "Andy will be down in a second. He just went up to make sure Trina was settled with Ashley before you got started. He didn't want to get interrupted."

"That sounds intense," I said with a laugh. I looked around. I was in a serious gym, about to have a workout session with my sexy, muscled man who no doubt knew everything there was to know about building muscle and getting into shape, something my body lacked. I only hoped I could walk tomorrow.

Just then Andy descended the stairs across the gym. So, that was the staircase up to his apartment. I had only used the outside, back stairs. His eyes locked on mine and his lips curved into a smile that left no doubt he was glad to see me. I probably had the same dumb grin on my face as well. I felt like a thirteen-year-old with her first crush.

"Hey, babe," he greeted me with a squeeze to my shoulder.

No kiss though. He was keeping work and our personal relationship separate. I respected that. "Hi," I said. "How was the rest of your day?" He knew I meant after we had talked after Margot left.

"Good, quiet. I got in a good workout this afternoon, so this time is all about you," he said with a wink.

"Look out, Kenzie, he's in personal trainer mode," Logan joked.

"Just remember this body hasn't seen the inside of a gym in too many years to count," I said it in a joking voice, but it was the truth.

"No worries, babe," Andy said. "I've got you." His confidence was sexy.

The hour spent with Andy was the most fun exercising I ever had. We started out doing ten minutes of cardio on an elliptical machine to warm up. Then he led me over to the weighted machines I hadn't used in years. I had no idea how to adjust the seats, how much weight to use, or how many reps to do. I didn't have to even think about it though, Andy had it all handled. He kept the weight light this time for him to watch me and instruct me, but promised he would increase the weight to my max next time. He was already planning the next time. We talked about what our days had been like, and even quietly whispered about the drug results and more about his conversation with Margot. I was so focused on him and our conversation I truly noticed no one and nothing else going on around me. Just being with him put me at such ease. I assumed he made all his clients feel this way.

After the workout, we sat in his office and continued our conversation, making plans for the weekend. We planned the entire weekend together. Logan popped in, just as we were getting ready to leave. Andy was going to walk me out to my car.

"You can walk okay? He didn't kill you?" Logan asked. He was joking. I laughed. "It was great to see you. Don't be a stranger," he said, his hand on my shoulder again. I saw Andy flash a look at him I couldn't decipher.

"It was nice to see you too. Take care," I said as I moved to the door. I was parked in the side lot. Andy led me out the door by the hand. I motioned back towards the building. "What was that about?"

"What, Logan?" He asked. I nodded. "I told you. Logan is as protective of me as Margot is of you."

He pressed me against my car, his pelvis against mine and he kissed me. I didn't care about anything, about Logan, or Margot. I felt him grow hard up against me as we continued to kiss, our hands stroking over each other.

"I can't tell you how badly I want you," he whispered in my ear.

The wanting was mutual. "Is there anywhere we can?" I begged but silenced myself when a man's voice coughed, and a large, dark figure walked past.

"Andy, ma'am," a deep voice greeted.

"Butch," Andy acknowledged him by name and told me he was one of the members. I was embarrassed. I wasn't normally a make-out in the parking lot kind of girl. "Come with me," Andy said. He led me by the hand to the back of the building.

Andy

The garage was the only place I could think of where Kenzie and I could be alone. I opened the side door and led her into the dark space. The only window that let any light in was the window on the door. The two-car structure was filled with shadows.

I led her up to the passenger side of my truck. I'd nearly made love to her in it Saturday night. I'd not lose that opportunity tonight.

"I can't wait till Friday night," I said. It sounded strangled, even to me. My cock was hard in anticipation.

She kissed me passionately, pressing her body completely against me. She agreed. I had us both naked as the day we were born in seconds. I took her right on the bench seat, starting with a good tongue-lashing. She tried to grab my cock for some oral reciprocation, but I stopped her. I was so aroused it wasn't going to take much for me to explode. I'd left the truck door open, so I could see her face and her body in the dim light as we did what we did. Seeing the pleasure on her face as she moaned and gasped was the biggest turn-on. I gave her two orgasms with my mouth before I mounted her.

She followed my instruction without question and raised her feet to the ceiling. Taking a handful of butt cheek in each hand I raised her up and rolled her in a way I knew would, at this angle, line my cock up with her g-spot and expose her swollen and sensitive clit to my parts for deeper pleasure. The orgasm that immediately tore through her, her insides milking my shaft with a steel grip, proved she liked it. Her guttural moans quickly became screams, which mine drowned out seconds later when an orgasm so powerful hit me, I saw stars and got dizzy.

We lay there holding each other, kissing and caressing for quite some time. I loved how she was comfortable in her own skin. It didn't matter to her that we were naked in a garage across the truck seat. She seemed as comfortable as she did in a bed.

She had to leave. We reluctantly said goodbye, but I would call her again once Trina was in bed. The registered sex-offender neighbor was still locked up. I could tell she was relieved by that. She promised she would be careful and text me after she was home and safely inside with the alarm system back on and armed.

When I re-entered the gym, I found Logan and Butch in the heavyweight room. It was my intention to check in quickly with Logan before retreating to my apartment to relieve Ashley. I wanted some time with Trina before I put her to bed.

Butch had become a friend shortly after he had joined the gym. He was a fireman at the station a few streets over. His crew covered the entire old downtown area, good people to know. His black hair grew longer every time I saw him lately. He wore it in a ponytail tonight, I wasn't sure how he got away with that at work.

"The first thing he says to me when he walks in," Logan said pointing to Butch, "was, since when does Andy Stevens get a piece of ass in the parking lot." He was laughing like a fool.

"Fuck you," I groaned at Logan.

"But then we saw you go into the garage on the security cam, and I knew you were getting it in the garage, probably across the front seat in that sweet truck of yours," Butch teased. His face was stone serious though. That made it all the funnier.

I burst out in laughter. "Go ahead, be jealous, boys. I think you can expect to see Kenzie around here a lot."

Butch's eyebrows shot up as he finished his lift, dropping the barbell loaded with weights back to the floor. "I've got to meet this woman who's made the cut to be granted that status."

"No, she hasn't met Trina yet," I clarified. "Soon, though, if things keep going the way they are." I saw Logan's glare of warning. I usually loved that he was as protective of Trina as I was, but with this, he was being a pain in the ass. He knew I wanted to find a good woman to marry and settle down with, to be a mother to Trina. Certainly, he knew it would happen sooner or later. I was wondering if anyone would make the cut as far as he was concerned. "Speaking of which, I'm going up to be with Trina now. You'll take care of everything." I said to Logan.

"You know I will," he answered.

CHAPTER 9

Kenzie

I was less nervous as I entered my house. Just knowing that my neighbor was still locked up helped a lot. I entered the proper code into my security system and knew that it was armed. No one would get in without me and the police knowing. That put me at ease. I was still dancing on air from my evening with Andy. Having sex in his truck! I felt like a teenager again.

I hadn't brought my laptop in. I didn't plan to do any work tonight. It was already later than I liked to get home. I needed to eat something and then Andy would call again after Trina was in bed. I planned to be up in my room when that call came.

Unfortunately, my evening didn't work out that way. I checked my work email on my phone after I sent a text to Andy letting him know I was safely in my house. The potential clients I'd sent the proposal to, wanted some minor revisions in terms by the next morning. That was when they were deciding. I retrieved my laptop, sat at my kitchen table and got to work while eating a sandwich.

My phone rang as I was putting the finishing touches on the revised proposal. It was Andy. I couldn't believe it was already that late. As I brought the phone to my ear, I couldn't help but smile as I said "hello."

"Hi babe, how's your evening been?"

"Not as I planned. I had to revise the proposal I did over the weekend. The client needs it by nine tomorrow."

"Do you want to call me back when you're done?" He asked.

I think I smiled wider. I closed the lid to my laptop. "Nah, I'd rather talk with you than finish it now. I've been working on it since I got home." I sat back in my chair and relaxed. "You already got Trina to bed, huh?" It was so odd. I'd never met his little girl, but I felt this fondness for her.

"Yeah, it took two stories tonight. It usually does when I'm not with her until right before bedtime. Ashley already had her in her pajamas, which helped save time."

"Ashley was the blonde behind the counter when I came in Saturday?" I asked.

"Yeah. She and Logan live above the gym too. They both help a lot with Trina."

"They live together?" I asked. That would explain why Logan felt comfortable telling her not to be a bitch when I was there.

"Ashley and Logan?" He said then laughed. "No, they aren't together. I can't even imagine what that would look like. They each have their own place."

I relayed how Ashley acted towards me and what Logan had said to her when I came in Saturday. He seemed surprised she acted that way, but not surprised by Logan. "I'm not trying to get her into trouble or anything, but if I was a woman thinking about joining the gym the once over, she gave me would have had me changing my mind. No, I'm not in the shape she is in and I know it, but I didn't need her eyes telling me either," I said.

"I'm glad you told me," Andy said.

"Please don't tell her I did. If I come work out with you again and she's there, I don't want her to think I was trying to rat her out or anything. I don't do girl drama and I sense there could be some there with her."

Andy chuckled. "You're pretty damn good at reading people I'd say. Ashley's come a long way, but she still has a way to go yet. And what's this talk about if you come work out again? Didn't you have a good time with me tonight?"

I felt the smile spread over my face. I may have even blushed as the memories of the hot sex in his truck came back to me. "Of course, I did. Okay, I mean next time I come work out with you."

"That's better," he said. He sounded quite satisfied with himself. I had to laugh at the edge his voice had to it.

Andy

After I said good night to Kenzie, I just sat in my recliner thinking about her and the time we had spent together. I wished we could have talked longer. I just loved the sound of her voice and the companionship talking with her brought me. I should have felt bad that I was watching her on her camera as we talked, but I didn't. I loved how she smiled when she had seen it was me calling, and at several times during our conversation. I could hear in her words how happy she was but seeing that beautiful smile on her face really got me. Logan had been right the other night when he told me I needed to figure this out and settle it. I knew she was it, and I knew I had to do something sooner, rather than later to make her a part of my life, a part of Trina's life. What I wouldn't give to have her here with me! We'd tuck Trina in together and then go to bed, ourselves. Now I was smiling at the thought of it.

The next morning, I asked Logan about the incident with Ashley that Kenzie had told me about.

"Yeah, don't you remember? Ashley was a total bitch Saturday morning. And it wasn't even the morning after one of her Ring Girl nights," Logan said. I didn't remember. I guess I didn't interact too much with her that morning after bringing Kenzie to her car.

"Have you ever seen her act that way to any other woman who's come into the gym?" I asked. I couldn't have her turning off and turning away customers.

Logan shrugged. "I don't know, but I was going to talk with you about her and what we can do to get her to stop doing the Ring Girl thing. The first Saturday and Sunday of the month she's always a bitch, either that or it just happens to align with her monthly."

I laughed. "Yeah, don't say that to her or any other woman."

It was true though. I had noticed a spike in her bitchiness after a Ring Girl night. I wasn't sure what went on when she did that. It was one of the last things from her past life she had held on to. I couldn't imagine the money was that good, but I could be wrong. I never asked, and she never talked about it. I just knew that the first Friday of the month she couldn't work. I'd have to check with Mason and Blake, who ran the MMA training in the basement of the gym about it. They were present at all the Friday night fights.

I personally couldn't understand what Ashley got out of it if it wasn't the money. To prance around half naked in front of a bunch of drunk, horny men who were ogling her tits and ass as nothing more than sex objects while she held a number indicating what round the fight was in, was beyond me. I should probably go check a fight out one night, just to see if it was as bad as I envisioned. I knew I would never want my daughter doing it, that was for sure.

"You going to talk to her about it?" Logan asked.

Now I shrugged. "I kind of promised Kenzie I wouldn't tell Ashley she told me, so I'm not sure how to talk to her about it without letting her know where the info came from."

Ashley was just coming down the stairs. "That's easy," Logan said. "Hey Ash," he called her over. "Andy's planning on taking the weekend off to be with Kenzie again. I just want to be sure you're not going to be as big of a bitch this Saturday as you were last week before I agree to spend that much time with you."

Ashley's face showed instant anger. Oh shit! Wrong move Logan! "Fuck you, Logan," she spat. I didn't blame her. I would have reacted that way too.

"Is there a problem I should know about Ashley?" I asked.

"No problem with me, boss," she said, but I could tell that there was a major problem she wasn't telling me just from her attitude. I paused, staring at her. I knew when you said nothing to her, she tended to fill in the silence. "You want to play with your new friend again all weekend it's not my business. Will you be up in your place again or are you staying at hers this weekend? If you're here, I don't get why you aren't covering the floor for at least a few hours. Being on with asshole," she said nodding at Logan, "is no treat for me."

So, that was it. She must have seen Kenzie and me leaving my apartment. Shit, I thought Ashley and I were past this kind of crap. "I put in well over sixty hours every single week and have never told you even once you couldn't have time off. I've rearranged my plans many times to cover for you. You're scheduled this weekend. It's Logan who's helping me out, so, what's the problem?" I pinned her with a glare I don't think I'd used since my Army days dealing with subordinates. I took no pleasure in it. But she had to know this was inappropriate and not her place to question me. Even though our relationship was way beyond just boss and employee, I was still her boss and she was still my employee.

She tossed a hand up between us dismissively. "Nothing."

Now I was really pissed. "Both of you, the office, now."

She huffed out a loud sigh and marched into the office. Logan and I exchanged looks that showed we were on the same page. I closed the door behind me. I pointed at Ashley. "If this is a problem between you and Logan let's get it out now. But if it's between you and me, and it's what I think it is, I'm just going to tell you once, back the fuck off."

"You don't understand, Andy," she said.

"Enlighten me."

Logan chuckled. "So, which is it, Ash? You got a problem with me or Andy, or are you on your period?"

Oh crap, he so did not go there! "Fuck you, Logan," she erupted. He deserved it. "I don't have a problem with either one of you, okay?"

"So, you have a problem with Kenzie then?" I said.

"Is that her name?" She just stared at me with the bitchiest expression. I was done with her drama. I don't do drama, period. She knew it. Her nose was really out of joint if she was acting this way.

"If you would have introduced yourself, like I did, instead of being a bitch to her, you would have known her name," Logan said.

"You were a bitch to Kenzie?" I asked. "What the fuck, Ash?"

"I don't know," she said. "Maybe I just need to get laid like you guys."

Logan laughed. "Have you looked in the mirror recently Ash? All you have to do is go somewhere and put it out there and I guarantee you'll have plenty of takers."

"Give us a minute, will you Logan?" He looked relieved as he left the office and closed the door. "Ash, I'm only going to tell you this one time. My personal life is none of your business. It has nothing to do with the work you do here or the time you spend with Trina."

"You know our relationship goes a hell of a lot further than boss and employee."

I nodded my head. "We both do. I owe you big time for what you did for me, but I also think you owe me for helping to get you out of that life and giving you the chance to turn things around, which you have. I'd never let you near Trina if you hadn't. I'm proud of you Ash, you know I am. Trina loves you and you're a permanent part of her life, no matter what my relationship status is. I am going to find the right woman to marry and be a mom to Trina, and even then, that won't change anything with Trina and you. As long as you want to be in her life you will be." Tears were in Ashley's eyes. "Kenzie just may be that woman," I added. "So, I would really appreciate it if you were nice to her."

"Seriously, after one weekend?" Ashley didn't hide her surprise.

"Yeah, after one weekend, daily phone calls, and she was here working out with me last night too."

"I knew it. When you came up, I knew you had just had sex," she said shaking her head.

"Ash, that is none of your damn business!" I exploded. "What the fuck do you think is going to happen when you act this way? I don't do drama, you know that. Logan and I are going to call you on it every time. That shit doesn't fly here."

She started to cry. "Andy, I'm sorry. I was just surprised. You haven't had a woman spend the night in a really long time. And she didn't look like just a pickup, a random fuck. She's got relationship written all over her."

"Stay out of my personal business, Ashley," I warned her. "Trina will be with my mom all weekend and I'll be at Kenzie's. Cover your shifts and do your job."

"Andy, I'm sorry."

I wrapped my arms around her and hugged her. "Talk to me next time, Ash. Don't let it bring out the bad in you. You're better than this."

She embraced me back. "Thanks, boss."

CHAPTER 10

Kenzie

My timer chimed on the oven and I rushed over. I inserted the meat thermometer and smiled as it quickly rose to the needed temperature. My pork loin was done. I checked the time. Andy was due any minute. I turned the oven off and pulled the roast from the oven, setting it to the back burners on the stove. In front of the roasting pan, my hollandaise sauce was done, the heat reduced to low. The asparagus was in the steamer, ready to be turned on when he arrived. I hoped he liked asparagus, not everyone did. I had beautifully prepared two bowls with gourmet salads. They were in the refrigerator with a bottle of white wine. I was excited to cook this dinner for us. I was excited for Andy to spend all weekend at my house.

I had left work early, comp time that was due me. I had taken a bath and shaved my legs, and other places too. I was dressed in my favorite lacy underwear set beneath a clingy dress with a plunging neckline that revealed the lacy edge of the bra. I felt sexy and very feminine. I had even arranged candles in my bedroom, had prepared a perfect night for us in every way.

My cell phone chirped, a text message from Andy. He was outside my garage on his bike. I opened the garage door and watched him pull into my garage. He parked next to my car. Wow! That looked so right. I closed the garage door as he grabbed a backpack from his saddlebag and walked to me. He moved with such confidence and strength. I knew I had really fallen for him. A moment of insecurity hit me, and the thought crossed my mind again how great he was, wondering what he saw in me. If this ended, it would really crush me.

"Hey babe," he greeted me with a kiss as he reached me. "Wow, you look great," he said, his eyes looking me over. He stepped into the kitchen behind me. "Damn, something smells incredible." He looked over the stove. "Babe, you didn't have to go to this much trouble, we could have just ordered a pizza." I'm sure I looked disappointed. He flashed a big smile at me. "But I'm glad you did." He peeled the foil up from around the roast. "This looks fantastic. You're going to spoil me. The only time I eat this good is when I eat at my mom's house. I cook the basics for Trina and me, nothing this fancy though." He dipped his finger in the hollandaise sauce. "Mmmm," he moaned.

I turned the burner on under the asparagus. "Hope you like asparagus," I said.

He nodded yes as he moved in and kissed me again. It was one of those kisses that weakened my knees and made me want to turn the stove off and take him to my room now. When he kissed me like that nothing else mattered and I felt no insecurities. I moaned my disapproval when he pulled away. He sat his backpack by the stairs and draped his leather jacket over the back of one of my kitchen chairs. I liked having his stuff at my house. I liked having him at my house. My eyes swept over every inch of him. He wore a dark green Henley shirt that hugged his incredible shoulders and arms. The color accentuated his vibrant green eyes, not that I needed anything to draw my eyes to his.

I opened the wine, and we ate our salads. Our conversation flowed easily as we ate the entire meal. It felt comfortable, but the underlying desire to go up to my room and enjoy each other naked was there every second. He was disappointed when I told him I couldn't come work out at the gym with him this week. I had an on-site in Phoenix. My flight left early Wednesday. I wouldn't be back until Saturday morning.

Andy

"Can't you come to the gym Tuesday or Monday to work out after work?" I knew I was being too demanding. It was just a surprise that I wouldn't see her until Saturday after she got back from Phoenix. I didn't like it.

"I can't Tuesday. I'm usually busy the night before getting last minute specs in for the install. We'll see about Monday," she promised. "I'm glad we have all weekend."

"I'm sorry. I didn't mean to sound like that. I was just hoping to see you midweek again," I said. She smiled, liking that I wanted to see her. She came to her feet and began to gather the dishes. I didn't want to waste any more time. I too rose and took hold of her, a palm to each side of her face. I kissed her like there was no tomorrow and pressed her against the counter. Our hands roamed freely over each other and I knew I had to take her to her room or I'd have her right there on her counter. I pulled her towards the stairs, still kissing her.

"The dishes," she moaned.

"They'll be here when we're done. They'll wait. I can't," I said.

I grabbed my bag on the way up the stairs. She pulled me into her bedroom. The bed was made with the covers pulled back and about a million throw pillows piled at the head of it. The sheets were a rich red color, sexy and inviting. A dim light on the table in the corner near the overstuffed chair in front of the window cast shadows everywhere, creating an inviting atmosphere in the room painted a rich, deep beige color. She lit several candles on the dresser tops as we entered. The glow was warm and set a sensual mood. She bit her lower lip as she smiled a lust-filled gaze at me from under her thick eyelashes, her face angled downward slightly. It was the sexiest damn thing I had ever seen.

I dropped my bag and took her into my arms. As much as I loved the sight of that clingy dress on her, I couldn't wait to get it off her. When I finally pealed it from her, the black lacy bra and panties that were waiting for me instantly hardened me. My hands groped over her, over the lace, taking in the sensation of it against her soft skin. My cock was uncomfortable in my pants. She wasn't helping any, the way her hands were caressing over it. I shucked my shirt and my jeans, leaving on the silky boxers I wore. The smile on her face as she gazed over me told me how much she liked what she saw.

I pressed her to the bed, loving how the black lingerie against the red sheets looked. I appreciated the work she had put into coordinating this, so everything was just right. The low lighting, the candles, the bed made turned down and ready for us let me know she was as excited for this time together as I was. I would make this a memorable night for her, her pleasure the focus of my existence for the next hour.

I began by lifting one of her legs from the bed. I slowly pressed wet kisses from her toes all the way up the inside of her leg until my mouth was at the prize, that sweet spot between her legs. I slid my tongue under her panties. I thought she was going to come from the slight contact I made with her. She gasped out and was already clutching the sheets. Oh, she had a long way to go before I would let her come. I wanted her to enjoy this, beg for it. I wanted to bring her higher than she had ever been. And then I did. I couldn't let her beg too much though. Watching her writhe beneath me, seeing her face agonized and on the edge of erotic bliss, I changed my mind and decided to bring her to repeated orgasms instead. Several times she screamed out, guttural sounds of intense pleasure quaking her body. I had two fingers buried deep inside her where my cock longed to be. She nearly broke them as tight as she squeezed as her orgasm hit her. I brought her back to that same level again and kept her there for longer than I had till now. Her back was arching off her mattress. Her breaths came in shaky draws with moans and cries for release, which I denied her. I slid up her, my boxers left behind, and I pressed in, into the drenched vise grip that was hotter than my cock could bear. Just feeling her around me brought me to the brink. I had to fight to keep myself from exploding.

I made love to her like I had never made love to anyone. I knew I loved this woman. I knew I wanted her in my life, in Trina's life. I wanted her in my bed every night. I knew I had to keep those thoughts to myself, for now. I didn't want to scare her off by moving too fast. I hated the idea of her being out of town. I hated that after this weekend I wouldn't see her again until Saturday.

I held her close to me, enjoying the sensation of her in my arms for long after we had both climaxed. It was comfortable and serene. That peaceful state was suddenly jolted by the abrupt wail of the alarm. Both of our phones that sat on the nightstands lit and flashed the red warning. I jumped up and pulled my jeans on. I kept my eyes on the door and quickly retrieved the gun from my backpack.

Kenzie gasped at the sight of the nine in my hand. "Andy?"

I pointed to her and barked an order for her to hide in the closet until I came for her. I knew I had shifted in my head to take on the threat, to do what I needed to do to protect her. The shocked expression on her face hit me like a punch. She didn't understand. I had to protect her, and this was how I did it, the only way I knew how to. I wouldn't hold her in my arms hiding with her. I had to take on the threat, head-on.

She grabbed her phone, and I saw recognition in her face that my phone had shown the alert too. I'd have to deal with that later. She moved to the closet as I made my way out to the hallway. The alarm showed the back door in the kitchen to be in alarm, but I searched every inch of the house anyway, checked every single lock and every single window contact. The police cruiser arrived as I finished. Thirteen minutes was their response time. That was pitiful and unacceptable. That was something else I would have to deal with later. I went back to her room and called her from the closet. She had a robe on. She clutched her phone to her ear.

"The police are here," she told me.

"Yeah, a cruiser just pulled up in front."

We went downstairs together. I left the gun in her room. After talking with the officer, we locked back up and rearmed the system. Kenzie was clearly shaken. If her alarm had to go off, I'm glad I was here with her when it did. After she was calm, I would have to advise her what to do if it went off and I wasn't there. I took her back to bed. I stripped the robe from her and discarded my pants. I held her, both of our heads on the same pillow. She trembled.

"Why'd you have a gun, Andy?" She asked after several silent moments.

"To protect you, Kenz. Did it bother you, seeing it?"

"You turned into a different person. I needed you with me." She clung tighter to me. "I was so afraid."

I took her face in my hands and made her look me in the eye. "Babe, you needed me to neutralize the threat. It's what I know how to do. I don't know how to hide in a closet."

"Just what did you do in the Army?" She asked hesitantly.

"I took care of business. I did what I had to do, just like I did tonight."

Kenzie

Andy's words replayed in my head. The sight of him with the gun in his hand stayed in my mind too. I wasn't afraid of guns. My dad had taught me to shoot, but it was a surprise to see one in Andy's hand after the alarm went off. Why hadn't he told me he had one in his bag? He had moved so quickly and with such confidence. I panicked, and he looked so calm. He took control of the situation. Yes, he did what I needed him to do. What would I have done if he hadn't been there?

I snuggled closer to him. Enjoying the warmth from his body that infused me. I felt safe. "You don't think it was just a critter hitting the back door, do you?"

I felt Andy's body tense. He breathed out heavily. "I don't want to say that cop didn't know what he was talking about, but no, I don't think it was a critter or a system glitch, the wind, or the boogie man." All the things the cop suggested was the cause, less the boogie man. Andy's voice was calm and quiet which unnerved me even more. "Babe, we need to install a lock inside your closet. If I'm ever not here, and it goes off, you need to lock yourself in your closet and call the cops."

"The system autodials them. They were the ones who called me tonight," I said, like it really mattered.

"I'll install a deadbolt tomorrow, make it more of a panic room."

"I don't want to panic," I said softly. "God, I am so glad you were here tonight. I don't know what I would have done." I would have frozen and panicked that's what I would have done.

"Well, if it was someone, they now know there is an alarm and that I am here. I don't think it will go off again tonight. Let's try to get some sleep," Andy said, nuzzling my neck.

If Andy wasn't there holding me, there would be no way I would be able to sleep, but because he was, I felt myself relax. He was right. If it had been someone, they certainly wouldn't try again tonight with him there and the alarm. I was hoping the alarm itself would stop any further attempts. Andy couldn't always be here with me.

I slept a lot better than I thought I would and waking in Andy's arms was wonderful. I loved the feeling of his hard body against me. Gazing into his sparkling green eyes I saw only passion and desire. Light poured into the room through the shears on the windows. I hadn't pulled the room darkening panels last night.

"Good morning," Andy said.

"Good morning, what time is it?" I knew I smiled at him like a lovesick preteen swooning over her idol.

"Just past eight," he answered, as he threw his leg over mine.

"I'll make us breakfast," I offered. He snuggled in closer to me, trapping me beneath him. I chuckled. He was making it impossible for me to get up.

"Later, I want you first."

I think I initiated the first kiss, but he took it from there. Before I knew it, I was moaning through my second incredible orgasm and he hadn't even penetrated me yet. He pulled my hand off his hard cock. He was panting and trembling on the edge, himself. He rolled onto his back and pulled me atop him. He groaned in ecstasy as I slowly slid down his swollen member. His hands gripped my hips, and he helped move me up and down, the two of us finding the perfect speed and rhythm to give us both the maximum pleasure. I reached my peak quickly. He was rubbing all the right places. I felt my entire body begin to quake. The wave that hit me was mind-blowing. I was lost in my own pleasure, but his grunts quickly matched the tone and volume of my whimpers which turned into screams. I collapsed over his chest and laid there mindlessly drifting in bliss. His deep kisses brought me back to my mind. When I was fully conscious again, I laid on my back. His bright green eyes gazed into mine.

I wished we could wake up this way every day. Even with everything going on, I hadn't been this happy in a really long time. Not only did I feel completely safe with him, he had to be one of the nicest people I'd ever met. I still wondered what he saw in me though.

The weekend flew by. We talked a lot, about ourselves, our beliefs, values, our dreams, and our wants for the future. We talked about his vision for his gym and I volunteered to come up with a marketing promotion for him that would attract more women to the gym. I was excited to work on it over the next week or so. I felt that I really had gotten to know him, know who he really was. Not only did he install a deadbolt to the inside of my closet door, but he also put one on the inside of my powder room off the kitchen. We cooked together, watched sports and a couple movies. We spent a lot of time in bed, a lot of it just snuggling and caressing each other. It felt right, perfect.

Andy

It was even harder to pull myself away from her late Sunday afternoon when it was time to get Trina than it had been the week before. As I drove to my mom's, I thought about what I had said to Logan last weekend about deserving this with her. I guess I hadn't realized how lonely my life had been until she was in it. It had been such a great weekend with her that I was seriously considering breaking my rule and bringing her with me to my mom's house to meet Trina. I of course did not.

Mom made dinner for Trina and me again. This was becoming a habit. A habit I hoped we could continue until Kenzie became a part of Trina's life too. Trina had a great weekend with Mom, so I didn't feel guilty about the time away from her. I smiled at the thought of being with Kenzie next weekend from Saturday when she landed after her trip until the last possible moment on Sunday. Maybe I'd have Mom bring Trina back to my place Sunday evening and put her to bed and sleep over, herself, so I could have all of Sunday night with Kenzie too.

Just like last week, Logan swung by my place after Trina and I got home. He filled me in on gym business, including that Ashley had gotten over her attitude and was decent to him. I was glad to hear that. There had been a time that Ashley got her nose out of joint over every perceived slight, Logan got better hours, more hours, fewer hours, whatever her gripe of the day was. I thought he wasn't going to ask about Kenzie at all, but as we opened our second beers while sitting out back on the deck in the warm evening air, he broached that topic, none too subtle.

"So, did you bang her out of your system yet?" He asked.

I couldn't help but laugh. I could only hope that one day a woman would get into his heart and mind like Kenzie had obviously gotten into mine. "Nope," I replied and then took a long pull of my beer. "I'm actually thinking I'm going to end up putting a ring on her finger." I could tell Logan was surprised. I couldn't stop the smile that was spreading over my face. "Man, she's it. I just know she is."

Logan shook his head and finished his beer. "She coming to work out again this week?"

"No, she's traveling this week for work. I won't see her again till she lands Saturday."

"That sucks," he said. "You decide on a timetable of introducing her to Trina? Should be sooner rather than later. If Trina doesn't accept her you know it won't work. I don't want to see this fail for you, man, but I don't want to see you get any more attached."

"Which is it Logan? Don't rush to introduce Trina to her or do it soon?" I laughed. "I think you spent too much time with Ashley this weekend. You sound all over the place."

"Fuck no, I don't. All I'm saying is if you're sure, you should move it to the next level."

"Thanks, yeah, I think so too. I damn near asked her to come to my mom's with me tonight. After next weekend, maybe."

Logan and I spent a few more minutes on the deck. It was a beautiful night, but I wanted to get inside and call Kenzie for our nightly call. I hoped we would still be able to talk every night while she was away. Logan was right. I needed to introduce her to Trina soon, for my own sanity. I was sure she would be great with Trina, but what if Trina didn't accept her for some reason?

Kenzie

I left work Monday a bit early and decided to surprise Andy and drop by the gym. I knew he'd be free because I had cleared the time with him for a planned phone call. I rounded the corner into the office and stopped dead. Andy and Logan held drug vials and needles, and packages of pills. My heart stopped. Son-of-a-bitch! I turned and bolted out the side door.

"Shit, Kenzie, wait," Andy yelled. He followed me out, calling to me over and over as I rushed towards my car. My hands were shaking as I unlocked my car and fumbled with the handle. Andy was behind me. I felt his hands grab my shoulders. He turned me to look him in the eye. "That wasn't what you thought," he said.

I don't even know what I said back to him if anything. All I could think was that Margot was right. It had been him. How could I have been so wrong? I felt my eyes burning and didn't realize the tears were spilling out until Andy begged me to stop crying, insisting it wasn't what I thought. He convinced me to come back inside, mostly because I knew I was in no shape to drive.

"Logan, tell Kenzie where this shit came from!" Andy demanded.

Logan looked at me with sympathy. "Kenz, sorry seeing this upset you." He was doing a drug search on-line. "I found this shit down in the MMA area in the basement. From the searches I've done so far, it appears to be steroids, hormones, and other shit to build muscle mass."

"I'm going to kill Mason and Blake!" Andy exploded. "They know that shit isn't allowed here. I run a clean place. I don't care if it's not banned in their fight club, it's banned in my gym!"

"Easy, Andy," Logan tried to calm him. "Honestly, Kenzie, this isn't Andy's shit."

Andy pinned me with pleading eyes. "Kenzie, please, listen to me. This isn't what you think. How could you think that?" In his eyes, I could see that he was hurt that I thought it was his drugs.

I fell against his chest and he held me. I cried, not knowing what to think. I wanted to believe him. I did believe him. That's why it hurt so bad. It had been such a shock to see him standing there holding the drugs and needles.

"Baby, tell me you believe me," he begged. "Here, sit down," he led me to the chair in front of the computer. "Look it up for yourself." He sat all the drugs in front of me.

I just stared at them. I fingered a few vials. They were what he said they were. Andy entered the information from the pills into the computer while I watched. The look-up confirmed what he and Logan had said. They were steroids, hormones, and muscle builders. I felt myself getting more upset. This time for wrongly thinking Andy was the one who roofied me.

"Give us a sec, will you, Logan?" Andy asked quietly. Logan left and closed the door. Andy turned the desk chair, so I faced him. He dropped down to a squat in front of me. "Kenz, do you believe me?" His eyes were probing mine.

I nodded. "I'm sorry," I forced out. I cried harder.

Andy took me into his arms and held me against his hard chest. By the time I calmed, we were sitting on the floor, me in his lap. My head was resting against his broad chest, his strong arms held me tightly. I felt terrible that I had thought for even a second they were his drugs, or he could have roofied me.

"Kenz, you thought I drugged you, didn't you?"

"I'm sorry, Andy. I never thought that but when I saw you and Logan holding the drugs, I just." My mind stopped working. I couldn't complete that sentence. I snuggled in closer to him, the only thing that felt right to do. I felt him press kisses to the top of my head.

"Babe, I didn't, I'd never," he insisted.

"I know, I know," I said. I angled up to gaze into his eyes. His showed he was very hurt that I could have thought that. "I never thought you drugged me," I repeated.

CHAPTER 11

Kenzie

It was later than I planned when I left the office on Tuesday. I felt tired and stressed. I'd been staying up later on the phone with Andy than I normally did, not that I was complaining. I really enjoyed our discussions and loved the companionship with him. I consciously pushed the trepidation I felt regarding tomorrow's trip to Phoenix from my mind. Also going on the on-site was Joe, one of the Network Engineers. I'd gone on dozens of on-site trips with Joe. Did I seriously think he was the one who roofied me? No, but I didn't necessarily not-suspect any of my coworkers either.

I was deep in thought when the light changed. I should have stopped, had enough time to, but I didn't. I sailed through as it turned red. My eyes caught sight of the car behind me, proceeding through the intersection as well. Had he been going that fast gaining on me? I didn't remember anyone behind me. *Okay, Kenz, wake up and watch what's going on around you.* That was when I missed my turn, yep, totally out of it. I turned right at the next intersection to go around the block, and so did the car behind me. It followed me all the way around the block and turned onto the same street I did as a matter of fact. That was odd. I couldn't see the driver. All the windows were darkly tinted. I felt foolish and paranoid, thinking for a minute it had been following me.

I was lucky that there was street parking right in front of the little shoe repair shop I was going to; otherwise, I would have had to go to the big public lot around the block which would take more time. I zipped into the space and was in and out of the store with my repaired boot in seconds.

When I pulled back out onto the street, I noticed that same car pulled out from a parking spot several ahead of me and again took up a place behind me. Okay, now I panicked. Just to be sure, I took a right on the next little side street, intending to go around the block to see if it followed. It did. Big mistake. The area back here was vacant. To the far side, a fence of a wrecking yard stood with junk piled up all inside the twelve-foot high fence, no sign of life. It ran the entire block.

I pressed my foot on the accelerator, the car that had been following me matched my speed, and it then accelerated faster. It came up beside me and sideswiped my car, trying to push me into the fence. I slammed my brakes on. It turned around and came towards me. My heart stopped for a minute, but my self-preservation instinct took over. I put the car in reverse, spun around and sped off, back the way I'd come. I knew there was a police station several blocks ahead on the main drag. I drove there only slowing down for stop signs but proceeding through intersections that were clear. I pulled up in front of the precinct going twice the posted speed, slamming my brakes to stop, and the car that had hit me passed me by and kept going. My heart was pounding, and my hands were shaking.

A uniformed officer came up to my car. "Ma'am, are you okay?"

I told him what happened through my open car window without getting out of my car, my voice rattling it off without a breath. He looked over the damage and tried to open my car door. It wouldn't open. He directed me to slide out of the passenger side and he then ushered me within the precinct. I was sat with a detective at his desk out in the bullpen area. He placed a call to Margot when I told him of the past episodes she was investigating.

Andy

I was nearly done with a private client, a woman I had worked with weekly for the last six months. Out of the corner of my eye, I caught sight of Detective Malone, barreling through the front door of the gym. She was on a mission. Her gaze affixed on me as soon as she saw me. I'd had just about enough of her. If she didn't have a warrant, I would toss her ass out.

"Stevens, have you been here all evening?"

All I could think about was Kenzie. There had to have been another incident. "Is Kenzie okay?"

"Why would you ask?" Margot asked.

"Because you're here, questioning me. Answer me, Margot. Is Kenzie okay?"

"She is."

"What happened?" I demanded.

"Answer me first. Have you been here for the past hour?"

"Yes, he has," my client answered for me. Her eyes were on Margot's gun and badge. "He's been here for the last two hours."

"And Mr. Logan, where has he been?" Margot demanded without missing a beat.

"He's taught back-to-back boot camps for the past two hours. There are over forty witnesses to that," I told her. "Now tell me, what happened with Kenzie?" The dread inside me was consuming. If she didn't tell me, I'd forget she was a woman and a cop.

"She was followed when she left her office. Someone tried to run her off the road. She's unhurt but is pretty spooked. She's at the ninth precinct waiting for me."

"Then what are you doing here?" I turned to my client. "I'm sorry, I have to go," I said.

"I understand," she said, her eyes sliding between Margot and me. I wasn't even sure what she could possibly be thinking.

"Whoa Stevens, she's waiting for me. You're not invited."

Just then my phone vibrated in my pocket. I pulled it out. It was Kenzie. "Babe, are you okay?" I asked answering it. I listened intently. She was more than spooked. She was completely freaking out. "I'm on my way. Sit tight." I turned to Margot. "I've been invited."

Kenzie

I don't think I had ever been as scared in my life as I was when I realized that I was being followed. And then when that car tried to run me off the road I knew what real terror was. Now that I'd given my statement and had time to collect myself, my hands stopped shaking. I glanced again at my watch. What was taking Margot so long? I knew she could have been on duty and at her own crime scene, which was why I had finally called Andy. I was relieved that he was on his way. I could have just taken an Uber home, but I really didn't want to be alone. I was really pissed there was damage to my car and I couldn't have it back to get it fixed until CSU was done with it tomorrow, not that I'd be able to deal with it tomorrow with my flight to Phoenix. This just added complication to the trip I was already nervous about.

Andy and Margot came through the door together. That didn't strike me as coincidence. I rose as they rushed up. Andy embraced me, and Margot was in cop mode, firing off question after question before Andy even had the chance to ask me if I was okay. The detective I had talked to came over and pulled Margot a few steps away. They quietly conferred. I didn't care what they were talking about. All I cared about was that Andy was holding me and I felt safe.

"I'm fine, now," I told him. "Thank you for coming. I'm sorry I pulled you away from work."

He pressed a kiss to my forehead. "Babe, no apology needed." He gave me another hug. "Are you done here?" I nodded yes. "Let's get out of here. I'm going to take you home to pack what you need for your trip tomorrow, then I'm taking you back to my place for the night. I'll get you to the airport tomorrow for your flight." I started to argue to tell him he didn't have to do that. "Kenzie, you're clearly shaken, and I don't want you to be alone. This wasn't a coincidence."

Tears filled my eyes. Just hearing him say what I thought was sobering. "Thank you, Andy," was all I could say while I shook my head yes. I didn't want to be alone.

"Miss Collins," the detective called as Andy and I began to step towards the door.

I turned back around to see an angry glare coming from Margot. I had forgotten for a minute she was there. That would have been so rude of me to leave without saying anything to her. I guess I was very shaken up. "I'm sorry, yes?"

"Detective Malone says she'll get your car for you tomorrow when it's released by CSU. I just need you to sign the release form giving your authorization."

"I can get it to your house, Kenz, and you can take care of the repairs when you get home," Margot offered.

"Thanks, Margot," I said nodding.

"What kind of damage was done?" Andy asked. The detective told him. "Kenzie, I can come get it here tomorrow and bring it over to my buddy that owns the body shop. He'll give you the best price you'll get, file the insurance claim, and everything. He might even be able to have it done before you get back from Phoenix."

"Really, you'd do that. I hate to put you through that much trouble," I told him. The look he gave me back showed me how ridiculous he thought my statement was. I smiled and nodded my head. "Thank you, Andy, yes, please do."

Margot was clearly unhappy as I signed the paperwork to have Andy called and the vehicle released to him. As we turned to leave again, Margot grabbed my arm. "Kenzie, you shouldn't be alone tonight."

"I'm staying at Andy's. We're just going to my place, so I can pack a bag for my trip tomorrow. I'll call you when I get back in town, Margot." I gave her a hug. "Thanks for coming. Figure this out, will you? I can't take much more," I whispered in her ear. She looked very concerned as I stepped away and left with Andy.

We stopped quickly at my house to grab the few things I'd need. I travelled so much I had it down to a science with the barest of necessities, my quart-sized baggie of fluids ready for travel at all times. For even a week I could get by with nothing more than a back pack and my laptop bag. I had Andy go through a drive-thru to get me a burger and fries. I was starving! I devoured it on the drive to his place. We pulled up in front of the back stairs to Andy's apartment and he took hold of both my bags. I followed him up the stairs not even thinking about his daughter.

When we went in, Ashley, the young woman who had been behind the counter that first day, sat on the couch snuggling with Andy's little girl. She was even more precious in person. Her big green eyes sparkled when she saw Andy. She jumped up and ran to him screaming, "Daddy!"

He set my bags down and scooped her up. After he gave her a big kiss, he turned her to me. "Trina, this is my friend, Kenzie."

"Hello Trina," I said. She was adorable!

Trina's big eyes stared at me. "Hi Kenzie. It is nice to meet you," her sweet voice said as she reached her right hand to me to shake hands. She didn't have a baby voice, but it wasn't a big girl voice either. It was the cutest. I was used to my sister's kids, who both had had speech delays and didn't speak in full sentences yet at four years old. She did. Her little voice sounded so grown up. And she had manners! Andy had done well raising her. I was impressed.

Behind them, Ashley stood up from the couch. "Ash, this is Kenzie," Andy said. I forced a smile. "It's nice to see you again, Ashley." I said.

She didn't look very happy to see me. She greeted me, but it wasn't an overly friendly greeting. Her eyes kept looking at my bags. The questions were all over her face. She wanted to know if I was staying the night and where I'd be sleeping.

"Thanks for staying with Trina tonight, Ash. I'll be home rest the night."

"Okay, boss," she said. She came up to Andy and Trina and gave Trina a big hug. "Good night, sweetie," she said. "I'll be home all night if you need anything." Then she let herself out through the door in the kitchen that led to the upstairs hallway.

"Kenzie will be staying the night with us, Trina," Andy said. He set her to her feet.

"Are you my mommy?" Trina asked, her eyes gazing at me

Andy was noticeably bothered by her question. "Trina, Kenzie is not your mommy. We've talked about this. She's my friend."

"Sweetie, why would you think that I'm your mommy?" I asked. I squatted down to her height.

"You could be, we both have black hair," she said with a smile.

"We do," I said, returning her smile. "And you have your daddy's green eyes."

"My grandma told me my mommy had black hair," Trina said.

I glanced at Andy. "I'm not your mommy, but I'd like to be your friend. I have been excited to meet you because I know how special you are to your daddy. You are a very lucky girl to have so many people in your life who love you."

Trina ran to the refrigerator and pulled down the family picture. She held it up to me. "That's me and my daddy," she said pointing to the two rough stick figures in the middle. "That's my grandma." She pointed to the short-haired blonde stick figure in a dress. "That's my Uncle Logan and my Aunt Ashley," she said pointing them out as well.

"That's a very good picture. You have a nice family," I said flashing a smile at Andy.

"Do you know my grandma?"

"No, but I have met your Uncle Logan a few times."

"He cusses a lot," she said laughing. "But I love to go to my Uncle Logan's room. It's out that door," she said pointing to the door Ashley had gone out of.

I looked at Andy and laughed. She was the cutest!

"Trina, it's time for bed, let's go to your room and Kenzie and I will read you a story."

"Is Kenzie sleeping in Grandma's room?" Trina asked.

Andy looked nervously at me. "You know how you like to sleep in my room after you've had a bad dream, so I can hug you better?" Trina nodded. "Well Kenzie just had a bad dream, so she needs me to hug her better tonight too. So, she'll be in my room, sweetie."

Trina nodded and turned to me. "My daddy will make it all better."

"I'm sure he will," I told her.

We read her two stories. Andy gave her a big hug and a kiss, tucking her in. She held her little hands up to me for a hug too. I glanced at Andy and then gave her a hug and I pressed a kiss to her forehead.

"Will you be here in the morning?" She asked.

"Yes, and we're going to drive Kenzie to the airport tomorrow morning," Andy told her.

"See you in the morning, sweetie," I said.

Andy turned her nightlight on, and we left her room, closing the door all the way. We went to the kitchen and Andy grabbed us each a beer from the refrigerator. "I figured you could use one," he said with a smile.

"Thanks," I said. I rubbed my tight neck. "Thank you for coming and bringing me back here. I really didn't want to be alone tonight," I confessed.

He wrapped his arms around me. "I'm glad you called. I wouldn't want you alone tonight, babe."

I gazed into his eyes. "I'm sorry you had to introduce me to Trina before you would have, because of this," I said.

"What do you mean?"

"You said you're careful and you don't introduce anyone you are seeing to Trina for a long time."

"No, I said I don't introduce her to anyone I'm not serious about," Andy corrected me. "And I haven't."

All I could do was stare into Andy's eyes. "I think you're pretty special, too. Thank you," I said, completely affected by what he'd said. He was serious about me, wow! I felt the same way. I was glad he was in my life. "She's adorable and you are an amazing father."

"I have wanted to introduce you. I want to spend more time with you Kenzie, if you want to spend time with Trina and me. I want you to be a part of our lives."

My heart squeezed in my chest. This was a huge step for him. I knew from what he had said before that he didn't open his life up with Trina to too many people. I nodded, a smile I could feel spreading over my face. "I'd like that. I understand you have to put her first, and I would never have pushed for more time with you, but I do want to spend more time with you both."

He snuggled in close. His lips were near my ear. "Let's go to bed."

"You want to show me this hug me better thing?" I asked flashing him a provocative smile.

He chuckled. "I guarantee you it will be very different from how I hug Trina better after a bad dream."

CHAPTER 12

Andy

I loved coming awake holding Kenzie in my arms, in my bed. The fact that Trina lay in the next room was icing on the cake. Kenzie would be a part of our lives now. There was no reason for her to not be here as often as possible. Kenzie moaned and snuggled closer to me. I loved the softness and warmth of her body up against mine.

My door flung open and Trina rushed in, jumping onto the bed with us. Good thing I had pulled on a pair of shorts and had Kenzie slip on one of my shirts after we had made love last night. I preferred waking to a naked Kenzie, but for now, until I taught Trina to no longer barge into my room, we'd have to be clothed in the morning.

"Good morning, angel," I greeted her with a kiss to her cheek.

She laid down next to me, her head on my pillow like she always did. Kenzie was on the other side. A smile crossed my face as I realized I snuggled with both my girls. I rolled my head towards Kenzie. Her eyes were open now, and she was staring at me with a beautiful smile gracing her lips.

"Good morning," I said softly.

"Morning," she replied.

Trina popped up as though she had forgotten about Kenzie being there. "Kenzie!" She leaned over me and wriggled her way between us settling in to snuggle with Kenzie. Now I really smiled. The sight of them laying there snuggled together, my two black-haired beauties, tightened my throat and brought moisture to my eyes. I knew I had to find a way to make this permanent, soon.

Kenzie's eyes locked onto mine. "What are you smiling like that about?"

I chuckled. I nodded to Trina. I didn't need to say another word. Her smile spread wider. Yeah, she appreciated it too. I could see Trina forming a strong attachment to her, fast, just like I had.

"Hey kiddo, what do you say we go have some breakfast?" She said to Trina.

Trina hopped up and pulled on her hand to follow her to the kitchen. Trina didn't let go of her the rest of the morning. We ate a quick breakfast. I liked how Kenzie helped get Trina ready to go, without even asking me. It was so natural, so comfortable. Had she asked permission to brush her hair or help pick out her clothes when Trina had begged her it would not have felt like she belonged here with us, like it was not comfortable for her.

I took hold of Kenzie's bags and led both my girls out the back door. We were laughing as we stepped onto the deck. Ashley sat at the patio table with a cup of coffee. The look on her face was downright bitchy. I shot her a scowl. We were not having that conversation again. And if we did, Ashley would not be a happy camper when I was done with her. To Kenzie's credit she was friendly and acted as though nothing was wrong with Ashley.

"See you later," Kenzie said with a smile to Ashley as we descended the stairs.

Kenzie

After we had pulled out of the driveway, I turned to look at Trina. She was listening to her music on the kiddie music player strapped to the back of the seat in front of her and she already had a book opened. Once I knew she was occupied, I turned my attention to Andy. "So, what's with Ashley? She clearly does not like me." I kept my voice low, so Trina wouldn't hear. I don't know why it bothered me so much, but it did.

Andy's eyes flashed into the rear-view mirror for a second, checking on Trina. He glanced at me. He looked thoughtful, his gaze back on the road. "She has some issues and you being a part of our lives has made her feel insecure." His voice was quiet too. "She'll get over it. It's not you. It's her."

"It's none of my business, but did you have a thing with her?" There, I put the question out there. If it wasn't that, I couldn't figure out why my presence bothered Ashley, or why Andy would put up with her crap.

"Not like you think. Look, Ashley stepped up and helped me big time when I needed it. I owe her because I wouldn't have Trina here with me if it weren't for her. I also helped her get out of the old life she had. She's like a little sister. I call her to task when she's straying and encourage her when she's doing the right things."

I didn't understand. "What did you help get her out of?"

"That's her story to tell, not mine. But going back to what I think you were asking, I've never slept with her, so it's not that kind of a jealousy thing she's harboring towards you. Give her time, she'll figure it out and get over it."

I sat back quietly and processed that. I was mad at myself for even asking. I didn't want to sound like the jealous girlfriend. I was glad to hear he and Ashley had never had a romantic relationship though. I knew I shouldn't even think about his past girlfriends. I glanced at him again. I was sure he had plenty of past romantic relationships, seriously, look at him. There had to be a lot of women left with broken hearts. That insecurity hit me again. I didn't want to be one of those women.

"Kenz, what?" He asked me quietly. I saw confusion and concern on his face.

I hoped I hadn't unconsciously said anything aloud. "Nothing," I said.

His hand took hold of mine. "Kenzie, you don't need to worry about Ashley. She'll get over it and even if she doesn't I don't care. That's her problem and doesn't influence me. If anything, it pisses me off how she's treating you. I'm sorry you even have to deal with her crap."

Now I felt bad that he was apologizing for my insecurities. I shouldn't have even asked. "No apology needed from you, Andy, really." I shook it off. "So, new topic, I'll text when I can while I'm in Phoenix, and I should be able to talk most nights after Trina is in bed."

"Like normal," he said with a smile. "We have a normal." He winked.

I giggled. We did, and I loved that we did. "Yeah," I agreed with a big smile.

"I'm glad you were at my place last night and this morning. You know, now that you've been there with Trina home, there is no reason you can't be more often." He brought my hand to his lips and pressed a kiss to my palm.

Zingers hit me in all the most intimate places of my body! "I'll miss you while I'm out of town," I whispered.

"I'll pick you up Saturday, hopefully in your repaired car."

"Yeah, thanks for taking care of the car, I almost forgot." How could I have forgotten? "I should leave a credit card with you to pay the bill." I dug into my wallet.

"Nah, not now. You can pay Eddie when you get back, I'm sure. Insurance will pay most anyway. I'll bring you by his shop after your home."

"I'm still waiting for the bill on the security system from your friend, Brian," I reminded him.

His smile was a guilty one. "He usually does his bills once a month. He'll get it to you, I'm sure."

"This has been an expensive few weeks. When I find out who caused all this I'm going to slap him with a bill for everything."

Andy

Yeah, she wouldn't be getting a bill from Eddie either. Whatever insurance didn't cover I'd take care of it in trade. I wished I could tell her to ease her worries, but I knew she'd never go for it. We hadn't talked last night about her safety going forward, but I had given it a lot of thought.

"You're not going to get the chance to bill the SOB because I just might kill him before he can even be arrested. Honestly Kenzie, he actually tried to run you off the road. That was a pretty bold move. We need to talk when you get back about protection for you when you're not with me."

I saw her face out of the corner of my eye. My statement frightened her, and she was shocked I had brought it up. I think she had consciously pushed the attack the previous night from her mind. I didn't want to scare her, but I didn't think this guy was done. She was still in danger I believed, maybe more now than before.

"I'm not the type of person who buries my head in the sand about anything, but could we not talk about that now? I really just can't," she said, her voice trailing off and not finishing her sentence.

She looked in the back seat at Trina. I had been watching her in my rear-view mirror. She was in her own little world with her music and her books. I took Kenzie's hand. "Babe, I'm going to keep you safe. I'm sorry if bringing it up upset you."

"No, that's okay. I just intentionally wasn't thinking about it. I've never been that afraid in my life, Andy. When I realized I was being followed and then when that car tried to run me into that chain link fence, and it was vacant back there, not a sole around. I really screwed up being there." She paused and shook her head. I saw tears gather in her eyes. I glanced at Trina again. She was still not paying any attention to us. "I just can't figure out why the hell anyone would be doing this to me. Why me? What did I do to cause any of this?"

"Babe, I'm sure nothing. You did nothing to cause this. You're a victim, here. Don't allow yourself to take on any blame for this." My voice was strong. For the first time Trina looked up at us. Shit! "Which book are you reading back there, Trina?" I called to her to distract her.

"Duke dog," she answered. "Kenzie, do you know the Duke dog story?"

Kenzie pulled it together quickly. "No, sweetie, I don't." She flashed a composed smile at Trina. "Maybe after I get back from my trip, we can read it together."

"Yay!" Trina cheered. "Will you come stay at our house again?"

Kenzie's eyes flashed to mine. "I'm pretty sure I'll be able to do that."

Kenzie

We pulled up to the departure curb at Blue Grass Airport. Both Andy and I got out of the car. I went to the side Trina was on and opened her door. I gave her a big hug and a kiss. "We'll read that book when I get back." Andy had the other side of the car open by my bags. He pressed me against the rear panel of the car, out of Trina's line of sight and he gave me an even better hug and kiss.

"I'm sorry if I upset you," he repeated. "I'll talk to you after Trina's in bed. Hope you have a good flight, and be careful, babe."

I kissed him again. "I will, I promise. Thanks for the ride, for everything." I didn't want to walk away from him. I wanted to kiss him again. I pressed one last kiss to his lips. I took both my bags from him. "I'll talk to you later." I waved to Trina and then stepped away and passed through the doors into the terminal.

Andy

After I pulled away from the curb, I called my friend Eddie who owned the autobody shop to arrange for Kenzie's car to be worked on as soon as it was released by CSU. He guaranteed he'd get it in right away and it would be done by Saturday. After I dropped Trina off at school and got to the gym, I placed a call to Margot.

"What is it Stevens? Is Kenzie okay?" She asked.

"Yeah, she got off without any problems this morning. Look, if you have a minute, I want to talk with you about what happened yesterday."

I intentionally left it unclear which part I wanted to talk about. I wanted to see her thoughts. Regardless what Kenzie said Margot liked her in a romantic way. The chick was clearly jealous of me. I wondered for a second how jealous she was. Would she be capable of doing these things to Kenzie to try and scare her closer to herself? Yesterday proved she was still trying to drive me away when she barged into my gym grilling me as to where Logan and I had been the past two hours. I didn't want to think that about her, but my thoughts were considering it.

"I am really worried. This was clearly an escalation of this guy's actions. I don't like that she's out of town. I don't like she is out of our sight. Stevens, I'm taking you on faith, that you had nothing to do with this and so help me God I will kill you if you had anything to do with this, but we have to keep her protected from here out. What happened to her last night, can't ever happen again."

"I agree with you one hundred percent," I said, relieved to some degree. If she had automatically jumped on Kenzie leaving with me or granting me the authorization to pick up her car and deal with it, that would have cemented my jealousy theory. "I don't want her alone after she gets back until this guy is caught." Margot was giving me the benefit of the doubt, I had to give her it to, "If I can't be with her, can you sometimes? She met my daughter last night, so there's no reason she can't be at my place now, but that might not always be feasible."

"Yeah, I'll work on schedules with you when its needed. She isn't going to like constant protection, you know that, don't you?" Margot said.

"Yeah, I do, but I think she was scared badly enough last night that she'll accept it for a while. If neither of us are available, I have a few members at the gym that do security work. I'd pay for her to be protected," I said, thinking aloud." Just then my private client walked into the gym. "Margot, I've got to go. I'll call you before Kenzie gets back, okay?"

"Okay, keep me informed of her movements too. I need to know where she is at all times after she's back."

I hung up hoping my instincts about Margot were right, that she had nothing to do with it. If she did I'd just given her a roadmap to Kenzie.

Kenzie

The entire Phoenix trip was uneventful. We got the client up with minimal fuss. My ATS partner on-site, Joe, interacted very little with me off hours. Normally we would at least get dinner together. I didn't ask, and neither did he. I'm sure he was spooked given my allegations that I had been roofied when we had all gone out. I couldn't blame him. If I were male, I would be careful too.

I had time every night to talk with Andy after Trina was in bed as planned. We racked up five hours over the first two nights. It was after ten, on Friday night. We had already talked for an hour. My flight left early on Saturday. He had my car back, all repaired. He said he didn't know how much it cost to repair that wasn't covered by the insurance. I'd have to talk with Eddie about it. I wasn't sure I believed him. I knew I needed to get to sleep. The alarm would go off way too early as it was. I was just about to say good night.

"Babe, I'm lying in my bed, thinking about you. I can't keep my hand off my cock. If you were here, what would you do to it?"

I'm sure I was blushing. I'd never done the phone sex thing, never sexted, sent or received naked pictures. I'd never thought of myself as a prude, sheltered or naïve, but I guess to some extent I was. I wasn't comfortable with it.

"Oh, Andy, you know what I'd do to it."

"Are you blushing?" He asked. He heard me giggle. "You are, aren't you?" He was teasing me. "You've never done this before, have you?"

"Okay, no I haven't," I admitted. He chuckled the sexiest sound. I didn't want to disappoint him or not be any fun, but I honestly wasn't sure I could do this.

"A phone-sex virgin," his husky voice said. "I get to pop this cherry. I'm glad I get to be your first." The phone line was quiet for a minute. If he was waiting for me to comment, he'd be waiting a long time. I had no idea what to say. "Okay, here's what I want you to do. Tell me exactly what you're wearing."

"You're going to be so disappointed. I have on a ratty old t-shirt and a pair of boy shorts panties. Nothing sexy."

He laughed again. "I can work with this. Okay put your phone on speaker." I did. "Now take your shirt off." I did that too. "Is it off?"

I giggled, not believing I was doing this. "It is."

"Okay, now lay down, put the phone on your chest, and close your eyes. Do exactly what I tell you to do and think about me while you're doing it. Your hands are my hands. My hands are caressing your cheeks. My lips could be hovering just an inch away, waiting to kiss you. Now both of my hands are ever so softly drawing lines down your neck, over your collar bones and down to your breasts."

I did what he said and followed his instructions, listening to his voice, envisioning him there, touching me. He had me caress my own breasts, both hands, run my fingernails over my nipples, followed by pinching both at the same time.

Then he instructed me to slowly run my hands down my abdomen, over my pussy, down my legs and softly up my inner thighs. Listening to his voice with my eyes closed I was actually getting off. When he finally had me reach my hands under my boy-shorts, I found myself dripping wet. I know I moaned aloud at the contact with myself.

"Oh, yeah, let me hear your pleasure, baby," he said. "Tell me, are you wet for me?"

"Yes," I admitted.

"Get rid of those boy-shorts, get them off, get naked for me," he said. I discarded them quickly. "Now you're lying naked?"

"I am, what about you?"

He chuckled that sexy laugh again. "Completely naked. And I'm hard for you. Is your hand between your legs?"

I laughed shyly. He had not told me to put my hand back after getting naked, but yes it was. "It is, and I'm circling it like you do."

"Oh, I like that. Now remember it's my hand. I want you to focus on nothing but how good it feels and keep going. My other hand is up on your breast. Don't stop until you're about to come, but don't come. Tell me when you're close."

I caressed and stroked myself, between my legs and my breasts. I completely forgot about everything but the intense pleasure I was feeling. As I was about to come I realized I was moaning and breathing heavy. "I'm close," I said in a breathy voice I didn't recognize as my own.

"Keep pleasuring yourself, but hold back, hold back as long as you can. That's my tongue, licking and sucking. I love your pussy, the taste, the smell, the softness, wetness, and heat. Oh yes, hold back, feel my tongue, feel me lick you like you've never been licked." I was moaning loud, nearly screaming out, holding back the release. My back was arching off the mattress, my breathing ragged. I listened intently to his voice. "Hold back, it will feel even better the longer you wait." I was nearly screaming now. "Yes, hold back, I'm touching you, feel my hands on you, my lips on you. I want you to come now, let it roll through you," he said.

I screamed as it hit me, a freight train slamming me, an orgasm so strong I was panting when it was done. "God, I wish you were really here," I said. My phone vibrated.

"Check your texts."

I pulled the phone to my eyes. It was a picture of Andy, or more specifically Andy's very erect cock with his hand grasping it. I felt the smile spread over my face. "Yeah, I really wish you were here," I said.

"Take a picture of your pussy for me. I want to see you wet," his voice was strangled. I heard movement. He was jacking off.

I took the picture he requested. Wow, yeah, I was really wet. I snapped a few more. One with my fingers buried in my pussy, another of my breast. I sent all three to him feeling very naughty. "Check your texts," I said. I still felt excited. I caressed myself some more.

"Oh fuck," Andy cursed. "Beautiful pussy, so wet. I want to bury my tongue and then my cock there. I want to feel you, so wet, so beautiful." His words got breathier the more he spoke. I heard his grunts, deep guttural sounds I knew well. He was bringing himself to orgasm. The sound of it turned me on. I was fingering myself ferociously now. I was close again. I wasn't quiet. "You're so wet, it feels so good, doesn't it? Oh, baby, run those fingers faster over your clit. I love feeling over every inch of your soft flesh, over your breasts, over those hard nipples. And that ass! Baby, I love your ass. I fantasize about your perfectly shaped ass. Faster," he said in tune with my whimpers and moans. "That's it, finger it, baby, don't stop. Feel how good that is. Scream for me," he urged.

My orgasm hit me, and I did scream out a deep grunt. I couldn't have come harder if he had been there touching me. "You did that to me," I told him when I had recovered. "I've never brought myself to a climax like that," I added.

"I've missed you. I can't wait to hold you and make love to you tomorrow night. You'll stay with me tomorrow night, won't you?"

How could I say no to that? "I've missed you too, Andy. This was, wow!"

He chuckled again. "Yeah, it was, wow. You sleep well, baby. Dream erotic dreams about me. I know I will be."

Andy

We hung up, and I took a shower. I made the mistake of looking at her pictures before getting in and seeing her wet pussy, her full breasts, I got hard again. I jacked off in the shower. I wanted to do something special for her tomorrow when she got back, plan a special night for us. She had never had phone sex before and I appreciated she played along. She had even texted me sexual pics. It took a great deal of trust on her part to do that and given what was going on with her, I was honored she trusted me that much.

I was also worried about her and her safety. I had given it a lot of thought since I had talked to Margot. She wouldn't like it, but she needed to be protected twenty-four-seven. I laid in bed thinking about it and how to go about it. I also felt this irrational fear of losing her and how devastating that would be. I thought about how special she was. She had questioned why her? Why this was happening to her? I laughed aloud a little. Obviously, someone else felt about her as I did, someone deranged who wanted her, stalked her, would roofie her, break into her house, even

89

try to run her off the road to have her. She was right. It had to be someone from her job, someone who interacted with her and wanted her like I did.

CHAPTER 13

Kenzie

As the plane taxied to the gate, I took my phone off airplane mode and hit dial. Andy was at the top of my favorites contact list now. He answered on the first ring. "Hi, we're just pulling up to the gate and I'm close to the front of the plane. It shouldn't take me more than ten minutes to get out front."

"Call me when you're there and let me know what vestibule you're near," Andy's voice said.

I couldn't wait to see him. I had missed him very much while I had been away even though we had talked every night. "I will. I'll see you in a few."

He pulled up to the curb in my car a few minutes after I called him. He got out of the car and came around the car to hug me. It felt so good to again have his arms around me. The damage to the car was repaired. He'd completely taken care of it for me. He didn't know how thankful I was, even though I told him over and over. I noticed Trina's booster seat was in the car as he took my bags and set them to the backseat.

"You don't have any plans for the rest of the day, do you?" He asked.

I felt the smile spread over my face. "No, I was kind of hoping to spend it with you." I didn't believe in playing games or acting coy. He had already put it out there that he wanted to spend more time with me. "I missed you while I was gone."

Now he smiled wide. He leaned over and kissed me. I don't know how long the kiss lasted, but I know I put everything I felt for him into it. We only stopped when a knock to Andy's window startled us and brought us out of it.

A cop stood there with an amused look on his face. "Hey, move it along. You're holding up traffic, here!"

"Sorry," Andy apologized. We glanced at each other and giggled. "Oops," Andy said. "I missed you too," he said as he pulled away from the curb.

Andy got off the expressway at an exit that didn't lead to either of our places. "Where are we going?"

"My mom's house. I hope you don't mind. She wants to meet you, and I really want you to meet her too. She has lunch for us and then afterward, I thought we could take Trina to the zoo. It's one of her favorite places. She'll be thrilled to show you her favorite animals."

"That sounds nice. I wish I knew I'd be meeting your mom. I would have dressed differently." I wore an old San Diego Padres t-shirt and a pair of blue jean shorts. I didn't have much makeup on either. I would have made more of an effort if I'd known I was meeting his mom today.

"Yeah, she's more a Cincinnati Reds fan, but maybe you could turn the t-shirt inside out," he teased me. "But if you really want to impress her you should wear a Stevens Street Gym tank," he added with a laugh.

"Cute," I told him. "Seriously, I hope she didn't go to too much trouble. I don't want to put her out at all."

Andy laughed. "My mom loves to cook and loves to have people to cook for. Trust me, she was eager to make us lunch and meet you."

We pulled into the driveway of a house on a quiet, tree-lined street. It was just the type of neighborhood I would envision Andy growing up on. The house was your typical brick-front ranch, with window boxes full of colorful flowers bordered by white shutters. The small front porch had a swing on it and flower pots overflowing with flowers that matched those in the window boxes.

We held hands as we walked up to the front door. It opened as we reached it. Andy's mom greeted us with a warm smile. She was a beautiful woman in her sixties with short blond hair, a petite frame, and the same sparkling green eyes that Andy and Trina had.

"Mrs. Stevens, it's nice to meet you," I greeted, putting my hand out to shake hers.

She engulfed me in a hug. "I'm glad to finally meet you too, Mackenzie. Please, it's Sheri. Welcome." She led us inside into the cozy living room and then gave Andy a hug too. Family pictures hung on every wall in groupings. You'd think it would look cramped and overdone, but it didn't. It gave the room a homey, warm feeling. My eyes wandered over many of the pictures. She handed me a small framed photo of a baby from the entry table, that I only then noticed had dozens of small, mismatched frames on it. "Andy," she said with a smile. "Wasn't he a cute baby?"

I smiled as I memorized it. "Yes, he was," I agreed.

"Oh, Mom!" Andy complained.

"Kenzie!" Trina squealed.

She ran at me from the doorway to the kitchen. "Hey Kiddo!" I greeted, lifting her up as she reached me.

She gave me a hug. "Are you coming to the zoo with Daddy and me?"

"Wouldn't miss it!" I replied with a smile. "I can't wait for you to show me your favorite animals."

"Daddy wants Grandma to come too, and he said maybe we could stay at a hotel with a pool, so I can swim but only if you want to and will stay with us, but Daddy said Grandma and I would have our own room, but I want to be with you and Daddy," she jabbered in one long sentence that following almost made me dizzy.

"Trina," Andy said, taking her from my arms, "I haven't even asked Kenzie about staying at a hotel tonight, but if we do, you and Grandma will have a room to yourselves. Kenzie and I will be up much later, and we don't want to wake you when we come in." He smiled at me.

Yeah, that would be the reason for the separate room! I glanced at his mom. "Are you okay with this?" I asked her quietly. Neither of my parents would be, accompany us to babysit so we could have adult time in a separate bedroom. Maybe if we were married, but certainly not after knowing each other such a short time. Maybe that was the difference between parenting a daughter and a son.

Sheri looped her arm through mine and led me to the kitchen. Andy and Trina didn't immediately follow. I heard Andy talking to Trina as we left the room. I hoped he wasn't reprimanding her for her excitement. Then I heard him tell her they needed to go to the bathroom and wash their hands for lunch and knew that wasn't the case.

"Mackenzie, honey," Sheri said in a soft voice. "Andy doesn't let too many people near that little girl, so if he's inviting you into their lives like this, I know he has to be serious about you." She positioned me in front of herself and pinned me with a thoughtful stare. "The only thing I'm going to say is don't continue with this if you're not as serious as he is. They're a package deal and you must be willing to step up and be a mother to Trina if you want Andy in your life. Nothing less will work."

"Wow, you really don't beat around the bush, do you?" I asked, surprised by her bluntness.

"I love my son and my granddaughter and don't want either getting hurt. Trina's already getting attached to you. If that isn't a destination you want to be heading, you need to take the off ramp right now. But if that's where you want to go, then I say don't hold back one bit. Andy missed you while you were away. He's planned a special day and night in Louisville. I love to watch Trina's excitement at the zoo and I will gladly babysit tonight for you and Andy to have a nice evening."

Wow, what a great mom. I shouldn't have been surprised. Andy had told me how supportive his parents had been through everything with Trina, from the second Andy found out about her through now.

"I happen to think your son is very special and I want to spend as much time as I can with him and Trina. Before he introduced me to her on Wednesday, I understood and would never have pressed for more time with him, away from Trina. She's his daughter. She has to come first in his life. I'd never try to change that."

"Love is an amazing thing. I had a wonderful man I was blessed to be married to for thirty-five years before God called him home. We had five beautiful children together and somehow, I never felt pressed to rank anyone as coming first. It all just fit and worked."

I nodded and smiled. Yeah, well, it was a family they had created together, a much different scenario than me coming into his and Trina's life. I wouldn't point that out though. "It smells wonderful in here," I said glancing at the covered baking dish on the stove. "I hope you didn't go to too much trouble making lunch."

"Mackenzie, don't hold back. You've been invited in. Step into the role and make it yours." She gave me a hug and then lifted the lid on the pot that was on the stove to reveal a perfect, flakey pie crust. "One of Andy's favorites, my homemade chicken pot pie," she said with a smile.

"I can see why it's one of his favorites. It looks and smells wonderful. Thank you, Sheri." I wasn't thanking her for the pot pie.

Andy and Trina came into the room. Trina ran up to me. She took my hand in hers. "Sit next to me, Kenzie," she said pulling me towards the table.

I smiled at Andy. I liked that she wanted me to be next to her. It was very important to me that she accepted me. If she didn't, Andy, and I didn't stand a chance. "Are your hands washed for lunch, sweetie?" I asked, knowing Andy had just brought her to wash them. She held them up, palms to me and nodded her head yes. "Okay, which seat is yours?" I asked at the table. Only one had a booster seat strapped to it.

"Don't be silly," Trina said. She pointed to the booster seat. "That's my chair. No one else will fit."

I laughed. She climbed up and into it by herself. She was far more independent than I thought she'd be. She pointed to the chair next to her. I turned back to Sheri and Andy. "Can I do anything to help before I sit down?"

"No, babe, sit. Mom and I've got this."

Andy sat a plate in front of me and took a seat across from me as he sat his plate on the table. His mom carried two plates as well, a smaller one for Trina and another for herself. A glass pitcher of lemonade and glasses were on the table. It looked freshly made. Trina grabbed my hand and her grandmother's. Andy reached his hand towards me and took his mother's in his other hand.

"I get to say prayers," Trina said excitedly. She smiled at me. "Thank you, God, for the food and my family. Thank you for Kenzie for my Daddy and me. Amen," she said plainly. I was impressed and touched. "Was that grace okay, Daddy?"

Andy smiled at me. "It was, Trina. You did a good job," he said.

"Was that okay, Kenzie? Daddy told me I couldn't say," she said, stopping herself with her hand over her own mouth. "I can't say," her tiny voice squeaked out between her fingers.

"That's okay, sweetie," I said. "I don't want you to go against anything your Daddy said." I pressed a kiss to her forehead.

We ate and made plans for the day and evening. "Yes, I'd love to stay in Louisville with you, your grandma, and your Daddy tonight," I told Trina, my eyes flashing to Andy's. "I'll need to stop at home first though and pack a few things."

Andy just nodded. After lunch, he took me into the living room alone. "About packing a few things, you don't need to, babe. I stopped over and got you a few things." He held me in his arms as he spoke.

"I don't understand," I said.

"Kenzie, last weekend, when your house alarm went off, you saw it on my phone too, I know you did."

I did, but I was confused with what that had to do with me needing to stop home and pack. We hadn't talked about it at all, but I didn't care that he had my system alarm on his phone. "Yeah, I kind of forgot about it, since then. Why are you bringing it up now?"

"Kenzie, I had Brian put your system monitoring on my phone. Your whole system, including the door locks. Don't be mad, but I wanted to be able to watch over you and be sure you were safe."

"Okay, wait, the locks?" I guess I didn't equate the alarm with the locks.

"If you were in trouble in your house, I want, I need to be able to get in and help you. I'd never enter if you weren't there without your permission, but I went in today and packed a bag for you. Just a few things. I found that blue dress and the heels you wore on our first date and packed it for tonight. I wanted to see you again in that dress and I have reservations for dinner for us at a place that dress will be perfect for. Please don't be mad or let it creep you out. Today was the only time I have ever entered your house without you knowing it and I only did it to surprise you with tonight in Louisville. After last night," he whispered, pulling me up against his chest, "I felt we were close enough I could. I know you had never done that with anyone. Correct me if I'm wrong, but that was even more intimate for you than the love we've made, wasn't it?"

Honestly, I didn't know how I felt about it, any of it. I had him stay all last weekend at my house, so he was welcome there. If his plans tonight would have been staying at my house, I would have been all for it. But he had taken it upon himself to have a key to my house without me giving it to him or me knowing it. I didn't like that.

"If you weren't in danger, I wouldn't have had Brian give me the access, baby. Please believe that. And you are in danger. I really don't think this guy is done. Margot agrees he's escalating."

"You talked with Margot about this? She knows you have a key to my house?"

"I talked with her about this asshole and what kind of threat she thinks he is. She's as worried as I am about him and what he might do next. No, I didn't tell her I had access to your house. She does know though that I planned to take you to

Louisville overnight. She wants to know your movements. We both just care about you, Kenz." He watched me carefully. I know my face contorted as various thoughts processed through my mind. "Am I wrong that letting me in as you did last night was a huge step for you, took our relationship to a different, deeper level?"

He was right. It was a very intimate expression, engaging in that with him last night. I'd imagine it was as baring as his trust of me, letting me in with his daughter. I thought about it in those terms. What required more trust, letting me get close to his daughter or giving him the key to my house. The answer was obvious. The key to my home was nothing compared to the trust required to let someone into Trina's life. When thinking about it in those terms I felt petty for feeling upset about it.

"Kenzie, I'm serious about you, am in for the long haul. I'd never abuse having the access, but I did it to protect you."

Andy

I couldn't tell what Kenzie was thinking. She looked disturbed and deep in thought. She hadn't moved out of my arms though. I took that as a positive.

"If you would have asked, I would have given you the key. I trust you that much, as much as you trust me to let me into Trina's life. I have to tell you, I honestly don't know how I feel about this, that you just did it and didn't tell me."

"Okay, we're ready," Mom said cheerfully coming into the room with Trina. She saw the serious expressions on both our faces. Her expression changed as she glanced between Kenzie and me. "I'll just have Trina go to the bathroom before we leave." She pointed to the hallway that led to the bedrooms and bathroom.

"You're still coming with, aren't you?" I asked her after Mom and Trina had disappeared into the hallway.

"Yeah, I am," Kenzie said with a forced smile. "Is there anything else you need to confess to me? Now would be the time."

Only that I am in love with you, though I knew it wasn't the time to tell her that. I wanted to tell her that at the perfect moment and now was not it. "No, but I did tell you. I didn't have to today, but I wanted you to know. I'm worried about your safety, babe, and so is Margot."

She thought about that for a moment. "Did you happen to go into my lingerie drawer and pack anything sexy to go under that dress?" She asked much to my surprise.

I chuckled nervously. "No, but there might be a gift box from Victoria Secret in my bag."

Now she smiled. "Really?" I nodded. She raised up on her tippy-toes and placed a kiss on my cheek. Then her lips came to my ear. "And by the way, I'm serious about you too."

I pulled her to me and kissed her, really kissed her. I held her tightly to me, loving the feeling of her body flush against mine. I think my hand may even have been clutching her ass.

"We'll just wait in the car," Mom said.

I heard the front door open and then close. I didn't stop kissing Kenzie until a few minutes later. She smiled with an embarrassed look on her face as our lips parted. "I think we just made out in front of your mom," she said. I laughed. Yeah, well, she better get used to it.

I went into Mom's room and grabbed her overnight bag from the bed. Then I led Kenzie to the car. Mom and Trina were in the backseat. I put mom's bag in the trunk. It was just past noon. It would take just about an hour to reach the zoo in Louisville. We still had all day.

Kenzie

The drive to the zoo and the afternoon there was comfortable and fun. I was so glad Andy arranged this with his mom there. It gave me the chance to get to know her and Trina better. I realized it also gave her the chance to get to know me better too. It couldn't be easy for her to trust an outsider with her granddaughter. Sheri was an amazing person. The love she had for her family was apparent in all she did. Andy had already told me all about his four younger siblings, but hearing how Sheri talked about her children, I saw the respect she had for each of them and it showed me that she was proud of the adults they had grown into.

She encouraged me to step into a role with Trina that I never would have presumed to take on my own this soon. At one point, Trina had to use the bathroom. Sheri asked me if I'd take her, rather than herself. Andy seemed surprised, but caught on. I saw the appreciation he had for his mom that she was promoting my relationship with Trina. I could see myself easily loving this little girl. She was a joy to be with. I loved to see her excitement, and she had such good manners. Seeing Andy with her all day made me love him all the more. He was a fantastic dad, patient and loving.

We spent four hours at the zoo which seemed to be Trina's limit. She was just beginning to get whiney when we headed towards the exit. Her grandmother's promise of going to the hotel to swim instantly quieted her protests of leaving. Andy had been so wonderful with her I wondered if anything would fluster or anger him. In the short time I'd known him I saw only the best qualities in him. I again wondered how he could be single and I also wondered why me. What did he see in me and why was I let into his world?

On the drive to the hotel Sheri asked me more about my family and favorite childhood memories. We'd touched on it some during the day. She was glad to hear I was close with them even though they lived so far away. I didn't know if Sheri knew about the incidents, so I didn't bring anything up. I felt bad because I had not talked to my parents too much since I met Andy. I didn't want to tell them about what was happening, and I didn't want to lie to them that everything was okay either, so I didn't call. My sister was busy with her two kids and her life in southern California, so we normally didn't talk but once a month. I hadn't talked to her either since I met Andy. No one in my family knew about him. I didn't confess this to Sheri though.

Andy

We got Mom and Trina settled in their room across the hall from Kenzie's and mine. Mom was going to treat Trina to a swim at the pool, and dinner at the pool grill, followed by more swimming. Trina loved to swim. She'd sleep well tonight! I blew up her arm floaties before Kenzie and I gave her a goodnight kiss and hug.

"Thanks, Mom," I said, giving her a kiss before I guided Kenzie out the door. If we didn't leave now, we may never leave. Trina was begging us to stay and go swimming with them and I think Kenzie was about to fold.

The room Kenzie and I were in overlooked the city. It was a beautiful evening. Kenzie looked out the window. We were on the tenth floor. The sun was just dipping below the city buildings. Sunset was about an hour away. The view was spectacular. But that wasn't what my eyes were on. I came up behind her and wrapped my arms around her. I nuzzled her neck with my cheek and pressed my entire body against her.

"We have just over an hour until we have to leave for dinner," I said as I pressed kisses to her neck.

"I have to shower," she said. "I have zoo dirt all over me."

"I can be ready in ten minutes, including a shower. How long will it really take you?" I ground my pelvis into her ass. She moaned out her approval.

"Thirty-five, if I don't shave," she said.

"Don't shave," I said, sliding my hand up her shirt to cup her gorgeous full breasts.

I had her naked in seconds. I did move her away from the window. I didn't want to give all of Louisville the show of my beautiful Kenzie's sexy body. I didn't care if she had zoo dirt or even animal crap all over her. After watching her with my daughter and my mom all afternoon, I wanted to make love to her now. Make that, I needed to make love to her right now. My heart had swelled by how natural she interacted with Trina and by how much Trina gravitated to her. I loved how comfortable she was with my mom too. She fit. There was no other way to describe it. She just fit.

My cock fit in her, too, very well, very erotically. I usually liked hours for us to be with each other. Twenty-five minutes was the fastest we ever wrapped up a love-making session. We'd make up for it later! After dinner, we had all night. We showered together, and I watched her do a quick makeup job. She didn't need any more than she put on. She was beautiful. I watched as she blew dry her hair and scrunched a product in it that made her loose, natural curls shiny. She slicked on a shiny gloss on her lips and grabbed her dress. She still wore only the towel. Fuck! I wanted to cancel dinner and take her back to bed.

"Underclothing?" She asked, pinning me with her beautiful, brown eyes.

I had been gawking at her as she got ready, blatantly gawking at her with lust. My lips curved into a grin. Yeah, she busted me. I grabbed the small Victoria Secret box from my bag and held it over my head. "It'll cost you a kiss," I teased.

Her lips came to a full smile. Her eyes sparkled at me as she came up to me and pressed one to my lips that brought my cock back to life. She stepped back and dropped the towel. "If you want more of this after dinner, it'll cost you that box you're holding over your head."

I loved how she teased me right back. I loved her style. I loved her. I decided I'd tell her tonight. I handed her the box and watched her remove the lacy little set I had picked out. It was in black and dark blue to match her dress. The bra was a push up style that I couldn't wait to see on her. The panties, if you could call them that, were lace, see-through, a fabric so sheer and so lightweight I'd have to be careful I didn't shred them taking them off her.

I watched her put them on. "Twirl around," I told her before she put her dress on. She did a sexy little spin for me, her eyes locked on mine, a flirty smile on her face. I had to readjust my cock in my pants. It was suddenly uncomfortable. I zipped her dress for her and fastened a simple gold diamond pendent necklace around her neck, hers. I wished I had gotten her a necklace too. She was ready with two minutes to spare. We stepped out of the room. She looked beautiful. I knew I wouldn't be able to take my eyes off her all night. While we waited for the elevator, I kissed her again, nowhere near done with her for the night.

Kenzie

We took the elevator to the revolving restaurant on the twenty-fifth floor. I had never eaten here, but it was well known for exquisite cuisine as well as breathtaking views of the city and the Ohio River. Andy had gotten us a table against the glass. I'm not sure how he pulled that off with very little notice. The sun was just beginning to set. It was a clear night. It was the perfect evening to enjoy the view.

Dinner was delicious and of course Andy's company made it special. We were so compatible it was scary. I'd always been a believer that when something seemed too good to be true, it was usually too good to be true. I had decided that I wouldn't hold back waiting for the other shoe to drop. I would be fully in every moment that I had with him and wouldn't hold back.

We shared a decadent dessert, enjoyed Bailey's spiked coffee like we had all night. Under the surface was the constant desire to take it back to bed. I had never wanted a man like I wanted Andy. I couldn't keep my hands off him as he unlocked our room door. This evening had been perfect. The restaurant had been incredible, the view, the food, and Andy's company. I knew I had really fallen for him.

We made love in the darkened room with the curtains open over the large window. The stars and moon were as bright as the city lights streaming through. The incredible things he did to my body had me gasping and crying out repeatedly. I ran my hungry hands over every inch of him, over every solid, muscular inch. My hand found its way to his rigid length. The sound of appreciation that came out of his mouth when I stroked him excited me. I loved how uninhibited he was, how vocal about his pleasure he was.

"Oh, fuck, Kenzie," he whispered. "What you do to me is incredible!"

He kissed me more deeply and lined his body parts up with mine, preparing to enter me. We were lying half on, half off the bed. This would be a new position, one that would give us both a good view of his cock going in and out of me. It was erotic to watch, having the visual along with the physical sensation. He wore a tortured expression on his face as he slowly slid in me, inch by incredible inch. My eyes bounced between his eyes and the view down below.

Andy

That had to be one of the hottest views I'd ever had, watching my cock fuck Kenzie's tight pussy. My eyes alternated between the erotic show and Kenzie's beautiful and animated face. As she watched too, which was a fucking turn-on, I saw pure lust and uninhibited excitement in her eyes. I loved how she threw her head back and her hooded eyes rolled back, how her mouth gasped open as I felt her pussy tighten in a vise grip around my cock when she came. The sounds that came out of her pushed me over the edge. I didn't last long. Before I wanted it to end, I was shooting my seed so deep inside her you'd think there was a prize for doing so. I didn't want to pull out and end the incredible contact, the incredible sensation of joining with this amazing woman. I kissed her again and then stared deeply into her eyes. This was the moment I'd been waiting for, the perfect moment to tell her I loved her.

Both our phones wailed out, the screens flashing red. "Fuck," I cursed and grabbed hold of mine. It was her system, the back door in alarm, again. The system reset immediately. The control pad in the kitchen had to have been manually reset out of alarm mode. I pulled up the camera feed watched it, rewound it and watched it again. Nothing. No one entered, the back door never opened. What the fuck?

Kenzie was already on the phone to Margot. She covered herself with a sheet on the bed. She was curled up into a nervous ball of energy sitting there with a scowl set across her face. "Yeah, be careful," she said before she hung up. "Margot's going to go over. She has my code." She rubbed her forehead. "Fuck, Andy, why is this happening?"

I sat beside her and wrapped my arms around her which was all I could do to help her. "I don't know babe. Whoever it is knew you were due back today, probably expected you to be there." She dropped her head against my chest and we reclined.

We didn't speak another word to each other. I just held her until Margot called her back an hour later. Margot quickly put her at ease. Nothing had been wrong at her place. The system was armed and showed no problems. The back door, all doors and windows were secure. I wasn't buying that it was a system glitch. I knew Brian Porter and his work too well. He didn't install anything flawed.

She wrapped her arms around me and snuggled in closer to me. Her body was tense. I stroked over her and held her for a really long time until she fell asleep. I wasn't sure what to do next. How could I keep her safe? I couldn't be there with her at all times and she had already said she wouldn't move in with me, yet. I smiled when I thought about it. She had said not yet. She hadn't said not at all. I loved this woman, and I wanted her with me, with Trina, always. Today had been perfect, her, me, Trina, my mom, all of us together.

The one thing I decided I would do was that I would call Brian Porter and have him check the system out. Maybe he could figure it out.

Kenzie

We met Andy's mom and Trina at the hotel breakfast buffet. I hadn't slept well. The house alarm going off again really rocked me. Andy told me he would call Brian Porter and have him look into it. I didn't think there was a problem with the system. I moreover believed something had breached my house last night even though we saw nothing on the camera feed. Everyone at work knew my travel schedule. I was still convinced it was someone at work. The more that I had thought about it, the surer I was. But I wasn't sure what to do next.

When we arrived back in Lexington, we left Trina with Sheri and met Margot and Brian Porter at my house. After a thorough system check Brian reported it clean. The camera in the kitchen area hadn't shown anyone enter the house, so the alarm and reset of the system looked like a hack-job to Brian. But why would someone set off my alarm and then reset it when I wasn't even there?

"Who at your job would have the skills to hack into the system?" Margot asked.

"Name any of the technical geeks and I'm sure they could," I replied. I turned to Brian, who stood there looking pretty pissed off. My eyes met his. "You really think my system was hacked and that no one was really here last night?"

He nodded, his ballcap bobbing. "I'm sorry, Kenzie, I do. It's a pretty secure system and has never been hacked before to my knowledge. Give me a day, I'll beef up the security protocols. The fucker won't get in again."

"You're not staying here until we're sure it's safe," Andy said. "Go pack a bag, you're staying at my place until we get this sorted out."

"And I'm not crazy about the idea of you going into work tomorrow, either," Margot added.

"I have to go to work and I can't stay away from my house indefinitely," I said throwing my hands into the air.

"Kenzie, this asshole tried to run you off the road and has hacked into your security system. He's got balls, and he's got brains and you need to take this threat seriously," Andy said bluntly.

I knew it and I didn't need to hear it. His words made me shudder. "Can't someone figure out where the hack came from, trace it back to him?" I asked.

"I'll have Cybercrimes look into it, but I suspect he's probably covered his tracks well," Margot said.

"Put me in touch with the investigator from Cybercrimes. I'll work with him," Brian Porter volunteered. "I know this system inside an out."

Margot nodded. "I think fear and intimidation were his goals last night. If he could hack into your system, he had to have known you weren't home."

"I don't understand," I admitted. "All along his motivation seemed to be getting me. That's why he roofied me and tried to run me off the road, right? Certainly, he knows scaring me with last night's hacking would keep me away from the house and keep me with Andy. It makes no sense."

Andy wrapped his arms around me and drew me in close. I felt his hard body behind me and he nuzzled me, his cheek to mine. "It's okay babe, breathe."

"Don't try to figure out what this guy is thinking, Kenzie, you'll drive yourself crazy. Let's go upstairs and pack you a bag," Margot said. "I agree with Stevens, you shouldn't stay here till we figure out the hack."

Someone pick me up from the floor! Margot agreed with Andy. I of course was still standing, but to hear her say she agreed with him was a shocker. I nodded and went up the stairs. Margot was right behind me.

Andy

Kenzie had an edge to her the rest of the day. She tried not to show that she was upset but I could feel the tension radiating from her. She was great with Trina though. Trina loved having her there and didn't seem to notice that anything was wrong. Kenzie and Trina made a salad, and I grilled steaks for dinner. We ate with Trina at the table on the back deck. It was comfortable, and I wanted this every night.

"I need to be up and gone for work by seven tomorrow," Kenzie said.

"Do you want me to drive you?" I offered.

"No, I want you to get back to your normal schedule. I want to stop imposing on you. I'll be fine," she insisted.

I covered her hand with mine and gave it a squeeze. Trina watched us closely. "We like having you here, don't we Trina?" I asked. She excitedly agreed. "And you're not imposing. You know I would really love it if you would L-I-V-E, H-E-R-E," I spelled it out. There was no reason to plant that concept in Trina's head, yet.

I still had not told Kenzie I loved her because of the way the mood had been broken the night before and because of how tense she still was. She smiled at my spelled-out statement. As long as she smiled I knew I had a chance of that happening. I was just glad that Trina was oblivious to everything.

"Why don't you work in the gym with my daddy?" Trina asked.

Kenzie smiled at her. "I have a different job, kiddo," she said. "Though that would be very nice to spend all day, every day, with your daddy."

I smiled at the thought of it. Wouldn't that be the best? I'd love for Kenzie to work at the gym. I wished in that moment that I could make that happen. Out of the mouths of babes! Yeah, that became my new end goal, for Kenzie to move in with us and work in the gym with me.

That night when we went to bed Kenzie was exhausted. Even though I wanted to make love to her, I could see she wasn't in the right state of mind for it. We snuggled under the covers and I held her tightly. I didn't escalate things, and neither did she. She seemed content to just be held. Before I knew it, she had drifted off to sleep. I laid there awake, holding her, for a long time. This was the first time we'd been together that we hadn't made love. That realization disturbed me.

She rushed out the next morning with barely a kiss goodbye. Trina was still asleep. I stood on the back deck watching the tail lights of her car pull away. She promised me she would text when she made it to the office and that she would be careful all day. She'd also let me know when she was leaving work to head back to my place. I hoped Margot and the Cybercrimes division could figure this out soon. It was really starting to wear on Kenzie.

Kenzie

I felt a new level of paranoia all day at work. Had one of my coworkers really hacked my security system for the sole purpose of intimidation and fear as Margot thought? If so, that was just cruel and crazy. The only saving grace was that no one knew about the car trying to run me off the road last week, or of the alarm going into alert on Saturday night. I was vigilant for anyone who seemed to know something or anyone who watched me to see if I was off at all.

Joe and several of the other guys still avoided too much conversation with me. I didn't blame them. Stoner-Todd, as I would now always think of him was more talkative with me than usual. I guess he had considered that we had bonded discussing his DUIs and drug use, either that or he was feeling me out to see if I had told anyone about him. Marcus and Lindy were out of town at an on-site in Chicago and my boss Dale, was out sick. He still ran the standing Monday morning staff meeting by dialing in.

A client I had brought up a few months back in Cleveland was having integration and training issues. While I had been out last week, Dale promised them I'd come on-site. He already had me booked on an early morning flight on Tuesday. *Great, just fucking great!* He also had me booked to give two demos later this week, I learned. I'd have to work my ass off preparing them while traveling. I hadn't even spoken with the potential client yet to get specific deliverables.

"You've got to be fucking kidding me!" Andy exploded to the news that I'd be heading back to Blue Grass Airport early the next morning. "I'm sorry," he calmed himself a second later. "I'm just worried about you."

"I'm traveling alone this time, so at least I don't have to worry about any of my coworkers."

Andy stepped close and embraced me. I let myself relax into him as much as I could. I was tense, there was no denying that. I was nearing my breaking point. You hear stories about women being stalked for months or years, moving several times in an attempt to keep their locations a secret. This had only been going on a few weeks and I was already at the end of my rope. I couldn't imagine it going on much longer, or how crazy I'd be by then. Margot had to figure this out, and soon.

"Babe, I can feel the stress in your whole body," Andy said softly, bringing me out of my thoughts. His hands kneaded my shoulders. "Get changed into some workout gear. We're going down to the gym. You need to release some endorphins."

I think I moaned out loud. Yeah, a workout was never the first thought I had when I felt stressed. It was usually eating something rich and sinful, a piece of chocolate peanut butter pie sounded good. I also should get some work done this evening, starting right now. Neither of those demos were going to program themselves.

"I know something else that releases endorphins," I said with my best lust-filled smile.

"You don't know how tempting that is," Andy said. "After," he added, his gaze focusing on me like the cat eying the canary.

He had already switched into personal trainer mode as Logan had called it. *Great, just fucking great!*

I will admit, after an hour and a half in the gym beginning with cardio, a full-body workout of weighted equipment, and even some punching and kicking a heavy bag, I felt better. I was dripping wet, sweat pooling in places of my body I didn't know it could.

When we went back up to Andy's apartment my intention was to get in the shower right away. Andy had other ideas. He took me up on my earlier offer, before we got in the shower, in the shower, and then after. We only got dressed when we did because Trina was due home. She had been at her friend Molly's house for a play date and had stayed for dinner. Andy and I hadn't eaten yet, well not dinner.

As I opened my laptop, Andy threw a couple chicken breasts on the grill. I sat out on the deck at the table to be near him and started to put the first of the demos together. Trina came home a few minutes later and gave me a big hug. I got no more work done. Instead we read her favorite story about Duke dog.

The remainder of the night went quickly and before I knew it we had tucked Trina in bed and Andy and I were snuggling together in his bed again. I didn't even remember saying good night before the alarm woke me at five a.m. Tuesday morning. I must have fallen asleep that quickly. Back to the airport was the last place I wanted to go. Reluctantly, I pressed a kiss to Andy's lips, embraced him, and pulled myself behind the wheel of my car. I watched him ascend the wood staircase, back up to the deck, before I put the car in drive.

Andy

I hated watching Kenzie drive away. Yesterday had been wonderful, her coming home to my place after work, us working out together in the gym, and then making love before dinner. When Trina came home, and Kenzie closed her laptop with a smile to focus on my baby, my heart melted. I knew she would always make time for Trina, no matter how busy her work schedule was. Later, it seemed so natural that we tucked Trina in together and read her a couple stories. Then we retired to my bed together, and I held her. Her form relaxed into me and just like that, she fell asleep, content and safe. It was so comfortable, so natural, and perfect.

Her job and this traveling bull-shit was the only part that I disliked. Before Trina had asked why she didn't work at the gym, I hadn't given it any thought. I wondered how I could make that happen as I watched her taillights turn the corner and disappear. Maybe that was too selfish to think, but I didn't care. I liked having her as a part of my life and as I told Logan, I deserved it. It had been way too long since I was with a woman who made me this happy. The last four years were about taking care of everyone and everything else in my life. Didn't I deserve to be a little selfish?

Kenzie

The week went by quickly and without incident. I talked on the phone with Andy and Trina every night while I was in Cleveland. I really missed them both. I got the client back on track, got both demos programmed and conducted one Thursday evening from the hotel with a company in California. I flew back Friday morning and would conduct the second demo from the office Friday afternoon.

I arrived at the office just after lunch. I went right into Dale Miller's office to report in. "Close the door, Kenzie," he said much to my surprise.

"What is it?"

"That cop came back earlier this morning with a warrant. The police's Cybercrimes division is accessing our network as we speak. Would you like to tell me what exactly they're looking for?"

This was news to me. Margot didn't reach out to me regarding any of this. "I don't know, Dale. Detective Malone didn't contact me at all."

"Were there any other incidents that I should be aware of?" He asked.

"I'm not sure I'm at liberty to say," I replied. Everyone who had been out that first night I got roofied was a suspect, including Dale.

"What the fuck is that supposed to mean?" He demanded.

"I'm not sure what the police want me to disclose or not, pending their investigation," I said.

He ran his fingers through his hair. He nodded towards the door, dismissing me. "I'm not even sure what to say to you at this point," he said.

"I'm sorry, Dale. Just trust me that if they got a warrant, it's important."

I left his office and went to my desk. I sent a text to Margot right away. I sent a second to Andy while I waited for her reply, which didn't come. Through his office window, Dale Miller stared daggers through me. I glanced around the office. No one else looked upset or nervous. No one stared at me like he did, so he must not have shared the serving of the warrant with anyone else.

An hour later, Margot and two uniformed officers came through the door and went straight to Dale's office. She closed his door. They were only in there a few minutes when the door reopened, and Dale led her and the uniforms to the locked Network room. Dale badged them in. A few minutes later they came back out, with Todd Johnson in cuffs.

I came to my feet and rushed to meet them as they led Todd to the door. "Margot?" I questioned. "What are you doing?"

"I'm sorry, Kenzie, you need to step back."

She led me to Dale's office and closed the door with just the two of us in there. I watched through the window as the uniformed officers led Todd Johnson out of the building, his hands cuffed behind his back. All our coworkers were on their feet watching the show. A few split their attention between Todd Johnson's arrest and me within the boss' office with Margot.

"It took some doing, but we traced the hack back to this company's server. Todd Johnson's credentials were used to remote in from his home IP address and that was the origin of the hack to your security system Saturday night."

I just stared at her in disbelief. Todd Johnson? I never would have suspected him. "Why, do you know why he did it?"

"I'm hoping I will after I talk with him at the station," Margot said.

"Do you need me to come in and give a statement?"

"No, just don't say too much around here, okay? I'll call you later after I interrogate him."

I watched her leave the office and then the building. I think I was in shock. I just stood there, staring out the window at all my coworkers. I felt tears fill my eyes. They got him. It was finally over. Then I realized all my coworkers were staring at me. No one had gone back to work. Everyone stood around almost traumatized.

Dale finally returned to his office, which I still stood in. "Your home security system was hacked?"

I guess Margot had told him that much. I nodded my head yes. "I can't believe it was Todd," I said.

He gazed out the window at all our coworkers, who now had moved into small groups and talked amongst themselves. "We need to head this off. They need to get back to work and not focus on this. I need to remind everyone that Todd is innocent until proven guilty. After he makes bail and comes back to work," he began, but I interrupted him.

"Are you fucking kidding me, Dale?" I said, my voice louder than I planned. Everyone in the office halted their conversations and stared my way. "Until he is proven guilty or innocent, he can't come back to work. Do you have any fucking idea what I've gone through these past few weeks? I was roofied, my house was broken into twice, someone followed me and tried to run me off the road, and then my security system was hacked. Until we know if it was Todd or not, I cannot be forced to work with him. You have to suspend him until the facts are in."

"Maybe you could just work from home, Kenzie?" Dale suggested.

"Fuck you, Dale! Either Todd is suspended or is the one who works from home or I will slap you and ATS with a civil suit so fast, your head will explode."

"Kenzie, calm down," Dale said.

"I am calm," I said in a voice I didn't recognize. "Continue with your prior thoughts and you will see fucking angry. Think about this and the allegations against him. Just the hacking alone is grounds for his immediate dismissal, using company resources to commit an illegal act. Suspend him, Dale, or I go public and I will ruin you."

Dale was shocked. "You are upset. I understand. Yes, of course, Todd will be suspended. You should take the rest of the day off, Kenzie, get some rest. I can see this has worn you down."

"I have a demo in twenty minutes. I'll think about taking the rest of the afternoon off when it's done," I said and then calmly left his office. My hands shook.

Everyone stared at me as I went back to my desk. An emotion was surging through me that I couldn't describe, a combination of shock, anger, relief, and sadness. Dale began walking up to our coworkers and speaking with them in small groups. They began to disburse after he had spoken with them. All the smokers headed for the smoking exit, cigarettes in hand.

I sent a quick text message to Andy informing him of my coworker's arrest. I told him I'd call him after the demo. Then I carried my laptop into the conference room I would use for the demo. Marcus Holland and Lindy Hall followed me in. Lindy had a cigarette in her hand, she was heading out with the other smokers.

"Kenzie, are you okay?" Lindy asked.

I shook my head no. "I'm sorry, I lost it. I can't believe they traced it to Todd Johnson. I can't believe he did any of those things to me."

Lindy hugged me. "I can't either. It has to be a mistake."

I wasn't so sure it was a mistake, but I still couldn't believe it was Todd.

"Knowing you, you probably wouldn't have believed it was any of us," Marcus said. "Did all those things really happen to you?"

I stared at him in disbelief. Did he think I was making it up? "Yeah, it's been terrifying."

"If you need anything, let me know," Marcus said. "I could come over tonight, if you don't want to be alone," he offered.

"Yeah, we support you, but that doesn't mean we don't support Todd too, you know, until it's proven. I don't even know how I'm supposed to feel about this, but I want to be here for you," Lindy added awkwardly. "I'm busy tonight though," she added.

I forced a smile. "I'm fine tonight, but thanks." Their offers were sweet, kind of. "I have to get ready for a demo. Thanks, guys. I'll talk to you later."

They left, and I was glad to be alone. I was emotionally exhausted. I just had to get through the next hour and a half and then I could leave, which I already decided I would.

Focusing was hard through the demo. It didn't help that it had been put together quickly and I hadn't had much time to confer with the potential client. I was surprised when it was done, and they asked for a proposal including the Statement of Work the next morning. They had decided to go with us on the spot.

"Will that be a problem?" The voice came through the speaker phone. "We're a twenty-four by seven operation and I want to get this put to bed tomorrow. If you can have it in my inbox first thing tomorrow morning. I can have it signed and returned to you by end of day. The partners are playing golf tomorrow and I can get it taken care of easily."

"Sure, that's not a problem," I replied. Fuck, putting it together tonight was the last thing I wanted to do on a Friday night after being out-of-town most of the week and dealing with Todd's arrest.

"Fantastic, thank you, Kenzie," his voice said. "I look forward to working with you on this implementation."

"Thanks, Scott, me too. I'll have that in your inbox tonight." I ended the call, signed off, and then hit dial on my phone.

Andy answered on the first ring. "Hi babe, are you okay?"

I could hear the concern in his words, but just the sound of his voice washing through me brought me peace. "I am now. I can't believe it was Todd Johnson," I told him. "I hope he gives Margot a full statement. I need to know why."

"It's over babe, and as long as he's locked up, you're safe. That's all I care about."

I knew I should feel the same, but I didn't. I needed him to confess and tell Margot why. Then it would be over for me. Until then, I would always wonder why he had done it and what I possibly could have done to deserve it or if I had done anything to encourage it. Even as I thought this, I knew it was crazy to feel this way. I should just be glad it was over, and he was in custody.

"Babe, you still there?" Andy asked.

I hadn't realized I blanked out on our conversation. "I'm sorry, yes. I was just thinking about it all."

"So, is that a yes? You'll be over right after work? This calls for a celebration!"

I hadn't a clue what he had said, and I wasn't going to ask. I moaned out my frustration. "No, that isn't a yes. I have to put together a proposal and a SOW for the client I just did the demo for. They will get it signed tomorrow. I have a solid three hours of work I have to do tonight."

"What? On a Friday night?" Andy complained.

"I know. I'm not thrilled with it either."

"Come over, you can do it from here and then we'll have the rest of the night," Andy urged.

I considered it for a few seconds. "I haven't been home, really, in a couple weeks. And it's safe now, so I should go home. Tomorrow is trash pickup day and I haven't had it out in several weeks. I should at least get it out. Tell you what, I'll go home tonight, get my work done and then I'll come over tomorrow morning and we'll have the rest of the weekend."

"Babe, I'm not going to complain about your job, but I really wanted to be with you tonight. You've been gone since Tuesday."

"Andy, I know, please, just let me do what I need to tonight and I'll see you tomorrow morning. Now that it's over I need to get back to a normal routine," I said. My voice sounded whiney even to me. "We'll have that celebratory dinner tomorrow night."

"You're sure you're okay to be alone tonight?" Andy asked.

"Yeah, I am. He's in custody and I'm safe. And I really do need to get this proposal done tonight. I'll talk to you later, okay?"

I heard the hesitation in Andy's voice when he replied. "Okay. Call me with any info from Margot, okay?"

"I promise I will."

By the time I left the office it was already past five, way later than I wanted to leave. After I left the conference room, I was the target of many of my coworker's conversations and questions. Evidently my desk was the place to congregate. I couldn't recall a Friday that my coworkers didn't race out the door as early as possible. Of course, it wasn't every day one of our coworkers was arrested at work.

And then Dale Miller stopped me as I was nearing the exit to apologize for his insensitivity when Todd was arrested. He explained he had just been shocked. Yeah, well, he wasn't the only one. He was trying to smooth things over with me and even asked if I was serious about filing a suit against him and ATS. Oh, so that was it!

I called in a food order at my favorite Chinese restaurant near my house and picked it up on my way home. As I sat the takeout bag on the passenger seat, Margot called and brought me up to date on everything involving the case. I was shocked so much had taken place in the few short hours since Todd's arrest. When I hung up and turned the car over, it was getting dark outside. I guess it was later than I thought.

I immediately dialed Andy as I shifted into reverse to back out of my parking spot. "Hi babe," I said. "Margot just called."

I relayed to him what Margot had told me. At first, Todd Johnson cooperated and answered questions, swearing his innocence. He claimed he had a twenty-four-hour flu bug Saturday and spent the day and evening in bed, so he had no alibi that he hadn't hacked into my system. His cell phone signal confirmed it had not left his home area all day. The night I'd been followed and nearly run off the road, his cell phone pinged in the same area I had been in, at the same time. He claimed he'd left his phone at work that night and it was still on his desk the next morning. He had no alibi for that night either. That Saturday night someone was in my house when Andy and I got back from our first date, his friends confirmed his alibi, that he was out with them, but later, hours after Andy and I had surprised the intruder in my house. He had no alibi for that early in the evening. When presented with these facts he lawyered up, still maintaining his innocence and actually suggested someone was setting him up.

"What does Margot think?" Andy asked.

"She's sure he's guilty. It doesn't help that he has two DUIs, a couple of prior charges for possession and they found drugs and drug paraphernalia at his house when they searched it. They're testing what they found, but she thinks he actually had some of the same drug I was given and was in my vitamins."

"That is pretty damning," Andy said.

"She suggested an angle I hadn't considered why he did it. Evidently, he fears another round of layoffs are coming soon and she thinks he considers me his prime competition ahead of himself to keep my job if one of us is going to lose theirs. I'm not sure why she thinks this. Todd and I don't even do the same thing there."

"That's weird," Andy agreed. "Is he still locked up?"

"Yeah, doesn't even go before a judge to be arraigned until tomorrow. Margot's not sure about bail or how much it would be. The evidence is pretty solid. I guess we'll find out tomorrow."

"If he gets out, I won't want you home alone, you know that, don't you?" Andy pressed.

A smile came to my lips. I liked how protective he was. "I do plan to be at your place tomorrow morning and for the rest of the weekend. We'll talk about it after the arraignment."

"Just be careful tonight, okay?" Andy said.

"I promise, and I'll call you later after I get this work done," I said as I pulled into my driveway. "I'm home now. I'll talk to you later," I said.

I pulled into the garage and carried my bags into the house. Entering the code into the alarm system upon entry had become second nature. I went back out and wheeled the trash and then the recycling bins out to the curb. Then I re-closed the garage and locked everything up for the night feeling relieved that Todd Johnson was in custody. I still couldn't believe it had been him. I ate my Chinese at my kitchen table and then unpacked my laptop from my bag.

Andy

I really wished Kenzie would have come over to stay. I loved having her at my place with Trina and me. But I knew she was anxious to get back to a normal routine. Todd Johnson was in custody, the fucking scumbag, and she was safe.

I pulled up her kitchen camera on my laptop and watched her unpack her laptop from her bag. It sucked she had so much work to finish up on a Friday night. As relieved as I was Johnson was in custody, I wished it hadn't distracted her day. If it hadn't, maybe she would have finished this proposal at work and she'd be with me instead right now. I respected that she had work to do and was so dedicated. She was good at what she did.

She had emailed me a concept for the marketing program to attract more women to the gym while she was out of town. It was good, and I planned to put it into action. She also had a whole social media side to it that I hadn't considered as well as a member newsletter that would help build the community I wanted to further at the gym with our clients. She had delivered what I asked for and more. The idea of her working at the gym with me solidified and I could see how it could work well.

I tuned into her camera feed several times throughout the evening, after tucking Trina in, and a few more times while I worked on some of the marketing plan she had sent. I would have to have her help with the social media stuff. I knew when I was in over my head. I checked on her again just before ten. She was still at her table working. I picked up the phone and dialed her, anyway.

"Hello," she answered. I watched on the camera feed how she smiled when she saw it was me. That still made me feel incredibly good, knowing it made her happy when I called.

"Hi babe, how's your night been? All quiet?"

"Yeah, and I'm just finishing up my work, about to hit send on the email to the client, good timing."

"You've been working on it all night?"

"Yeah, this one couldn't be the standard boiler plate verbiage. I had to meet a lot of custom requirements from them, otherwise it wouldn't have taken this long."

I watched her tap on her keyboard and then she shut the lid to her laptop. "I'm sorry, babe, that was a sucky way to spend your Friday night."

"Yeah, please believe I would have preferred to spend it with you and Trina."

I watched her run her fingers through her hair, yawn and then she rubbed her eyes. She looked exhausted again. "If you want, I could see about getting Logan to take Trina for the night and I could be there in a half hour," I offered.

Her face lit with that beautiful smile of hers again. "That's sweet of you, but really, I'm beat. I'm probably going to just go up and go to bed when we get off the phone. I'll be over early tomorrow."

"Okay, babe," I said. I preferred to be holding her in my arms tonight, so she'd really sleep soundly, but I wouldn't push it. "I'll let you go then, so you can get to bed. I'll see you tomorrow."

"Thanks, Andy," she said. I watched her yawn again. "I'll come up the back when I get to your place tomorrow, and I'll text you, so you know I'm there."

After we hung up, I watched her move around the kitchen for a few minutes and then she turned the lights off on her way into the front hallway. I brought up the feed from the upstairs camera and watched her go into the room, closing the door behind her.

Just then, Logan knocked at my hallway door.

"Come in," I called. Since when did he knock?

"Hey," he greeted, stepping into the kitchen. "Is Kenzie here?" He asked, plopping down in the chair across from me.

"No, is that why you knocked?"

Logan grabbed us two beers from my fridge. "Well, yeah, I'm trying to be respectful. Give me some credit."

"They traced the hack from Saturday night and arrested the scumbag who's been harassing Kenzie today. It was one of her coworkers," I told Logan.

"Really?" He asked, clearly surprised. He held his beer up to me. I tapped mine against his. "Here's to a normal relationship now."

I smiled. It was a relief.

"So why isn't she here? On a Friday night?" Logan asked.

"She had a shit-ton of work to get done tonight. She's safe, so she went home. She's coming over first thing tomorrow morning and will be here rest the weekend." I took a long pull from my beer. "I asked her to move in," I told Logan. After a few second silence, a silence during which his eyes were probing mine. I smiled wide. "Trina loves her."

"And did she agree?" Logan asked.

"She didn't say no. She said we'd talk about it after all this crap was over."

"And it's over now," Logan said, finishing my sentence. "Man, that's great, really."

I smiled wider. "Thanks. I really love her. She just fits so well, with me, with Trina, even with my mom. She did a marketing promotion for the gym, here let me show you. It's great."

The laptop screen had gone dark. I brought it back to life and as I turned it to show Logan, the camera feed of her upstairs hallway flashed back into view. In the darkness I saw a figure move across the hallway, open her bedroom door and go inside.

"What the fuck? Did you see that?" He did not. I rewound the footage, and we both watched it again. It was clearly a man entering Kenzie's bedroom in the darkness. I dialed 9-1-1, my chest tight. I reported it as I pushed my feet into my boots. I grabbed my nine from on top of the refrigerator. Then I called Margot as I rushed to the back door. "Stay with Trina," I barked at Logan. I grabbed my bike keys and was out the door, relaying what I'd just seen to Margot as I ran down the stairs. "I called 9-1-1 before you, and I'm on my way!"

CHAPTER 14

Andy

I pulled my bike up alongside Margot's car when I arrived at Kenzie's less than fifteen minutes after I had pulled out of my driveway. I miraculously hit all green lights, not that it mattered. I wouldn't have stopped for any reds. I opened the bike up, going well over eighty the whole way. If a cop would have tried to stop me, I wouldn't have pulled over. Thankfully, I didn't encounter any cops.

I drew my nine as I approached the front door. It was open a crack. As quietly as I could, I entered and crept up the stairs. My heart pounded harder than it had in any situation I'd been in over in the sandbox. This was Kenzie's life at stake, which meant more to me than mine. When I reached the top stair, and stepped into the hallway, I heard voices.

"Not happening, Holland," Margot said.

"Drop it or she dies," a male voice yelled. I'd heard on the edge before, and this guy was on the edge.

I heard Kenzie scream. It was a sound that made my stomach drop and tightened my chest. I breathed in that cleansing breath you take before you go into a shit situation where you know the adrenalin will be pumping, where you'll have to take care of business. Whoever this asshole was, the only way he'd be leaving the room would be feet first.

I crept near the door and peered in. I couldn't see Kenzie or the Tango from my position, but I saw Margot, gun aimed at the bed, which was just out of my line of sight. If I hadn't seen him, he hadn't seen me either.

"Now," his edgy voice yelled. Kenzie screamed again, and Margot dropped her gun to the ground.

I took another cleansing breath and crept closer. If Margot saw me she didn't react. I breached the door and took in the asshole, gun to Kenzie's head, holding her from behind on her bed, them both on their knees.

"You?" He said to me in surprise.

I didn't hesitate. I squeezed the trigger.

The scream that came out of Kenzie was something I would never forget, no matter how long I lived. Seeing the blood all over her stopped my heart. Jesus Christ, had she been hit?

Marcus Holland fell to the bed. Kenzie stayed on her knees. Her eyes went to her shoulder, covered in blood, to the bed, to the wall behind her, also covered in blood, and finally to Holland's lifeless form beside her. She was trembling and crying. Margot and I both went to the bed. I wrapped my arms around Kenzie and pulled her in close, directing her to look at me, not Holland.

"It's okay, babe, look at me, not at him. I love you, baby. It's okay. I've got you." I pulled her in and held her. "I love you Kenz, I've got you and am never letting you go."

Margot checked Holland. She shook her head at me. Yeah, he was dead. There had been no doubt in my mind.

"I shot Holland," Margot said. "You got that, Stevens?" She took my gun from me, grasping it to leave the appropriate prints.

"GSR?"

"Was at the range in these clothes when you called. I'm covered in it," she said. "Trust me. It'll be easier this way."

A figure came through the door. It was a good thing my gun was no longer in my hands. I would have shot first and asked questions later. It was Logan. He was beside the bed in a second. "What can I do?"

We heard the sirens in the distance.

"Quick, trade shirts with Stevens and wait downstairs for the uniforms. Tell the truth about the rest," she ordered. She turned to me. "Scrub those hands and arms, get the GSR off."

Logan already had his shirt off and took the identical Stevens Street Gym t-shirt from me. He was out of the room before I had moved to the sink.

"Kenzie," Margot said cradling Kenzie in her arms. "I shot Holland, had no choice. He was about to kill you. You understand?"

"I don't know. I don't remember," Kenzie cried with a shaky voice. "He said he loved me and was going to take me away. How could it have been Marcus? Why didn't I know? I trusted him." She cried harder, trembling as I took her back into my arms.

A flurry of activity followed with the arrival of the uniformed officers, other detectives, paramedics, CSU, and finally the coroner. It all played out in slow motion before my eyes. This was Margot's crime scene, not my battlefield. I wasn't in charge. It was hard for me to disengage and respond only when spoken to. I sat in the plush chair in the corner of Kenzie's room holding her in my arms while all the activity took place around us.

After photo's, finger prints, GSR test of Kenzie and me, my shirt, and Margot, thank you, Margot, the lead detective finally allowed us to dress Kenzie in non-bloodied clothes. Her nightgown was placed in an evidence bag. The paramedics examined her and certified her as non-injured, but wanted to take her to the hospital. Her heart was racing, and she alternated between being upset and withdrawn. She was clearly in a state of shock. She declined transport. I backed her up on it. No, she would be in my bed tonight. I'd take care of her and keep her safe.

She couldn't get through giving a statement. The lead department investigator, Detective Simmons wanted to get a minimum of a statement from her before he let her go. I was about to deck the guy. How many times did Kenzie have to tell him she couldn't do this now, or that she didn't remember? My shirt, correction, Logan's shirt was soaked with her tears.

"I can't, please," Kenzie begged. "He's dead, all the blood, Margot had to shoot him. He was going to kill me," she said, which finally satisfied the investigator.

He met my gaze and I think he knew I was about to stop him and take her home with or without his approval. He couldn't have known how close to beating the crap out of him I was. "I'm sorry, Ms. Collins. That's enough for tonight. We'll talk again tomorrow after you've had a chance to rest."

Logan was in the kitchen when I led Kenzie down the stairs. The police hadn't bothered with him too much. Margot handed Logan Kenzie's purse and car keys, telling him to drive us in her car. She then told Logan to roll both our bikes into Kenzie's garage. She'd make sure they were locked up. She'd be over early in the morning but would text first.

As Logan backed out of her garage I suddenly realized that with Logan here, I didn't know who was with Trina? "What are you doing here? Who's with Trina?" I asked in a panic.

"Like I'd leave Trina alone?" Logan replied. Yeah-duh! He never would. "Butch was in the gym. His ass is in your recliner. You think I'd not have your six? No way in hell I'd let you walk in here without backup."

Logan was a good friend, had my back in the sandbox, had it since. "Thanks, man," I said. I held Kenzie securely in my arms. She had relaxed and was dead weight.

I appreciated that Logan had taken it upon himself to follow me to Kenzie's. As out of it as Kenzie was, I couldn't have driven. She needed me to hold her. Logan pulled up alongside the back stairs and I goaded her out of the car. Thankfully, she made it up the stairs, otherwise, I would have carried her. Butch sat in my recliner and got up as we entered.

"Kenz, this is my friend Butch," I said as he approached. So many people had talked with her and examined her at her place that his presence didn't seem to faze her. She didn't say a word, she just clung to me as though I was her lifeline. She'd gotten quieter as we drove home, her breathing erratic. "Butch, I'm glad you're here. The paramedics looked her over, but she's gotten more withdrawn since we left her place."

He was doing a visual assessment, I could tell. "She should be at the hospital, Andy. She's clearly in shock," Butch's calm voice said.

"No, hospital," Kenzie whispered, grabbing my arm more tightly.

Butch's stare spoke volumes. As an EMT he knew the hospital was the best place for her, but I would not make her go. "Let's get you into bed, babe," I said.

I led her down the hallway. Butch was right on my six. I held her steady as I peeled the covers back. She nearly collapsed as I helped her lay. As soon as I backed off, Butch came in close to her. He took her pulse and I could see his eyes were evaluating her closely. He looked concerned. Logan joined us. He stood at the foot of the bed. My bedroom had never had so many people in it. Thankfully, Trina was a sound sleeper.

Butch glanced up at me. "I watched the camera feed from her place on your laptop. I'm assuming the worse based on the activity I saw." I nodded. "She injured anywhere at all?"

"No, that asshole didn't hurt her," I said.

"Kenzie," he said putting his face in hers. "Do you hurt anywhere, at all?"

She shook her head no. Her eyes showed panic. I knew her heart was racing. "No, not me."

"You got anything on you, you can give her to take the edge off, slow her heart rate and help her sleep?" I asked.

Butch gave me a hard stare. Yeah, we'd been through this before, he wasn't a pharmacy, nor was he a doctor, just an EMT, and firefighter. He was a professional that didn't like to cross the line, even for a friend. He was also a good guy who would do what he could to help. She was scared and refused the hospital. I'd take good care of her. He knew that.

"You still have that bottle of Benadryl I had you pick up for Trina last month?" Butch asked.

"Yeah, in my medicine cabinet." I pointed towards my bathroom. Logan stood closer; he moved within and grabbed it.

"I told you, a bathroom medicine cabinet is not the best place to keep meds, bro," Butch said. His eyes reprimanded me.

Logan handed the bottle over with the medicine spoon. Butch measured out the dose and fed it to Kenzie. He told me the max dose and frequency to give it to her through the night. "I'm on at the firehouse overnight. Call if you need me." He gripped my shoulder and then left. I heard the apartment door that led back down to the gym open then close.

I turned to Logan. "Thanks again, for coming to her place." He nodded, his eyes fixed on Kenzie. "Can you take Trina to your place for the night? I don't want her to come in here and see Kenz this way."

"Yeah, I'll text you before I let her come back in the morning."

"Thanks," I said. I told Kenzie I'd be right back and followed Logan into the hall. He scooped Trina up and I opened the door to the hallway for him. I entered the code on the lock to his apartment and I placed a kiss on my sleeping baby's forehead. Then I hurried back to my apartment. I grabbed a bottle of water for her from the refrigerator and locked up. Kenzie's eyes were glazed over when I re-entered my bedroom. I stripped to my shorts, and slid in beside her, taking her into my arms.

I dosed her with the Benadryl through the night and she got several hours of sleep in between doses. I held her all night, sleeping for an hour here or there. The scream that had come out of her when the shot was fired haunted my dreams. The second that I didn't know if she'd been hit or not replayed through my thoughts. I knew I would never let her go. I was in love with this woman and I had nearly lost her.

My cell phone chirped a new text message waking me. The sun was streaming through the partially opened curtains. Kenzie slept in my arms. Her face looked peaceful. I grabbed my phone. It was Logan. Trina wanted to come home. It was eight o'clock. I felt Kenzie stir. I found myself looking into her eyes.

"How are you?" I asked her.

She nodded, forcing a brave smile. It didn't reach past her lips. "I'm," she paused. "I don't know," she admitted. "I think I slept some."

I nodded. "Yeah, in between Benadryl doses," I said. "You look better than last night."

She nodded again. "It's really over?"

I embraced her. "It's over, babe," I said.

"I can't believe it was Marcus," she said. "He's really dead?"

I nodded again, my eyes locked onto hers. She looked incredibly sad. "I had Logan take Trina to his place last night, but she's awake and wants to come home. Are you up to seeing her?"

Kenzie nodded. "Yeah. I won't cry or freak out or anything."

I sent Logan a text and asked him to bring Trina back. Kenzie stowed all sadness as soon as Trina bound into the room and then onto the bed to lay with and snuggle with her. Logan stood near the foot of the bed with me. He had Tripp teaching the boot camps this morning and the twins, Mario and Marco were running everything else. He'd handled everything. I appreciated him taking care of the gym.

"Ashley?" I asked.

"Last night was the first Friday of the month. It was her Ring Girl night. I know better than waking her early after it," Logan said with a smile. "She won't like it, but I'll call her in for the afternoon shift." He nodded at Kenzie. "I think we'll all be pulling extra shifts to help cover you for a few days, not complaining, just stating a fact. I'll just take care of everything in the gym until you tell me to stop."

I gripped his shoulder, overwhelmed with gratitude. "Thanks, man, I'm going to take you up on that."

"Don't even think about the gym. I'll make sure all is covered, even your private clients. You take care of her. That's all you need to focus on."

Kenzie's phone rang. It was Margot. I held the phone up to her. She waved me off. "Hi Margot," I greeted, answering it.

"Kenzie?" She asked.

"Yeah, she wanted me to answer. What's up?"

"How is she this morning?"

"She's hanging in there. Got some sleep last night."

"Good. Hey, I hate to do this so early, but Detective Simmons and I are nearly to the gym. He needs to conduct interviews with both of you and Mr. Logan." She was acting way too formal. She must have been in the same car with the guy. "I know there are back stairs up to your place. I'm assuming you'd prefer we don't come in through the gym."

"Yes, thanks, Margot. There is a drive behind the side parking lot. Follow it back. Logan will be on the elevated back deck waiting for you." I disconnected the call and nodded to Logan. "Looks like Ashley's getting woke early, after all. They want to talk with you too."

"What, now?" Kenzie demanded.

"Yeah, they're nearly here."

Logan left to wait on the deck. I had to dial Ashley twice before her groggy voice answered. "Sorry to wake you, Ash, but we had a crisis. I need you to come take Trina."

"Ugh! Andy, can't Logan," she began.

"Now, Ash! This is urgent." My voice was more demanding than I had intended. Trina sat straight up, a frown curving her little face. I disconnected the call.

"Daddy?" She questioned.

That was not what I intended, to scare my little girl. I know she didn't understand anything going on. I preferred she would be gone before the cops came in.

"It's okay, sweetie," Kenzie soothed her before I even could. She wrapped her arms back around Trina and pulled her closer.

"Why is Daddy mad at Aunt Ashley?"

"He's not mad at her sweetie, he just needed her to know it's important she come now."

I stood in the bedroom doorway, waiting. Ashley came in the hall entrance at the same time Logan led Margot and Detective Asshole in the back. Ashley, besides being tired and probably hung over, looked very confused seeing the two badges coming into the apartment with Logan. Margot and the detective looked equally perplexed that she was entering my apartment at the same moment they were.

"Logan, what the fuck? You can't watch Trina?" Ashley complained.

Logan went in close, his face in hers, and barked a reply that was much less patient than I had been. "Kenzie was attacked at her place last night. The cops killed him in Kenzie's bed. Andy and I were there when it happened. We have to give our statements. Is that a good enough reason for you to be woke this early, princess?" His voice was caustic and laced with sarcasm. Calling her bitch would have sounded less brutal than how he said princess.

Ashley's shocked eyes flew to mine.

"Ash, Trina's in my room with Kenzie. I just need you to take her to your place until I let you know she can come home."

I heard Margot tell the other detective that Trina was my young daughter. His face softened. I heard Trina protesting going with Ashley, loudly. I went back into my bedroom.

"I stay with Kenzie!" Trina yelled. Her arms were locked around Kenzie's neck.

"Trina, you have to go with Ashley," I said, trying to reach out to her, intending to pluck her from the bed. She grabbed more firmly onto Kenzie.

"Sweetie," Kenzie said softly, her quiet voice was sweet and loving. "I know you love to spend time with your Aunt Ashley. I need to talk with my friend Margot, and I need to talk with her alone, sweetie. It's an adult conversation. But as soon as I'm done I want you to come back and we'll read that Duke dog story. It's my favorite now."

Ashley stared at Kenzie and Trina and nodded. I knew Ashley had to see how good with Trina, Kenzie was. Even this morning, after the worse night of her life, Kenzie was gentle and loving.

Kenzie

Trina gave me another hug and then went to Ashley. Ashley smiled the first friendly smile at me. When I looked up past Ashley and Andy I was surprised to see Logan, Margot and Detective Simmons were all clustered in the doorway. Margot's look was soft and supportive. When it came to kids, Margot was a marshmallow.

"How about we talk in the kitchen?" Andy said, pointing back to the apartment. "You up to that Kenzie?"

I nodded and silently got up. No, I really wasn't up to it. But I knew the police were only doing their job. I just hoped I could give the detective the information he needed. I was nervous too now that it was the next day. Would he question me about my relationship with Marcus? I mean, why would he do what he had done? Would the detective think I had encouraged any of this behavior?

Andy

"We were able to pull the security footage and other data from the system this morning. Thank you for providing it," the detective said to me.

I nodded. I wondered if Simmons had slept at all. He was in the same clothes. I didn't think he had. Margot was in different clothes. I also wondered if she had slept. I doubted it.

"I actually would like to start with you, Mr. Logan. I see from the notes you were not tested for GSR last night. Where's the shirt you had on last night? That it?"

"Yes, it is," Logan said.

Margot flashed a concerned look my way. I wasn't worried. There was no way Logan would still be in a shirt covered with GSR. He and I both had a dozen of these t-shirts. As I expected, the test was negative. Simmons took his statement, taking down Butch's information to verify. Then he dismissed Logan.

"I'm going to check the gym," Logan said then left.

"Miss Collins, did you know Mr. Stevens had tapped into your security system?" The detective asked.

"Please, its Kenzie, and yes I did. He had my permission to have access. He's my boyfriend. Why are you asking? He had nothing to do with Marcus Holland."

"Just dotting my I's and crossing my T's," he replied. "I read the file of the multiple incidents over the past month that Margot was investigating," he said casually. "I've already been to Holland's place. His notes confirm he was behind all of them, and more that you probably just didn't notice."

"His notes?" I asked.

"Marcus Holland was a serious stalker, had been for over a year based on what we saw at his place. He kept extensive notes on his plans, actions, and everyday interactions with you," he told Kenzie.

Kenzie held her hand up. "Please, stop. I don't want to know, not right now anyway. I just can't." She shook her head. Tears filled her eyes. I took her into my arms. "What about Todd Johnson?"

"Holland had detailed notes on how he framed Johnson, even slipped him something to make him sick and keep him home all day and night when your system was hacked so he wouldn't have an alibi," Simmons said.

"He's already been released," Margot added. "We won't pursue any charges related to the drugs we found at his home."

"Miss Collins," Detective Simmons said, "how did Marcus Holland get into your home last night?"

"He must have slipped into the house when I got home. I took the trash and recycling out," Kenzie said. Tears were spilling out of her eyes and rolling down her cheeks. "That was the only time a door was open, unlocked."

My gut clenched. That bastard had been inside with her all night. I should have been there. I shouldn't have listened to her and stayed away. I'd never ignore my instincts again.

An hour later Simmons had all the information he needed. He seemed satisfied. I only wanted to hit him once, when he asked, none to gently, if Kenzie had ever had a sexual relationship with Holland. Just the insinuation that she had encouraged Holland at all made me angry. Kenzie remained calm. She told the truth which was all she could do.

Margot gave Kenzie a hug and then she and Simmons left. I made Kenzie breakfast, which she only picked at. I encouraged her to call her parents or her sister. She refused. While she was in the shower, I called my mom, and told her what had happened. I asked her to come over. I wasn't sure if I was going to send Trina home with her, or if I just wanted her there for Kenzie. I figured if Kenzie couldn't have her own mom there, mine would be the next best thing.

Kenzie

At first, I was mad at Andy for calling his mom, but as soon as she embraced me and held me, I knew I wanted her there. Even at my age, just having a mom there to tell me everything was okay was just what I needed.

"Why won't you call your parents, Mackenzie?" Sheri asked.

"They're away on a cruise this week," I replied.

"And your sister?" Sheri pressed.

"She has two little kids. They need her more than I do. I have Andy," I said. It was true. I had Andy to hold me and take care of me. He knew I had been in trouble and he called Margot and came himself, to help me. I felt tears flood my eyes.

"That you do, babe," Andy said.

The remainder of that day and the next moved in slow motion and were an emotional blur. Sheri stopped back over twice as did Margot. Logan came in to check on me a few times as well. At my prompting, Andy kept Trina home with us. Having her there grounded me, making me focus on something other than myself. When Trina was cuddled up with me, I couldn't allow myself to show the crushing anxiety or   fear   that   irrationally   hit   me   often   those   first   few   days

CHAPTER 15

Andy

It had been a few days and Kenzie hadn't left my apartment. She wouldn't even sit outside on the deck with me. I'd seen PTSD. I knew the signs. Kenzie was clearly suffering from it. She was sitting on the couch, reading Trina a story. Even with this shit she was going through, she was amazing with Trina and Trina was clearly getting attached to her. It was Monday morning, and we had a half hour until Trina's school started. I text messaged Beth, who was due to stop by in fifteen minutes to bring Trina to school for me, and told her I would get her to school myself. It was a beautiful day for a walk and Kenzie needed to be pushed.

"Kenzie, I thought we'd walk Trina to school today."

"Yay!" Trina cheered. She hugged Kenzie. "I want you to see my school."

Kenzie's eyes showed panic as they flashed at me. With Trina hugging her and thrilled with it, I knew Kenzie would not say no. "It's time you got back in the swing of it Kenz," I told her. "I'll be right with you." I knew Trina didn't have a clue what I meant.

Kenzie nodded bravely. "I'm sorry," her frail voice replied.

"No need to be. One step at a time." I gave her a supportive smile. "You know you can stay here as long as you want."

"Stay Kenzie," Trina begged, her little palms on either side of Kenzie's face. She turned to me. "Daddy, make Kenzie stay with us forever."

I chuckled. Yeah, that was exactly what I wanted too, but not this way. Kenzie needed to recover and be strong again. She needed to be able to go home and be okay alone before she stayed with us forever. I wasn't sure how I'd explain it to Trina when she left, but she would have to understand that Kenzie would be back, so she didn't feel abandoned by her.

"Nothing would make me happier, angel, but that isn't something we're going to talk about right now."

I held both Trina and Kenzie's hands as we stepped out onto the back deck. "Breathe," I whispered, leaning in close to Kenzie. She dropped my hand as we reached the stairs. I thought she was refusing to go down.

"Trina needs your hand more than me. I'm fine," she said in a brave voice.

She wore her sunglasses, so I couldn't see her eyes. She followed us down the stairs. I was proud of her. I knew this wasn't easy. PTSD was very real, and she had been through a trauma. She was doing this for Trina, I knew, and I appreciated it more than she would ever know.

Trina was thrilled as the three of us strolled down the sidewalk side-by-side holding her hands. Every few steps we flew her in the air. Her giggle warmed my heart. My little girl was so happy. Kenzie seemed to do better with every step we took, but I had no way of knowing if she was falling apart inside and just covering it well or not. As we walked the two blocks to Zion Lutheran, Trina never stopped telling Kenzie all about her school, her teacher, and her friends. When we reached the crowd of moms dropping off their kids, Trina excitedly introduced Kenzie to everyone she knew. Kenzie handled it well. She seemed comfortable in the crowd.

"Beth, Beth, this is my Kenzie," Trina said enthusiastically when we made our way to Beth and her daughter, Molly.

Beth giggled. She shook Kenzie's hand. She, of course, had no idea what Kenzie had been through. "Trina has told me all about you," she said with a smile, her eyes going back and forth between Kenzie and me. "It's nice to meet you."

Kenzie smiled. "It's nice to meet you too." She was relaxing and seemed more normal than she had since it happened Friday night. I was glad I had pushed her.

Beth leaned in close to Kenzie. "This is huge for her, having you in her life. You must be very special for Andy to let you in this way with Trina."

"She is," I said. Kenzie's smile was nothing short of mesmerizing. In that moment, she looked like the old Kenzie.

"She's a very special little girl," Kenzie said. "I feel very lucky to be in her and Andy's lives."

Kenzie

Andy insisted I sit out on the deck with him after we got back from walking Trina to school. I did feel more relaxed than I had since it happened, and I had to admit, it felt good to be outside. With him next to me, I felt safe. On our walk to and from school, I felt safe. The sun was warm on my face and a gentle breeze blew in the sweet scent of the magnolias that were blooming by the garage. I felt guilty though. He had spent every minute with me since it happened. I knew he had work to do.

"What can I do for you Kenz?" He asked, bringing me out of my own thoughts.

"You're doing it. I'm sorry I'm so," I paused. I didn't even know how I felt. There were so many emotions swirling around my head. It was overwhelming.

Andy brought my hand to his lips and kissed my knuckles. "No sorry needed, Kenzie. Just keep trying to move forward. You're suffering from PTSD, you know that, right?"

I'd heard his words, but the meaning didn't fully register with me right away. "Do you really think so?" I asked. I knew I sounded stupid.

"Babe," he said scooting his chair closer. He wrapped his arm around me. "Trust me. You are."

Tears stung my eyes. I thought I was done crying. I didn't want to feel this way. I didn't want him to have to worry about me, or feel he needed to stay with me. I didn't want to be a burden to him. Talk about pathetic. He'd run as fast as he could from me if I didn't stop this.

"I don't want to feel like this. Please don't give up on me, Andy."

"Never babe. I promise." He kissed my cheek. I turned my head and his lips met mine. When he kissed me like this or held me, I melted into him. I didn't think about any of it. "It's over. He's dead. You're safe now."

"Then why can't I," again I paused. I couldn't even put it into words. "You know, I don't even remember what happened after Margot and you came into the room. I heard the gunshot, but I don't remember anything else, just all the blood. That's it."

Andy pulled me into his lap. I felt him kiss my temple, my cheek, my forehead. "Your mind is protecting you right now. You'll remember when you're ready to deal with it. That's how it works."

Andy's phone vibrated, and he checked his text message. "We'll come back out later, and I definitely want us to walk back to Zion Lutheran and pick Trina up after school, but I need to go down to the gym. That was Logan. He needs me for a few minutes. You'll be okay inside alone for a few minutes, won't you?"

"Of course, and I'm sorry you even have to ask," I said.

I came to my feet and went with Andy to the door. He made a point of showing me he locked the door after we entered. He settled me on the couch and handed me my cell phone. He promised he would only be gone a few minutes and that he'd lock the door into the hallway when he left. This was literally the first time I had been alone since it happened except when I had gone to the bathroom, but even then, Andy stood right outside the door for me. I knew I had to get a grip and do anything I had to, to move past this. I couldn't expect Andy to do this for much longer.

I watched the clock on my phone while he was gone. At exactly the eight-minute mark I heard the lock code beep in the door and it opened. Andy stepped through the door followed by another man. A man I had never seen. At the sight of him, everything changed. I felt like I was suffocating. My chest tightened, and I had to clasp my hands in my lap, so they stopped shaking.

Andy

When we stepped through the doorway and Kenzie saw Tony follow me in, panic hit her and took over. I rushed to her, sat beside her and took her in my arms. "Kenzie, this is Tony, Dr. Tony Wilford." She looked confused.

"She's not breathing, Andy," Tony said. "Kenzie, I'm a therapist who specializes in treating PTSD. I want you to close your eyes and concentrate on my voice while breathing. Breathe in for a count of five, four, three, two, one," he slowly counted aloud. "And now exhale for a count of six, five, four, three, two, one. And again." He repeated the counting several times until Kenzie was breathing with his counts. "That's good," he said. He had a soothing voice. "Now open your eyes." He wore a pleasant expression.

"I'm sorry. I was just startled. I wasn't expecting you, Doctor," Kenzie said.

"That's quite alright," Tony replied. "You can call me Tony. I try to keep things informal." He motioned to the chair across from Kenzie. "Do you mind if I sit down?"

Kenzie nodded but still looked confused. "I, I don't want to feel like this anymore," Kenzie said. Her voice sounded frail again.

"Good, you realizing there is a problem is the first step. Wanting to fix it is the second. That's where I come in," Tony said. His voice was confident. "Andy told me what happened and how it has affected you. Will you let me help you work through your feelings?"

"I'm sorry. Who are you?" Kenzie asked.

"Tony's been a client of mine for a couple of years," I said. "And he's one of the best trauma counselors in the Lexington area. I asked him to come see you."

"When? You've been with me every second since it happened."

I smiled. "Okay, I text messaged Logan to call him." Kenzie nodded. "Will you talk with him, Kenzie? He can help you work through this and move forward." Kenzie nodded again.

"You said to Andy since it happened. Since what happened, Kenzie?"

"You said you knew." Kenzie was clearly getting agitated.

"I know the condensed version, but I want to hear the whole story from you and I want you to tell me how you feel."

I took Kenzie's hand. She was trembling. She blew out a breath and I saw a resolve take up residence on her face. "How do I feel? I can't even put all the emotions into words. I'm overwhelmed by them and feel like, I don't know. Like I'm dying. I know sometimes I feel panicked, for no reason at all. And sometimes I just feel numb." Her trembling fingers came to her face, and she wiped a tear away that had dripped out of her eye. "And I'm tired, just exhausted."

"Those are all signs of PTSD, Kenzie," Dr. Wilford said. He opened a leather portfolio he was holding and flipped a few pages. "Kenzie, I want to go through a list of symptoms with you. I need you to tell me if any of this applies to you, okay?" Kenzie nodded. "Andy, I want you to merely nod yes or no if you have noticed any of these."

Then he began. We both answered or nodded yes to fatigue, anxiety, blocking of memories, emotional numbing, and lack of concentration. Kenzie said no, and I nodded yes to withdrawal, edginess, and jumpiness. To my surprise, Kenzie said yes while I shook my head no to flashbacks, shame, and guilt. We both said no to nightmares, sleeplessness, irritability and physical discomfort.

"Okay, that's good," Tony said, making a few notes. "As you probably figured out, those are all symptoms of PTSD. You have enough for me to say you are suffering from PTSD, not that I doubted Dr. Andy's diagnosis," he chuckled a little, the smile widening on his round face. I'd never seen him work. There was a reason he was one of the best. "We'll take this slow and talk about it. You're in a safe place and anything you say will remain confidential. I want you to know you can tell me anything. I won't judge you no matter what you say. Would you like Andy to stay or to go?"

He gave her the option. He had told me before we came up that he would, and I had promised I would abide by whatever Kenzie wanted. He had explained that he would give her as many options as he could to help her regain the sense that she was in control. Kenzie noticeably stiffened. Her hold on my hand became tighter.

Her pleading eyes drilled into mine. "Don't leave," she said.

"He won't leave, Kenzie," Tony said. "Okay, now in your own words, tell me what happened. Take your time, there's no rush."

Kenzie's voice was shaky at first, but it got stronger, the longer she talked. "A guy I worked with, Marcus Holland, he um, I considered him a friend. He broke into my house and held a gun on me, in my bedroom. He was shot there. The blood was everywhere. I remember hearing the shot. It was loud, like an explosion, but I can't remember what happened, can't remember anything after Margot and Andy came into the room, just seeing the blood. Why can't I remember?" Tears were streaming down her face. I held her and kissed her cheek. It was killing me that she was going through this.

"Your brain is protecting you. You may remember in time when you're ready to deal with it. You might not ever remember. The brain is amazing. You need to try not to force it. In time, if you haven't remembered the episode and you feel you need to, we can do some therapy to try to recover the memories if you'd like. But for right now, I want you to try to accept it for what it is. Your brain will let you remember when the time is right. There are other things you need to work through first." He gave her a supportive smile. She nodded. "Why was he there? What did he want?"

"He wanted me to go with him. He said he loved me and we were meant to be together." She paused, and her eyes stared at the ceiling. "He said he was going to take me away to someplace no one could take me away from him. God! How come I didn't see, didn't know?"

"Didn't see what? Didn't know what?" Tony pressed.

"How he felt? That he wasn't normal. How could I not see that he was a threat?" Kenzie was crying hard now. I held her more tightly. "Even after I was roofied, and I was sure it was one of the guys at work, I didn't suspect him."

"Is that what you feel ashamed of Kenzie? Why you feel guilty, because you didn't see that he was a threat, didn't suspect him?" Tony asked.

Kenzie nodded, her eyes closed tightly. "And guilty that Andy has to go through this and have me here like this."

That shocked me. My God! Had I done anything to make her feel that way? "Kenzie, no," I said. I stopped mid-sentence as Tony was waving me off.

"Kenzie, you hit the nail on the head with that statement. He wasn't normal. He was fixated on you and conjured up a two-sided love affair that wasn't there. People that suffer those kinds of delusions aren't normal. And they're experts at concealing who they really are. Professionals cannot even diagnose them most of the time before they act. You would never have known. They're that good at not letting on what they're feeling. He was delusional. I want you to hear what I've said and believe it because it's true."

Kenzie's breathing had become erratic again. Tony went through the breathing technique again until she was calm. She looked exhausted. I wasn't sure how much longer Tony was going to let this go on. He had told me when he arrived he had cleared two hours to talk with us. I didn't think Kenzie could take much more.

"Andy, do you have any water? I could use a bottle. What about you, Kenzie?" He asked.

She nodded and breathed out heavy. "Yes, please," she said looking at me with pleading eyes.

Tony watched her closely as I moved away from her. Her eyes stayed on me. "You feel safe with Andy, don't you?" He asked.

I saw the corners of her lips tug upward. "It's the only time I feel safe, when he's holding me. I don't want to feel this way." Then she dropped her voice down low, and I barely heard her, but I did hear her. "I don't want to drive him away or worse, I don't want him to stay with me because he pities me."

My heart sunk in my chest and it ached. I would never leave her and would always want to stay with her. I knew that I was in love with her. I had said those three words to her for the first time as I was holding her after the shooting. I didn't know if she remembered, and I hadn't said them again since. After learning that Holland had said he loved her I didn't want to freak her out. I'd have to run that by Tony and get his opinion if it would be okay to tell her or not.

"Two waters," I said cheerfully as I handed them the bottles. I pretended I hadn't heard.

"When you walked Trina to school today, Andy said you appeared better. How did you feel? Were you faking it for Trina's sake?" Tony asked.

"I was nervous, going out. It was safe to stay here since it happened. Going outside, and the thought of being around other people was scary. I was afraid they knew or would guess something was wrong with me, something had happened to me," Kenzie began. "But once we were walking with Trina, and she was so happy, I got more comfortable. And surprisingly, in the crowd of kids and their moms, mostly moms, a few dads, I felt hidden, anonymous, you know?"

"I do," Tony said. "Trina, she's something else, isn't she?"

Kenzie beamed a genuine smile. "She's the sweetest little girl. I've already fallen in love with her." I felt the smile spread over my face. She loved my daughter. From watching her with Trina I had guessed it, but to actually hear her say it, it was indescribable! Kenzie chuckled a little. "Earlier today, Trina told Andy to make me stay with them, to not let me leave. It was so cute."

"She loves you, Kenz," I chimed in.

"You both do," Tony said, much to my surprise. "Isn't that right Andy?"

Kenzie's eyes met mine. "I do, I love you too, Kenzie," Tears formed in her eyes, but she didn't look panicked by my statement. Tony nodded to me. "And I'm never going to leave you. You don't have to worry about that. As far as you feeling guilty for anything regarding me, don't. You're worth anything we have to do to get you through this. Logan and Ashley can run everything downstairs. They don't mind and neither do I. *You* are what's most important to me."

She wiped her tears but remained quiet for the longest time. Tony patiently waited. "I don't deserve you, Andy, and you don't deserve to have to take on this crap."

"Well, you got me, so it doesn't matter," I said. Tony nodded to me again. "I love you, Kenzie. We're going to get through this together."

Kenzie shuddered in my arms and cried. "All I could think about when Marcus had that gun to my head was that I was going to die, and I'd never get to tell you how I felt about you." She cried harder. "God, I love you so much. Thank you, thank you for knowing I was in trouble and coming to help me."

I held her as she cried until she was calm. I felt emasculated that she was going through this and holding her was all I could do to help her. I couldn't make it go away, I didn't prevent it from happening. I wondered if she would ever fully recover from it. I wanted her whole. I selfishly wanted her whole, so we could get married, so she could be a mother to Trina, and I wanted to have more children with her.

"I want to touch on one more thing before we wrap up for today," Tony said. "When you said that Trina had told Andy to make you stay with them and not let you leave, you said it was cute. It was along the same lines as what Marcus Holland said to you, but it didn't scare you coming from Trina?"

"She's a little girl, of course, it didn't scare me."

Tony smiled. "You're going to be just fine, Kenzie. It's going to take a little time to feel normal again and work through this, but you are going to be just fine. I can tell. I've worked with a lot of people suffering from PTSD and there are definite signs the ones who make it through relatively quickly have, and you have them."

Kenzie seemed relieved to hear that. I sure hoped he was right. He handed Kenzie three pieces of notebook paper with large writing on it. I read each one along with Kenzie. The first read, 'Marcus, and Marcus alone is responsible for his actions. I could not have known how mentally ill he was.' The second read 'None of what happened is my fault. I'm only responsible for what I do from here out to recover.' And the third read 'Trina and Andy, love me. I won't feel guilty for the time Andy is spending with me. I will get strong to be a part of their lives. Marcus will not take any more time away from me.'

"Whenever you have thoughts that you should have seen Marcus for what he was or feelings of guilt about anything, I want you to pull those sheets out and read them until those thoughts and feelings have turned around. Even if you aren't thinking those things, I want you to read these pages four times a day," Tony told her. "And if you're having any anxiety causing your breathing to be shallow or your chest tight, I want you to do the breathing I showed you. You may have to help her with that Andy."

I nodded. No wonder Tony was the best trauma counselor in the area. Three simple statements to read and reprogram your thoughts. It was genius! Then Tony handed me a prescription bottle.

"It's Xanax if Kenzie's having a particularly rough patch of anxiety. But use sparingly, no more than three a day. I think you can get through this without it, but I want it available if needed. I'm letting Andy hold on to them, Kenzie, as often when someone is feeling crushing anxiety they can't keep dosages straight."

Kenzie

I didn't like the idea of using drugs to get through this. I nodded but was sure I would not take any.

"Four times a day I also want you to sit and meditate for a minimum of ten minutes each time. I want you to block out anything bad. I want you to visualize and focus on a happy scene. Maybe what your life will look like when you are through this. Happy times, even if it is as simple as you and Andy walking Trina to school, going out to dinner, or going back to work." He handed me a journal. "And I want you to journal your feelings twice a day, shortly after waking, and before you go to bed."

I shook my head. "I'm not really a journal type of person," I said.

Tony chuckled. "You are now. You'll be surprised how much this will help. It can be as simple as writing, I had no nightmares last night. But if you have any problems

131

blocking out bad thoughts while meditating, I want it in there. I want a minimum of one sentence, twice a day." I took the journal from him. "Kenzie, how long was Andy gone for when he came to the gym to meet me?"

"Eight minutes," I replied.

"Andy, start with four times a day. I want you to be in a different room than Kenzie is in or downstairs for eight minutes. We'll increase the length of time when you're ready, Kenzie. When he's gone might be a good time for you to meditate." The thought of set times for Andy to be away from me made my breath catch. "You've already done eight minutes, you know you can, and you are safe here. You can do this, Kenzie," Tony said. He sounded so confident. I wasn't.

"Oh, and you two are to walk Trina to and from school every day this week. The exercise and being out in the fresh air will do you good, Kenzie. And tell Andy when you're ready for real exercise down in the gym. That will do wonders for you too."

I was feeling overwhelmed. He wanted me to do so much. But I said I didn't want to feel this way anymore, and he was an expert. I'd give it a try.

"We'll do it together, babe," Andy said. Had I said my feelings aloud?

"Kenzie, we will have another session tomorrow. Would you like me to come here or would you like to try to come to my office? It's your choice."

I'm sure Tony could see the panic in my eyes at the thought of going to his office. "Here, please," flew out of my mouth.

He nodded. "Oh and do you need a note or anything for work?" He asked. I was confused. "A medical justification to be out all week, and maybe next week too until you're ready to go back?

I hadn't really thought about work, the time I was missing, or when I'd go back to the office. I knew that Margot had notified my boss of what had transpired, and he wasn't expecting me back for an extended time. "Not yet, I'll let you know," I answered.

"Very good," Tony said, coming to his feet. He reached his hand to me and placed it on my shoulder. "It was nice to meet you and I will see you tomorrow. Andy is going to walk me back down to the gym now. This will be the second eight-minute separation for today. Why don't you give the meditation and visualization a try?"

I thanked him, even though I didn't want Andy to leave me again, but he was right. I had already spent eight minutes apart from Andy, and I didn't die. I could do this. I pulled my legs up and tucked them underneath me. I closed my eyes and focused on Andy and Trina, thinking about how much she giggled as we had walked her to school.

Andy

As soon as I closed the door to my apartment, Tony pinned me with his eyes. "I'm glad you called for me, Andy. You were right about the PTSD."

"I'd know, I've seen enough of my brothers suffer from it after we got back."

"You need to push her to do everything I said to do." He pulled a piece of paper from his portfolio and handed it to me. He had the instructions written out. "She has the potential to snap back from this relatively quickly if she faces what happened and learns coping strategies. You acted fast enough calling me in. Often, I don't get consulted until weeks or months after the trauma and by then, the dysfunction is already entrenched."

I nodded. I would make sure she followed the instructions to the letter. I wanted her better. "Hey one more thing, Tony," I said as we reached the outer door. I dropped my voice down low. "Kenzie has wanted to get intimate, but I've held back, not sure if she was ready. It's upsetting her that I won't make love to her. Do you think it's okay too?"

Tony laughed. "She needs the connection with you. As long as she doesn't become agitated or upset, carry on with your relationship like it was before the trauma. That too will help her move past it."

I'm sure I looked like a kid on Christmas morning. I checked my watch. I had two minutes left before I was due back. We had several hours before we were due to pick Trina up. I'd take her to bed as soon as I got back upstairs. We decided on the same time for Tony's visit the next day. I ran back up the stairs and re-entered my apartment right at the eight-minute mark. Kenzie was seated on the couch sitting with her legs folded beneath her. She looked peaceful. Hearing me, she opened her eyes.

"I did it," she said with a smile. "I thought about Trina's laughing as we walked to school this morning. I pictured her face, smiling as she introduced me to everyone."

I took her in my arms and kissed her more passionately than I had in the past two days. I arched my back, pressing my erection into her stomach. With the thought of taking her to bed, it had formed before I had even entered the apartment. "I'm so proud of you, babe. You're not mad I called in Tony, are you?"

"Not fair, asking me if I'm mad at you when you kiss me like that and poke that into me."

I chuckled. She seemed so much better already. I knew she had a way to go yet and there would be ups and downs, but for the moment, I had my fun and flirty Kenzie back. "Oh, I'll poke it into you alright," I said. "Doc Tony gave permission, said engaging in what we did before it happened would help get you through it. So be prepared, Missy, as Logan would put it, I'm going to bang your brains out," I said with a perverted laugh. She laughed as well. "Four times a day seems a good starting point," I added.

Kenzie laughed harder as I lifted her in my arms and carried her to my bedroom. The love we made was connecting and passionate. I could see and feel her fear and anxiety slip away. This was just what she needed. As I held her afterward, my hands caressed over her soft skin, I knew I never wanted to let her go. We fit together perfectly, physically and emotionally, she had my heart.

"I love you, babe," I whispered to her.

She kissed my chest where her face rested. "I love you, Andy. I was thinking about you and Trina when Marcus was holding the gun on me. If I would have died, you and Trina would have been the last things I thought about."

I squeezed my eyes closed. I didn't want to think about that again and I didn't want her to think about it either. "No more of those thoughts, babe," I said. "You need to do everything Tony says to do to get through this. I'm going to push you if you like it or not, but I need you to know everything I'm going to do will be because I love you. We can't move forward with us until you've moved past this."

"I did hear you say you loved me after Marcus was shot. You were holding me and put your face between my eyes and all that blood. And you told me you loved me," she said. "I'm sorry I didn't tell you then that I loved you too. I just wasn't able to say anything."

"I understand. You don't have to apologize for that. It was the worst possible moment for me to say that for the first time, but it just came out because I do, and I was so relieved you were okay."

Kenzie gave a forced chuckle. "I almost told you I loved you so many times over the last few days but started to doubt you said it when you didn't say it again."

"After hearing that Marcus Holland said it to you, I didn't want to freak you out."

"You're not Marcus. I love you and I trust you completely. Please don't hold anything back from me, and I promise you I won't either." Kenzie held up her hand with all fingers except her pinky bent down. "Pinky swear," she said.

I chuckled and locked pinkies with her. "I promise."

She snuggled in close against me and I listened to her breathing even out. Her body completely relaxed against me. She was asleep. I'd let her sleep until the last possible moment to go get Trina. She needed it. She had to be mentally worn out. I wished I could take it all away from her.

CHAPTER 16

Andy

As I knew would be the case, the next few days brought ups and downs with Kenzie's recovery. She did everything Tony asked her to as many times a day as he had prescribed. My time away from her grew to fifteen-minute increments, six times a day, and she handled it just fine. Tony came to my apartment for the next several days, conducting his sessions there. After the second day, he convinced Kenzie to talk with him, without me present. At Tony's prompting, I got in a good workout down in the gym each day during that hour. That was a huge step for her, to trust him to be in there alone with her. I was very proud of her. She was trying so hard and facing what had happened. Our walks to take Trina to school or to get her afterward became a special time for us. Margot stopped by every day as did Logan, and my mom.

It was Friday morning, and we had just returned from walking Trina to school. I felt the edginess in Kenzie as she took hold of her purse and the journal Tony had given her. Today would be her first appointment at Dr. Tony's office. I'd drive her there, walk her in, and get her settled. While she would meet with Tony alone, I was meeting Margot at Kenzie's house. It had been released, the crime scene no longer locked down by the police. Kenzie hadn't taken a single Xanax yet though today may be the first for that. I slipped the bottle into my shorts pocket.

"Babe," I said, taking her in my arms. "You're up to this, going to Tony's office."

"I know. It's time. My world cannot be your apartment and walking Trina to school. Thank you for pushing me."

"I'm here for you, you know that," I reminded her.

"Yeah," she said nodding her head. She blew out a deep breath. "I'm as ready as I'll ever be."

I held her hand as we went out the back door. She walked bravely up to the passenger side door of her car and got in. I wondered if she even remembered the drive back to my place that night in the back seat of this car.

Kenzie

Andy held my hand as we drove to the office complex on the other side of Lexington where Doc Tony's office was located. We took the stairs to the third floor and entered the unassuming office door merely marked Anthony Wilford. A woman who appeared in her early twenties sat at a reception desk to the right. The small waiting room to the left looked more like a comfortable family room in anyone's home decorated in warm earth tones.

"Hi Andy," she greeted warmly. "You must be Kenzie. I'm Jamie. It's nice to meet you."

"Hi," I replied feeling anxious. "It's nice to meet you too."

"Hi, Jamie," Andy greeted. "Is Tony running on time?"

"Yes, he should be out soon. Please make yourselves comfortable." She motioned to the seating area. "Kenzie can I get you a water or a soda?"

"No thank you, I'm good," I replied. I said that over a few times in my mind. I'm good. Yes, I'm good. I'm out of the house, am across town and I didn't even feel anxious on the drive over. I could do this. I could get back to my life, soon. I wanted to get back to my life.

I was lost in my thoughts when the door to the inner office opened. Tony stepped into the room escorting out who I assumed to be another patient. He was mid to upper twenties, military cut hair, and appeared to be in worse shape than me, emotionally.

"Good job today, Tyler. I'll see you tomorrow, same time, right?" Doc Tony said.

The man nodded at Tony, then at us, and left silently.

Tony smiled warmly at me. "How are you doing today, Kenzie?"

"I'm doing good. Very little anxiety coming here," I reported.

"Good to hear," Tony said motioning me into the door he had come out of.

"Okay, babe, I'm going to go now. You'll be fine," Andy said confidently.

He gave me a quick kiss and then left. I swallowed the moment of panic that hit as I watched his back disappear out the door. I took a deep breath and went into Tony's inner office. It was a comfortable space decorated in subdued shades of blues and greens. I settled in on a big, overstuffed chair.

The hour and half long appointment went well. Today, Tony made me identify it by name, an attack, an attempted kidnapping by an obsessed stalker who was obviously mentally ill. We even said it in separate choruses like a weird round of Row Row Row Your Boat, and ended up laughing.

"See, they're just words. Saying it for what it was can't hurt you, Kenzie," Tony said. "I think it's time we talk about you going back to your house, in phases."

"Andy was going there now to meet with Margot." Tony nodded. Of course, he knew. I knew Andy was texting him on a regular basis. "They've offered to take care of the mess. I appreciate it. I know I can't go into my room and see the blood."

"I've seen the crime scene photos, that's probably best."

"I still don't remember the shot or too much of what happened after Margot and Andy came in. I mean I remember hearing it. It was so loud, but the rest of it is kind of a blur."

"And that's still perfectly okay," Tony assured me. "How about when Andy comes back, I have him drive you by your house on your way back to his place? You won't go in it yet, just sit out front for a few minutes?" I nodded. Yes, I could do that. "And then tomorrow I'll meet you there for our session. The three of us will go in together. I won't want you to go upstairs yet, just stay on the first floor," he suggested casually.

"I honestly can't imagine sleeping there by myself ever again," I confessed. My chest tightened. I closed my eyes and did my breathing and visualization drill he had taught me.

When I reopened my eyes, he smiled and nodded. "Very good, Kenzie. You've learned the skills well. You're going to be just fine going in, probably won't even need me, but I'll be there."

"Yes, I do want you there. So, you said in phases. What exactly will that look like?"

Tony chuckled at me. "Managing it like a project, I see." He stared at me intently for a second. "You will dictate what you're ready for, but usually, I'd suggest a drive by first, followed by entering and walking through the first floor, maybe have lunch in your kitchen next. A later visit will include going upstairs, maybe entering the master bedroom, maybe not. Depending what you're up for. Maybe the next step would be you're there all day with, and then without Andy there. You'll sleep there with Andy in bed with you, and when you're ready, he should sleep in the guest room, with the ultimate goal of sleeping alone in the house like you did before the attack, but again, the timetable you will dictate."

I merely nodded. That could take months! No, I wouldn't let it take months. Andy deserved better than that. He deserved me pushing myself to get better and move past this much faster. I met Doc Tony's eyes. "I want to push myself. I want you to push me. He's dead. I'm safe now. I want to move forward."

Tony smiled. "One step at a time."

Andy

I pulled up in front of Kenzie's house. Margot was already there. She opened the front door as I approached. "How'd Kenzie handle going to the Doc's office today?"

"She handled it. I'm so proud of her, Margot. She's done everything Doc Tony has asked her to. She's doing everything she can to get past this."

We went in and I followed Margot up the stairs. "Has she remembered the shot yet?"

"No, not yet. Tony said she may not ever remember, there's no telling." I answered. "She accepts what you told her."

The feelings that assaulted me as we entered Kenzie's bedroom overwhelmed me. Made me feel like I needed some trauma counseling, myself. Fuck! I wasn't expecting to feel anything. What hit me first was the memory of that scream that came out of Kenzie as the shot took Holland out. The blood everywhere sickened me. It wasn't like I'd never seen blood before. I had, had seen way more of it than I cared to remember. The bed was toast. There was no plastic mattress liner on it, I knew, so the blood would have soaked the mattress. The bedding would all have to go in the trash and the wall would have to be scrubbed and re-painted. The rug had been somehow spared though.

Margot and I got to work, stripping the bed. The pillows weren't even salvageable. Wearing masks and gloves, we crammed everything into large biohazard bags Margot had brought. We carried the mattress downstairs and left it on the garage floor with the bags atop it. Both Logan's bike and mine were still parked there. We'd have to get over and get them. Margot had a special biohazard company coming later that afternoon to remove the stuff.

Then we pulled the bedframe with the box spring on it out and washed the blood from the wall with a bleach water and detergent solution specifically made for biohazard situations. It cleaned up well, but we still decided to repaint it with Kilz primer followed by the room color paint, that Margot knew was in the garage. I'd come back tomorrow, during Kenzie's session and do that.

We hadn't discussed the shooting, hadn't really had any time alone since it happened. "Are you back on regular duty yet?" I asked her. I knew she was on mandated desk duty until the shooting was fully investigated.

"I will be soon. Simmons just wrapped up his investigation and ruled it a good shoot. Now I just have to pass the psych eval to be ruled fit for duty. I have an appointment with the department shrink for that this afternoon."

"Why'd you do it?" I asked. I didn't need to spell it out. Her gaze told me she knew exactly what I meant.

"Kenzie's great with your kid," Margot said. "But she's your kid, and she needs you to be there for her, her and Kenzie both. This was easier."

"Not for you."

Margot shook her head. "The shoot was justified. I wouldn't have done it if it wasn't. And you didn't need to go through any of the shit that would have come. It was an easier justification for me than you."

I nodded my head. "Doc Tony said we should consult Kenzie about any replacement items, bed, comforter, whatever. She may or may not want the same things in here."

"Do you really think she's going to return and live here?"

"She has to be able to be alone and come home, but long-run, no, Trina and I want her with us." I smiled.

Margot laughed. It wasn't a sarcastic laugh, it was more a knowing laugh. "She's really good with your kid, Stevens," she repeated.

Kenzie

I felt the most unusual emotions assault me as my house came into view. Andy parked in front of it but left the engine running. He silently took hold of my hand. As if I noticed it for the first time, my eyes hung on the bush that was next to my garage. I wondered if that was where Marcus had waited for me to get home, so he could slip into the garage unnoticed. My trash and recycling bins were not at the curb. Someone, probably Margot, had returned them to the garage.

I took a deep breath as my eyes went to my bedroom window. I felt sad that Marcus had lost his life in that room. The moment he had come into my room and I knew I was in danger flashed into my mind. The darkness, the quiet suddenly shattered by the bedroom door opening, a soft sound that was so loud and terrifying. He was on the bed with me so fast. I don't think I even screamed. I don't think I was able to get a sound out, my vocal chords had been constricted. And then realizing it was him, the flash of the metal barrel of the gun, his hand gripping my arm, the fear multiplying.

"You're okay, I could never hurt you, was the first thing he said. What a ridiculous statement! He really didn't know the impact of what he was doing to me. He had been so mentally ill he didn't get how wrong his actions were. How could he have been so fucked in the head but still acted so normal?" I said aloud, not intending to.

"I don't know, babe," Andy replied softly.

"I wish someone would have realized how sick he was, so he could have gotten help. He wasn't all bad. There were good parts too. I choose to forgive him, for me, so I can move on and have a normal life." I smiled a teary-eyed smile at Andy. "Doc Tony at his finest."

Andy chuckled. He squeezed my hand. My eyes returned to my house. As Doc Tony had told me to do, I forced myself to visualize happy times in the house. The first one that came to mind was the weekend Andy had stayed here with me. His bike pulling into the garage and parking next to my car brought a small smile to my lips. That had looked so right, felt so right. All weekend with him there, in my bed, in my kitchen, watching TV with me on my family room couch flooded my brain. I kept the memory of the alarm going off away with conscious thought.

Then the memory of Andy and I entering through the front door that night after our dinner date at Madeline's place invaded my thoughts. The realization that someone was in my kitchen, Marcus was in my kitchen, tampering with my vitamins. A bone-chilling shiver ran down my spine as I realized that if Andy and I hadn't gone out that night, I would have been there, alone and vulnerable. Marcus could have just knocked on the door and I would have let him in.

"Babe?" Andy's concerned voice said.

"I'm fine," I insisted.

I forced a happy thought. The day I closed on the place and took possession. Mom and Dad were in town, to help me paint and move in. I remembered the excitement and the pride, in me and playing across both my parent's faces. I still had not talked with them about any of this. I felt guilty about that. I pushed the guilt from my mind. Mom and I planted flowers out front. They were blooming. I smiled as I took in the many colors of the perennials dotting the flowerbed in front of my windows. Mom had been so happy to share her love of gardening with me, in my yard. I was so proud I had purchased my own house.

"You ready, Kenz?" Andy asked.

"One more minute," I replied, conjuring up one more memory. My sister, Katie had come to visit when her youngest, Kayla was a baby. Her son, Owen was a rambunctious toddler, running around and squealing. She handed Kayla to me as she chased after Owen, to put him in time out for doing something, I didn't remember what. I walked around with baby Kayla in my arms and remember seeing the smile Katie gave me. 'Wow, that looks good on you. You need to find a good man, Kenz and make yourself one of those,' she had said with a laugh. I giggled to myself and then I gazed back at Andy. I'd found my good man. Now I just needed to move past all this. "Okay, now I'm ready."

CHAPTER 17

Kenzie

Doc Tony's car was waiting in front of my house when Andy and I pulled up. He got out of his car as we did from mine.

What did my neighbors know? What did they think? Police had been in and out of my place for days. They had to have seen the coroner come and go, taking with them Marcus' body. I'm sure yellow crime scene tape had been up. Things like this just didn't happen in this neighborhood. Were any of them watching us now, watching me walk up to my house for the first time in over a week? It wasn't that I cared about neighborhood gossip or what anyone thought of me. I knew I had done nothing wrong.

"Kenzie, are you all right?" Doc Tony's even voice asked.

I hadn't realized it, but I had stopped walking. I was several strides back from my front porch standing still. Andy's hand was on the small of my back. I nodded bravely and walked to the door. I entered the code and opened the door. The smell of paint assaulted my nose. Andy had come back over alone the previous evening and painted my bedroom. Sheri stayed with me and Trina at Andy's while he had been gone.

"Wow, that's still strong," Andy said. "I'm going to run upstairs and open the windows for it to air out." He disappeared up the stairs.

"Can we open some windows down here too, Kenzie?" Doc Tony asked.

"Yeah." I agreed, my eyes still glued to the staircase which loomed like a monster out of a little child's nightmare. And I was that scared little child. I knew it was silly to feel this way. I closed my eyes and took a deep breath.

Doc Tony nodded proudly at me for how I handled it. I smiled and moved further into the house, into the kitchen. I opened the sliding door in the kitchen, again thinking how I needed to get curtains for it, definitely before I moved home. My gaze settled on the six coffee mugs sitting upside down in my dish drying rack beside the sink.

Doc Tony chuckled. "Margot and her cop friends made themselves comfortable, it would appear," he said.

"I bet there are donut wrappers in the trash," Andy's voice joked from behind us as he reentered the kitchen.

We all sat at the kitchen table. We talked about how I felt being home, redecorating my bedroom, and next steps. Doc Tony encouraged us to stop by a mattress store on our way back to Andy's and get me a new mattress, so it would be there and in place when I was ready to go upstairs. Tony thought it best the bedroom was completely put back together before I went up there for the first time. I also told them I wanted curtains on the back door, there in the kitchen. Andy promised to put them up for me as soon as we bought them.

We stopped at a department store as well as the mattress store on the way home and I picked out new pillows, bedding, and the curtains. This was my first shopping outing, and I didn't have a panic attack doing it. I knew I was doing better. I wouldn't have been able to do this even a few days before.

When Andy and I returned to his place, we went down to the gym and enjoyed a good workout which was becoming a daily routine for us. Some days we worked out together, others I worked out while he took care of business, but he was never out of my range of sight, which I appreciated. Today, Andy worked near me with a client, a private training session. Watching him work from the outside like this made me love him all the more. He was the best at what he did. I hadn't been wrong when I had thought that he must put all his clients at ease, as he had me. He had a way with people that was amazing to watch.

The next day, Doc Tony met us at my house again. After he made sure I was okay, he left, leaving Andy and me there to have lunch, watch a movie and spend the majority of the afternoon there, just like we had that weekend he had spent with me. I only felt anxious once when Andy went to the bathroom. It was the only time that afternoon he'd left my side. Otherwise, it was comfortable. I felt capable of being there. When we left, I was excited to go back to the gym for a good work out. It was amazing how much it helped me regain my confidence. It was good for Andy too, allowing him to get back to work more than he had been since it happened.

The mattress was delivered the following day. Logan came with us that day. He stayed and helped move the mattress upstairs. He and Andy were up there a good half hour, but I was okay sitting at my kitchen table. When they came down the stairs, Logan gave me a hug, told me he would see me later that day at the gym. He rode his bike home. Andy's was still in my garage. I was perfectly comfortable on the first floor of my house now, but I knew I had to push myself to get better.

"I want to go upstairs," I said.

Andy nodded. "Not into your room though, not yet, per Doc Tony. He wants to be here when you do that. But we can go up, in the hallway and the spare bedrooms."

Amazingly, I had no increased anxiety going upstairs or into any of the rooms up there. I did feel my heart skip a beat when I gazed at my closed bedroom door. "I want to go in, Andy," I said, staring at the door.

He wrapped me in an embrace. "Please, tomorrow, with Doc Tony," he said.

Kenzie

Doc Tony let me lead the three of us up the stairs. I hesitated at my closed bedroom door. I glanced back over my shoulder at the hallway camera, thankful it had been there, and that Andy had been watching, had seen Marcus Holland come into my bedroom. My heart pounded as I reached my hand to the door knob. My hand shook.

I stepped in, relief flooding me. The curtains were open. The room was bright, not dark as it had been that night. My eyes landed on the bed, on the new comforter in rich shades of burgundy and cream that dressed my new mattress. I'm sure my plain taupe comforter had been ruined. This one looked good, accented the deep beige of the wall paint, which my eyes focused on next. I knew the wall behind the bed had been repainted. You couldn't tell, it looked the same as it always had. Andy had done a good job. I looked around for anything out of place. Nothing was. The room was tidy even though dozens of strangers had been in here. I'm sure I had Margot to thank for the room looking so orderly.

At Doc Tony's prompting, I walked around the room. I sat in my big chair by the windows. I used my bathroom. I went into my closet. The deadbolt Andy had installed drew my attention. If Margot and Andy hadn't come, would I have been able to get inside the closet at some point and lock Marcus out? I shared this thought with Doc Tony and Andy. Andy volunteered to teach me to defend myself. We'd start that afternoon. Tony thought that was a good idea and would help to empower me.

Doc Tony then prompted me to sit at the foot of my bed. As I did and stared at the door to the hallway, I think I stopped breathing. That was when the events of that night flashed back through my mind, a blur of images and fear I couldn't stop. They were a jumbled distortion of feelings of terror, sounds, and images that attacked me all at the same time.

"Kenzie, breathe," I heard Doc Tony's voice through the haze that assaulted my senses.

He knelt in front of me. We did my breathing technique together, and I felt calmer. "That was a powerful sensation," I said. "I didn't expect for that night to flash before my eyes like that," I whispered. My eyes landed on Doc Tony. "We've talked about it many times, what happened in here that night and how I felt about it, about the fear and how I felt such a lack of control while it happened." Doc Tony nodded. "That's why you wanted to be here when I came in. You knew I'd feel like that."

Doc Tony smiled. "You're doing great Kenzie. You lived through it, survived it. You're strong. He's dead, he's gone, and you're not going to let him rob you of any more of your life."

I nodded, feeling his confidence. But then a sudden sadness overtook me.

Andy

Tears flooded Kenzie's eyes. "Damn it, Marcus, why'd you have to do it? You didn't have to die," she said, her voice laced with sorrow.

I held Kenzie as she sobbed, sobbed for the death of the man who had stalked her, terrorized her, and would have taken her away and kept her tied to his bed. I shuddered at the thought of what would have happened to her had I not seen that fucking scumbag go into her room. I felt no sorrow for his death, for doing what had to be done.

Doc Tony's eyes were locked onto mine. I hadn't even realized that tears were in my eyes too. I choked my emotions back. This wasn't about me or my feelings and emotions. This was about Kenzie and hers. I knew in that moment, though, that I needed a few sessions with Tony too. I had unresolved feelings about the attack, an insecurity that I wouldn't want to let Kenzie out of my sight for fear of losing her. I nodded to Tony. He smiled knowingly.

Kenzie

Over the next several days I spent a great deal of time at my house. Andy even left several times each day, leaving me there alone, per Doc Tony's plan. The first night I sat on my bed in the dark I panicked. Andy and Tony were there with me. My breathing and affirmation statements that I had survived, and that Marcus was not going to take any more of my life from me, got me through. The night finally arrived that Andy and I would sleep there together, in my bed. I was doing very well by this point, had almost no panic attacks at all. That night was comfortable, I was ready for this. We even made love in my room that night, incredible, intense, emotional love.

The next night was a little rougher. Andy slept in the guest room. The night after that was the hardest. Andy slept in the family room on my couch. I barely slept. Two nights later, he did not stay at all. I was alone in my house. That was the hardest. I didn't sleep at all. It took a few nights of being there alone to feel okay, and to sleep.

Over the course of a few days, almost everything returned to normal, kind of. I went to the store by myself, I even went to the nail salon for a manicure and pedicure. I found the only time I felt panicked when I was out and about was when I was alone, when I felt vulnerable that someone could take me, with no one noticing. Tony gave me new affirmation statements to recite in my head during those times.

I hadn't been with Andy and Trina or to the gym in two days, again, per Doc Tony's recommendation, and I missed them. I missed my daily workouts at the gym. I missed my life with Andy and Trina, walking her to school, tucking her in bed, snuggling with Andy, and of course the incredible sex. We'd talked about me moving in, but Doc Tony cautioned us that it was best that I be fully back in control of my life and able to be home and back to work alone, before we made that move.

I was scheduled to go back to work tomorrow, something that made me feel anxious. I had been thinking about it a lot the last few days. How would my coworkers react to me? And Todd Johnson, how would he react? He'd been arrested. I felt terrible about that. I ran to the store to pick a few things up before it got dark as I still felt insecure going out alone in the dark. Hell, I felt insecure in my own house in the dark when I was alone. I even left a light on in the bedroom all night.

I made a wrong turn down the personal isle and a realization hit me. *Oh Fuck!* I grabbed a box from the shelf that hadn't been on my list.

Andy

I felt nervous. Something was off in Kenzie, had been for a few days. Maybe I had pushed her too hard to go back to her house alone. I hope she understood that was to shake her from feeling afraid. It wasn't because I didn't want her with me.

"Thanks for coming over. You're earlier than I thought you'd be," I greeted her as she came through the door to my apartment. I knew I was grinning like a fool. It had been a few days, and even though we talked at least a half-dozen times each day, I had missed her so badly. I had so many questions on how her first day back at work went, but I'd let her tell me on her own. I wouldn't assault her with a barrage of questions.

"Yeah, I left work early," she said lacing her fingers through mine.

I led her out to the back deck. "Let's talk out here. It's a beautiful day and I don't want to be inside." I kept hold of her hand but leaned onto the railing with my forearms. My eyes went to the brick house a block or so over. I wanted her to see it from here when I told her.

"It is beautiful out here today." She beamed that smile at me that I loved.

"I've missed you the last few days," I told her. "I got used to you being here."

"Yeah, me too," she whispered. "But I did need to go back and know I could be there, without being afraid. Thank you for pushing me."

"I love you Kenzie, that's the only reason I did it."

"I know, and I appreciate that you did. I love you too, Andy."

I loved hearing her say those words. It made me feel incredible. I kissed her cheek. My eyes went to our joined hands. "I've missed holding you in my arms when we go to sleep and I've missed waking up next to you." I heard her breathe out heavily and my eyes darted to hers. I don't know what I expected, but I didn't expect to see them sparkle like they were.

"I've missed that too. I've missed seeing you and Trina every day."

"How'd it go today?" I asked, watching her closely for her reaction.

She looked away. "We'll talk about that later, okay?"

I let it rest. I nodded my head. I knew she had been anxious about going back to work. She'd tell me in her own time. I was excited to tell her my news, well to tell her hopefully our news. I couldn't hold back any longer.

"I was talking with Beth today, you know the woman who drives Trina to school some days," I began. "And she told me about a great house down the block from hers that is about to go on the market. It's walking distance to Zion Lutheran if I want to keep Trina there for kindergarten, and to Meadow Elementary, which is a great public school."

"I didn't know you were thinking about buying a house," Kenzie said. She looked confused.

"I've always known that at some point this apartment won't be the best place for Trina. I want a neighborhood with other kids, a yard for her to play in, and sidewalks for her to ride her bike on." I paused. Kenzie smiled and nodded. "The thing is, it's a desirable neighborhood. Houses rarely come on the market and they sell quickly."

"So, what are you going to do?" Kenzie asked.

I couldn't contain the smile that I knew was spreading over my face. "I went and looked at it earlier. Beth is friends with the owner. She hasn't signed with a listing agent yet and I can get it with no realtor involved, will save both the owner and me the commission. It's a great house, will be a great place for kids." I pointed to the house. "See that brown brick two-story with the green flag?" She saw the one I was pointing out and smiled. "That's it, two blocks away, not even."

Kenzie seemed a little disturbed by this. "That's great," she said. "So, are you going to make an offer?"

"The thing is Kenz, I want to do this right." I brought her hand to my lips and pressed a kiss to the back of her knuckles. "I love you and I only want that house if you are living there with me and Trina. I know we have only known each other for two months, but I know I love you and I know that isn't going to change. I don't like waking up without you next to me. I don't want to do that anymore; regardless what Doc Tony recommends." I pointed to the house again. "I want to buy that house for us, for you, me and Trina. I have no right to ask you to change your entire life for me, but I can't change mine too much. I have to be near the gym and I need a situation that will make it easy to work and be where I need to be for Trina during the day. Your house is over a half hour away and you travel for work. That won't work, Kenzie. But if we do this, I want to do it right. I love you. Marry me." I stared into her eyes, probing for her answer. Before she spoke. I wasn't sure what I saw.

"I'm pregnant, and I quit my job today." Kenzie pulled a pregnancy test from her pocket. The stick was blue. She stared back at me, her eyes pleading with mine.

I was numb. Pregnant? Wow! My head was spinning. Joy invaded all my senses and all I could think about was Kenzie holding a little baby, our baby. It kept me from answering. I know there had been a long silence as her words, I'm pregnant, swirled through my mind.

Kenzie

"Say something," I begged, after a really long silence. Andy said nothing. I'm sure he had to be as surprised as I was.

A grin formed on Andy's lips that involved his whole face. His stunned eyes sparkled like emeralds. "Marry me."

"Say something else that tells me how you feel about me being pregnant."

"I want to know the second you think you're pregnant with our next baby and I want us to watch the stick turn blue together."

That's when I lost it and the tears flooded my eyes. Andy had his arms wrapped around me before the first tear hit my cheek. I had cried so many tears in the past few weeks I didn't think I had any left in me, but these were happy tears. I couldn't remember now why I had worried about telling Andy I was pregnant. I should have known he would be thrilled.

"Hey," he said, pulling back so he could look in my eyes. "No more tears. I love you, and I am excited that we are going to have a baby together." He stared at me expectantly. "So, was that a yes, you'll marry me?"

I laughed and dried the tears from my cheeks. "Yes, that's a yes."

I hugged him, and we kissed one of those passionate, melt your clothes off types of kisses. After several seconds, the kiss was so deep I knew I wouldn't stop kissing him until we were naked. The erection that poked into my stomach told me he felt the same way. He picked me up and carried me into his place, right to his bed and we made love like we had never made love before. Not only was it incredibly orgasmic, but it was connecting and sensual, every stroke every kiss silently communicating the intense feelings and emotions we both felt. If there was such a thing as 'we made a baby' sex, that's what it was, intense, passionate, deep, meaningful.

Afterwards, we lay holding each other, his eyes staring deeply into mine. Neither of us spoke for the longest time. After another soft kiss to my lips, Andy smiled. Damn! Was he handsome! And he was mine. He was going to be my husband. He was the father of my child. I was the luckiest woman alive! Even the fact that I was alive was his doing.

"I'm going to call the owner of that house. I told her I'd bring you by when you got here this afternoon. You'll come see it, won't you?"

My smile spread. I nodded against the pillow. "Yes, I'd love to see it."

"And then we'll go buy your ring. I want it on your hand today," Andy said with a bigger smile. I nodded again, so happy I was unable to speak. "I'm sorry I didn't have it when I asked. I planned a big thing, ring in hand, down on one knee, all of it. But I knew when I looked at that house earlier today that I only wanted it if you would marry me and be there with Trina and me right away. I also knew that I couldn't take you to see it without you knowing I wanted you there as my wife."

"No apology needed. I think you did it the most perfect way. I don't need any of those things. All I need is you Andy, and Trina. I love you and you're all I need."

His hand found its way to my abdomen. "And our baby," he said with so much emotion I almost cried. "Why didn't you tell me you thought you were pregnant?"

"I was nervous, and sure I wasn't. I only figured out yesterday afternoon that I was late. I ran to the store to pick up a few things and threw a pregnancy test in my cart as a last second thing. I could have died when it turned blue this morning." I chuckled at myself.

"How late are you?"

"Just over two weeks. I've never been irresponsible when it comes to taking my birth control pills but with everything going on I had skipped several days and had to double up on the pills more than once. It's my fault, but I didn't mean for it to happen." I knew my voice was pleading for forgiveness.

"Don't be sorry for one second. I'm not," Andy said forcefully. "I want you and this baby. As a matter of fact, I don't ever want to wake up without you beside me again. After we see the house and buy the ring, let's go to your place and pack up a few things. Move in with me today."

"What about Trina?" I asked.

"Trina will be thrilled. She loves you and has missed you. She doesn't understand why you're not here with us anymore."

"I love her as if she were my own. I promise you, I will be a good mother to her," I swore.

"I know you do, babe, and I know you will be the best mother she could ever have." He kissed me and again we were on the brink of physically expressing our love. Andy pulled back and gazed into my eyes thoughtfully. "I don't want a long drawn out engagement, if you're okay with that. We can have any kind of wedding you want, but I don't want to wait. I want us married as soon as possible, are you okay with that?"

I felt my head nodding. No thought was required. My vision blurred from the tears that were in my eyes. I kissed Andy, the only answer he needed. We made love again. It was even more exhilarating than the last time.

CHAPTER 18

Andy

I called the owner of the house and asked if I could bring Kenzie by in about a half hour. We took a shower and then slowly walked hand-in-hand to what I hoped would be our house. I wanted to be married before we closed on it if Kenzie liked it. Though I was sure she would. It was a great family house. Trina would love living two doors down from her best friend, Molly. I was more excited than I think I've ever been in my life.

Kenzie

Andy introduced me as his fiancé. I smiled at the sound of it. The smile stayed there as we toured the house. The house was a dream. The entry was a two-story open area with ceramic tile. The grand staircase leading up to the second floor had intricately carved light wood banisters. A large modern kitchen was in the center of the first floor with stainless steel appliances, a lot of counter space, cabinets galore, an island with a wet sink and breakfast bar, and even a bay-windowed eating area. A first-floor laundry room that went into the three-car garage was off the kitchen as was a large family room with a fireplace. A screened-in porch led to a fenced in backyard. A den, powder room, formal living room, and dining room made up the front of the house. All the colors were neutral, just waiting for someone to color it their own. I envisioned some bold colors for the rooms.

The upstairs had an incredible master suite with a den that Andy and I both agreed would be a wonderful nursery until the baby was old enough to move into his or her own room, which really meant until we were comfortable enough to have the baby that far away from us at night. The large bathroom had a separate shower and a large whirlpool tub with a skylight over it. The closet was as large as the third bedroom at my house. The three other bedrooms were good-sized, and the hallway bathroom had double sinks set into a long counter, something my sister and I would have killed for as teens sharing a bathroom.

The owner left us alone in the upstairs hallway under a bright skylight and said to take our time looking around. She'd be in the kitchen when we were done. I was in love with the house. It was in a great family neighborhood and walking distance to the gym and schools.

"How much does a house like this go for?" I whispered to Andy.

"I've got it," he said.

"Andy, I quit my job today," I reminded him.

"We don't need your income to qualify for a mortgage on this, don't worry," he assured me and pressed a kiss to my cheek. "The only question is, do you love it? I want to make her an offer right now if you do."

I was stunned. Just like that, he'd make an offer. How could he afford a house like this? We had never talked about finances. I really didn't know how well the gym did or didn't do. But if he said he had it, I believed him. I smiled wide. "Yeah, I love this house. I can see us here."

He beamed. He kissed me passionately, right there, and then laced his fingers through mine and led me down the stairs.

The owner, Sue Flemming, poured us each a glass of iced tea as we sat at the table out on the screened porch. A soft breeze blew the warm air in. "The morning sun comes in here," she said. "I have my coffee out here every morning. I'm going to miss this house. It's been a great place to raise our family."

"Why are you moving?" I asked.

"My husband got transferred to his company's headquarters in Atlanta. He's already there. I stayed here so the kids could finish out the school year before moving them."

"This is a beautiful house," I said. "I can see why you will miss it."

"The neighbors are the best, too." Her eyes swept to Andy. "Well, you know Beth. The others are just as nice."

"We want to buy your house, Sue," Andy said. "You name the closing date, whatever works best for you and your family." He smiled wide. "I haven't talked to my bank yet, but I know the loan won't be a problem. The sale would only be contingent upon a home inspection, which I can't imagine there will be any issues. From what I can see you have maintained this place well."

"That would be great to just know it's sold and not have to mess with showings or anything." She smiled at me. "I'm so glad you liked it. After talking with Andy, I wanted him to have this house." Her gaze went back to Andy. "After you left earlier, I called my husband, and we talked about the price we discussed. We accept your offer. We'll still come out ahead, not having to pay a realtor and we both really appreciate your flexibility, allowing us to set the closing date. This is going to be hard enough on my kids, moving away from all their friends, not having to uproot them to something temporary in the area to finish the school year out, helps a lot."

I was shocked. Andy had already talked price with her and made an offer. He saw my face and smiled. He told me the amount which I appreciated, otherwise I wouldn't feel as though I was an equal in this relationship. I was surprised though. It was a lot more than I thought it would be, almost triple what I had paid for my house. Could Andy really afford this house?

"Just have your lawyer send the contract over and I'll have my attorney look it over," Andy said, pulling me out of my thoughts. "I'll have the mortgage guarantee over to you by end of day tomorrow."

"That's great," Sue said. "Thank you both. You're getting a great house."

"We'll be very happy here, I'm sure," Andy said. "Thanks, Sue. I look forward to working with you on the sale. I'll want to have the home inspection by the weekend, if that works for you."

"Standard contract language is usually within three business days," Sue said. "Can you line it up that fast?"

"Yes, I can get it done that quick. I'm sure there won't be anything major. Beth has told me how good of people you and your husband are. I know there can't be anything wrong with this house that you know of. Hopefully we won't find anything you don't."

Andy and I stood and shook Sue's hand and just like that we had bought a house, a great house, the perfect house! We walked back to the gym, hand-in-hand just as we had walked the almost two blocks to the house.

"You happy?" Andy asked me.

I knew my face had to be beaming as much as his was. "More than you know," I answered. "That's a lot of money, though."

"I've got it, don't worry," he replied. "It's what this neighborhood goes for." He chuckled. "I want us married and back from our honeymoon before closing."

"Can we pull a wedding together that fast?" I asked.

"I'm sure my mom would love for it to be in her back yard, if you're okay with that. Or will you want it in Florida by your parents?"

My parents, oh my God, I hadn't even thought about my parents. "No, here. I never lived in Florida. This is my home, our home."

We mounted the stairs up to his apartment. I paused on the deck, gazing at the house. How in the hell was I going to tell my parents all of this? And why hadn't they entered my mind during any of this, not while taking the pregnancy test, not when accepting Andy's proposal, not when looking at the house. I felt terrible. I had to be the worse daughter ever.

"Babe, what's the matter?" Andy asked.

"My parents are just going to love this," I moaned. "Surprise, a wedding and a baby!"

"Have you mentioned me at all to them?" Andy asked.

"I only spoke with them a few times, briefly, since we met. I didn't want to get into anything that would worry them, and I didn't know how to tell them about you without it leading to other questions because let's face it, what happened to me and our relationship are intertwined in a way I don't know how to separate. To tell them about you, I would have had to either lie to them about everything else or tell them and worry them."

Andy nodded his understanding, but he looked hurt and I felt bad about that. "Kenz, all the bad stuff is over. That asshole is dead and its only happy times ahead for us." He smiled. "We're getting married, having a baby, and we are buying a great house that we are going to live in together. These are things you have to share with your parents, and soon. The danger is over, and I think you need to tell them all of it."

"Do my parents really need to know that some maniac stalker roofied me, and then broke into my house, twice, threatened to take me away or kill me and was shot to death in my bed by Margot? That is not something I ever want my mother to have to think about. And you don't know my dad! The Marine in him will want to kill someone. He's going to be so pissed I didn't call him when it started."

"It goes a long way to explaining why everything moved so fast with us, though. Your dad is not going to be thrilled I got you pregnant only knowing each other such a short time. Trust me, I'm a dad, I know. If he also knows I protected you, just maybe he'll forgive it."

"So, we tell them everything so that my dad doesn't hate you?"

"No, we tell them because they love you, Kenzie and you don't lie or withhold information to the people you love. Besides, when they are up for the wedding, which I'm sure they will be, they're probably going to hear about it from someone. Shouldn't they hear it from you? From us?"

I blew out a disgusted long breath. He was right, and I knew it. And I also didn't want my dad to hate Andy. He was right about that too. My dad wouldn't be thrilled with the situation and would see him as nothing but a douchebag that knocked-up his daughter. The only way he wouldn't think badly of Andy was if he met him and saw for himself what kind of guy he is. "I can't even imagine how that conversation would go. It just doesn't seem right to do that in a phone call."

"So, do it in person."

"What, just fly to Florida?" Andy nodded. "It's not that easy," I protested.

"Make it that easy."

"Just like that? What, pretend we don't have a wedding to plan in a very short amount of time, that I don't have a house to sell, and never mind the fact that I no longer have a job, so I shouldn't be spending money I'm not making!"

"Those are all BS excuses and you know it." Andy pressed a kiss to my forehead. "We've already agreed our wedding will be small and very simple, and I guarantee my mom will gladly handle any detail you don't have time for. Once you sign on the dotted line to list your place, you have nothing more to do, which really Kenz, you don't need to sell it. Don't decide right away, rent it out for a year if you want and decide later. What happened there is still too fresh in your mind to decide if you want to sell it or not. And as far as you spending money that doesn't matter either. We're a team. What's mine is yours. Work, don't work, I don't care. If you want to take time off and just be a mom for a little while, I can afford that. Besides, you already came up with a kick-ass marketing program for the gym." Andy said proudly. "So as far as I'm concerned a trip to Florida is a cheap payment for your services rendered."

I ran my fingers through my hair and they came to settle on the back of my neck. It was stiff. Andy was right again. I couldn't have any part of this conversation with my parents over the phone. It had to be in person. "Come with me? You and Trina. They live an hour from Disney. We can go for a long weekend and take Trina to see The Mouse a day or two. I can't expect them to be okay with us getting married if they haven't met you."

Andy nodded his head in agreement. "I was thinking the same thing but didn't want to assume you wanted me there for the conversation with your parents."

"As you said, we're a team. Of course, I want you there. And the truth is Andy, I need you there," I said. He took me into his arms and held me tightly. I loved how safe I felt with him. "What about the conversation with your mom?" I asked when I pulled just far enough away to gaze into his eyes.

Andy smiled wide. "My mom already loves you. She will be thrilled we're having a baby and getting married. I suggested the wedding in her backyard as I know she will insist on it."

"Okay, so Florida next weekend?" He nodded. "I'll have to call to be sure they'll be home. They go on a lot of cruises."

"Will you tell them Trina and I are coming or surprise them with us?"

"Yes, I'll tell them. I have to so my dad locks all his guns up. They're hidden in accessible locations all over the house. He's used to putting them away when my sister and her kids visit. Besides, it wouldn't be right to spring two additional house guests on them."

Andy reached into my back pocket and pulled out my phone. He handed it to me. "Call them right now, then I'll book our airline tickets."

Andy

I knew Kenzie was nervous about calling her parents. After she hit dial on her phone and brought it to her ear, I sat and pulled her to my lap. I laced my fingers with hers on her free hand. I wanted her to know that I was there with her and she wasn't doing this alone.

"Hi Mom," she greeted. "Good, how are you and Dad?" Her eyes stayed locked with mine as she listened. I could just barely hear a woman's voice through her phone. "Hey, are you and Dad going to be home next weekend? I'm planning on coming down next week, Thursday."

"Yes, we will, honey," I heard her mom say. "Is your on-site in Orlando? When will we see you?"

I saw Kenzie swallow hard. She blew out a breath before she spoke again. "I actually would like to stay with you, if that's okay."

"Of course, dear," her mom said excitedly. "Will you be here for dinner Thursday night?"

"Yes, and Mom, someone is coming with me. His name is Andy and I've been seeing him. We're bringing his four-year-old daughter too, and if it's okay, we'll all be staying at your house. We thought we'd bring her to Disney a day or two while we're in."

"Oh, okay," she stammered. "How long are you all staying?"

"Until Tuesday morning, if that's all right," Kenzie said. I squeezed her hand.

"This sounds like a serious relationship. Why am I just hearing about him, dear?" Her mom asked.

Kenzie's face lit in a wide smile. "Yeah, Mom, it is. He's a great guy." Her mom started to ask more, but Kenzie interrupted her. "Look, Mom, I've got to go. I'll let you know what time to expect us Thursday. Give my love to Dad."

"Oh, sure. I'm sorry. You're probably at work. Love you, Kenz," I heard her say.

"Love you too, Mom," Kenzie said and then quickly disconnected the call. She breathed out heavily again.

"That went well," I said. "Now the fun part, let's go ring shopping!"

Kenzie laughed as I pushed her up and stood beside her. Not long after we were standing in front of a glass topped case with many sparkling diamonds beneath it. We walked the couple of blocks to the neighborhood jewelry store. As a member of the Downtown Merchants Association, I tried to frequent the other member stores as often as possible. Sure, I could probably get a better price at a chain jewelry store in the mall, but I knew I wouldn't get better service or a nicer ring anywhere else.

Merv grabbed two more rings that Kenzie pointed out from within the case. Every ring she picked out was stunning after the first low priced one she asked to try on. I appreciated that she wasn't trying to break the bank, but honestly, I didn't want some little rock on her finger. I wanted it to be as big as my love for her. After figuring out she gravitated to the French-cut Halo design, she hesitantly tried on the one from the price-range I was thinking. I could see her eyes light up when she saw it on her finger.

"That's the one," I said into her ear. Merv smiled at me and nodded.

"Oh, Andy, I don't know. It's so big." A.K.A it's so expensive.

Merv already removed the matching wedding bands from the case and set them to the velvet box on the counter. He was putting the others away. "That's a good quality diamond. And the band fits. It was made for you," he said with a smile.

"I can tell you love it," I said to her. She nodded. "Babe, I've got it."

Kenzie

I couldn't take my eyes off the ring. I know the lights in jewelry stores are made to show off the jewels, but I couldn't get over how much it sparkled. It was beautiful! Andy slid his credit card back into his wallet. He paid for the engagement ring and my wedding band, his was being sized. He put a deposit on it.

"We should get enough miles off this purchase to cover one of our tickets for the honeymoon," he told me, whispering in my ear. "We just have to figure out where we want to go."

We left the store and walked a block to a little Italian restaurant that had a cute outside patio. "We have over an hour to kill before we need to get Trina from school. Let's get an appetizer and a bottle of champagne to celebrate. Then we'll go to my mom's and tell her our good news."

"Perfect," I said.

We sat at a small table off to the side. It was a perfect day, in all ways. Andy tipped his glass to mine. "To our new life," he said.

I felt tears in my eyes again. I'd never been this happy. "I love you more than you could ever know," I said.

"Don't cry again," he said with a laugh.

I laughed too. We sipped our champagne and made plans. If we could pull it off, we decided to try to have the wedding in just over a month. I didn't want to be showing yet when we married.

"Oh, before I forget, you don't mind, do you?" He held up his phone. "I need to call my bank and get the mortgage started."

I listened quietly while Andy gave all the information to his loan officer at the bank. Hearing the number again that he had agreed to pay for the house added to what he had just spent on rings and airfare to Florida made me feel terrible. I had just quit my job and wasn't contributing a thing financially. He also told the banker the mortgage loan would be in both our names. I rattled off my social security number when prompted.

"Babe, I can afford it," Andy said again. He was off the phone and had seen the look on my face, figuring out what was disturbing me.

"This has been one very expensive day for you," I joked, trying to lighten things up.

"As a business major, I assume you know how to read financial statements?" I nodded. "I'll show you mine tonight. Maybe then you will relax and enjoy this."

"Oh, babe, I am enjoying this," I protested while reaching across the table to take his hand.

"I have enough in the bank to buy that house outright if I wanted," he said with a smile.

"You do?" How was that possible?

His smile spread, and he nodded. "I spent very little the entire ten years I was in the Army. I was an E-eight when I got out, made over five thousand a month those last few years. My dad was great with money, invested it very well for me." He saw my relief. "Now will you relax?"

I looked at the ring and smiled wide, feeling very relieved. "Aruba," I said.

"What?"

I laughed a little. "I want to go to Aruba on our honeymoon, now that I know you can afford it."

Andy laughed a full belly laugh. "Aruba, it is," he said when he had calmed his laughter.

Andy

"Yay!" Trina squealed throwing her arms around Kenzie's neck. I knew she would be happy Kenzie was going to marry us and live with us forever.

We had decided that we would wait to tell her about the baby brother or sister she was going to get for a little while. She climbed up in her booster seat and put her own seat belt on. Next stop, my mom's house, then Kenzie's to get some of her things. I was half tempted to ask Mom to keep Trina tonight so Kenzie and I could have more alone time to properly celebrate our engagement, but I wanted Trina to have tonight with her too.

We pulled into Mom's driveway and Trina was out of her seat faster than I was. "Trina, remember, we aren't going to tell Grandma right away about Kenzie," I reminded her. She nodded.

When we got to the door, the three of us walking together, Mom opened the door. "This is a nice surprise," Mom said with a big smile.

"Kenzie's going to marry us and stay with us forever!" Trina shouted.

Kenzie laughed.

"Trina, we weren't going to say anything right away, remember?" I said.

"Don't, Andy," Kenzie said taking hold of my arm.

"Come in, and congratulations," Mom said. She gave Kenzie a hug then me. I had already gotten used to Kenzie getting the first hug from my mom when we saw her.

"Let's go out back," I suggested. We sent Trina to the swing-set, and we sat at the table on the patio. "I asked Kenzie to marry me earlier today," I told Mom. Kenzie showed her the ring, the smile on her face beaming pure happiness.

"Oh, honey, that's beautiful," Mom said.

"I wasn't sure if she would say yes or not. I was so happy when she told me she was pregnant." Mom looked confused. "You're going to be a Grandma again," I told her quietly.

Mom's eyes shifted to Kenzie. "You're pregnant?" She asked with a big smile.

"I took the test this morning. I didn't even have the chance to tell Andy I suspected it. I love him so much Sheri, and he is such a good father."

Mom embraced Kenzie in a long hug. "That he is."

"We're not telling Trina about the baby yet," I said. Mom chuckled understanding why. "And we bought a house today. That's kind of what brought it on today, but you know I was planning to propose soon."

Mom appeared stunned for a moment. "A house? Where?"

I chuckled. "In that great neighborhood behind the gym. It's less than two blocks away. It all just kind of fell into place."

"It's a great house, wait till you see it," Kenzie excitedly told my mom.

"I am so happy for you both," Mom said sincerely. She turned to Kenzie. "What about your family, honey? Have you told them?"

"Next weekend. Andy, Trina and I are flying down to tell them. They don't even know Andy and Trina exist, well they didn't before I called today. They still don't know anything that's been going on with me, the attack, nothing. I didn't want to worry them."

"Oh, Mackenzie," Mom said taking Kenzie's hand. "I can see how this is tearing you up. I know you are close with your parents. Why didn't you tell them any of this yet?"

"I just couldn't from here, Sheri. Dad would have gone ballistic, still may when he finds out."

"What, that you're pregnant?" Mom asked. Kenzie nodded. "Honey, just give him time. No parent cannot be affected when they learn they're going to be a grandparent." She flashed a smile at me. She was happy for us and thrilled that she was going to be a grandma again. I also saw a little sadness there. I'm sure she was thinking about my dad, wishing he was here to share this with us.

"And he's going to be pissed I didn't call him when it was happening, but I didn't think it would end like it did, and I had Andy, so I didn't need him here and I didn't want to worry him."

"Just give him time, Mackenzie. Now tell me your wedding plans," she said glancing between the two of us.

Kenzie smiled wide. She gave Mom the date we picked. Mom immediately insisted we have it here in her back yard as I assumed she would. We accepted her offer. We spent the next half hour discussing details. We were all on the same page. It would be simple, small, and fun for our guests. Fuss would be kept to a minimum.

I was pleased it was what Kenzie wanted though I shouldn't be surprised. I couldn't imagine Kenzie wanting some over-done, over the top affair.

Mom offered to keep Trina overnight, but I declined. "I want Trina to have this first night with her new Mommy and know that she is now a permanent part of our lives."

"We're going to stop by my place when we leave, and I'll get a few things I need. I'll move in slowly, but I'm moving in tonight," Kenzie told my mom with a big smile.

"No, babe, not slowly," I said. "I'm bringing a few guys from the gym with me over there Saturday and we're moving everything you need. I'm not giving you any chance to change your mind."

Kenzie laughed. She thought I was joking. I wasn't. There was no way I would let her out of my arms now!

Kenzie

I sat with my back to the brick wall. I played my new affirmation phrases over a few times in my head and focused on my breathing. I wouldn't say I felt comfortable exposed and alone this way, but I was functioning. It was a step, a big step. I acknowledged pride in myself for exposing myself this way. I knew that Andy was one phone call and five minutes away, but I was determined to not need him.

I enjoyed the warmth of the sun beating down on me, on my face and bare arms. The light breeze kept everything cool. The sounds of traffic and people living their lives reinforced I was ready for this, as the surrounding bustle was uplifting, not alarming. It was going to be a beautiful day, and I told myself I was thankful to be sitting here enjoying it. I was the only customer sitting outside the little bistro on its patio. The server, Dave, brought my coffee and the decadent chocolate scone I'd ordered. As he backed away, Madeline came into view behind him. I came to my feet and embraced her. She knew nothing about what had happened. I hadn't talked with her since the night Andy and I went to dinner at her restaurant, a million years ago.

"I was so glad to get your text!" Madeline exclaimed. "We need to do this more often."

She sat next to me and the server came back close to take her order. Her eyes went wide at the sight of him and a flirty smile curved her lips. Until I saw Madeline's reaction I hadn't even noticed his appearance. He had dark hair in a man-bun, a dark shadow across his face and over his lip. He was sexy in a rugged way that I knew Madeline would like. He turned away after he had taken her order, but I could see him stealing glances towards her.

"I've missed you," I said with a big smile. I was so excited to tell her about Andy, the pregnancy, and the wedding. I had not decided yet how much I would tell her about the attack. Doc Tony had assured me I would know at the time what I wanted to share, and it would come naturally. She would be the first person outside the narrow world I'd lived in since it happened that I told. She'd be a warm up for the conversation with my parents.

"Tell me about what you've been doing since I saw you. And are you still with that gorgeous man?" Madeline had a lusty grin curving her lips.

I giggled, and I think I probably blushed. My left hand sat on my lap under the table, out of her view. "Andy, and yes I am."

"Things are going well with him?" She asked.

I set my hand to the table between us and led her eyes with mine to it. "He proposed earlier this week," I said with a huge smile.

Madeline grabbed my hand and examined the ring carefully, squealing with delight. "I'd say things are going very well!"

"What he didn't know was that I took a pregnancy test that morning. I hadn't had the chance to even tell him I suspected it," I confessed.

"Pregnant?" Maddie demanded. "You're pregnant?"

I nodded nervously. She would be the first person other than Andy I told. I hadn't even told Margot yet. Madeline came to her feet and hugged me again. As we both retook our seats, the server came with Madeline's coffee and muffin. Madeline immediately ordered a glass of champagne for each of us, insisting it was necessary.

"We're going to have a small wedding in Andy's mom's backyard in about a month. We'd like you to cater it, and I would be honored if you would be one of my bridesmaids."

"Oh, Kenzie, of course! I could close the restaurant that day and you could have it there if you want."

"That is such a kind offer, but Andy's mom wants to do this for us. I wouldn't have the heart to tell her no."

"Well the offer stands if you change your mind," she said with a smile. "So, what kind of menu do you want?"

I laughed. This was the Madeline I knew and loved. "Whatever you want to make, just appetizers and finger food if you want, flatbreads or a full meal served buffet or plated. Your choice. I trust you. Just work it up and get me the bill. We'll pay you in full before the day of. We're expecting between fifty and seventy-five people if that helps make your decision on the menu."

"Okay, give me about a week to come up with the concept," she said. Then she raised her champagne glass into the air that the server had just sat in front of us. "To you, your new life with your hunky man, and your baby. I wish you all the happiness in the world, Makenzie."

I took a drink and felt the tears flooding my eyes. "Thank you," I squeaked out after I had sipped the champagne. I hid how emotional I felt. I wasn't ready to tell her about the attack yet. "What about you? What have you been up to? And will you have a plus one for the wedding? You still seeing that Mike guy?"

Madeline laughed, and her face contorted into an exaggerated distasteful smirk. "No, Missionary Mike, will not be a guest."

"Oh, I'm sorry," I said.

"Me too. There was potential there, but the man just couldn't step out of his box. How is Andy in that department?" She asked, waggling her eyebrows. "With that body, I sure hope he doesn't disappoint."

I laughed, and I'm sure I turned fifty shades of red. "I have no complaints."

"Does he have any friends?" Madeline laughed freely. "Hunky friends, that will give me no complaints either? Seriously, if I never have missionary sex again, it will be too soon!"

I laughed harder. Being with her made me forget all about the attack and my own fears. It was like we were sixteen again and talking about boys and sex at the beach. I remember how we would sneak her sister's Cosmo magazines and read them with wide eyes, shocked by a lot of it, wondering if people really did those things. I remember we were each the other's confidants after our first times, second times, and third times during endless weekend sleepovers. Later, we were each other's alibis when we snuck away to be alone with our boyfriends, so our parents wouldn't suspect. Mackenzie and Madeline were always together, joined at the hip, as my father used to say. Seldom did anyone ever check to ensure we were where we'd said we were.

"So, you're not seeing anyone then?" I asked.

"Only in my wildest dreams, and believe me, I have those!" Madeline laughed. "I'm hooked on this book series that is a-maz-ing! If only I could find a man like the lead characters in this series." She made a motion fanning herself and her lips curved into a lusty grin. "There's no missionary sex happening in these books, I'll tell you that!"

I couldn't help but laugh. We chatted about light topics laughing and reminiscing. We talked more about the wedding and other details. I told her of our trip to Florida to visit my parents and tell them about the wedding and the baby. She cringed, knowing my dad.

"I haven't even told Margot or my sister about the baby or the wedding yet," I told her.

"I am honored that I was the first to hear," she said, popping the last bite of her muffin into her mouth.

That was one of the things I loved about Madeline. She was a curvy girl, always had been, but was not self-conscious about it. I had other friends who were stick figures and would never eagerly devour a huge muffin like Madeline would.

"Maddie, there's something else," I suddenly felt anxious. I was going to tell her. "Margot knows this, but no one else does."

She grabbed my hands across the table. "Kenzie, what is it?"

"Wow, I don't even know where to start." I figured it out a few moments later, and it all spilled out. The roofiing, the break-in, the Peeping Tom neighbor, being run off the road, Marcus, the shooting, all of it. Madeline sat there stunned, her hand clutched to her chest. I breathed out the heaviness in my chest when I was done.

"My God, sweetie, I don't even know what to say. I'm sorry. That had to be so frightening."

"I've been seeing a trauma counselor. Andy called him."

"Does the counselor think it's advisable to marry Andy so soon after all this happened?" Madeline asked, much to my surprise.

"He's a friend of Andy's," I said with a little laugh. "And he understands Andy is my rock. I wouldn't have gotten through any of this without him."

"Why rush into it? I think even your dad would be okay with waiting to be sure. What's wrong with just living together for a little while?"

"That's not the example we want to set for his daughter."

"He has a daughter?"

I smiled automatically and brought up a picture of Andy, Trina, and me on my phone. I handed it to Madeline with a big smile on my face. "Her name is Trina. She's four years old."

"She's adorable. My God, Kenzie, she could be your child. She looks like a mix of you both."

I laughed. "Yeah, she does. She's so excited she has a mom now, and I am thrilled to be her mom. Andy is such a great dad. She's the best kid!"

"What happened to her real mom?"

"She's no longer in their lives, gave up all rights after Trina was born."

"How could any mom do that?"

"I don't know. I love that little girl and have only known her a short time. Andy and I have already talked about me adopting her at some point."

Madeline was surprised. "Your life is going to change so much, Kenz. You ready for this?"

I know I was smiling wide. "I am. I can't tell you how right it feels to be at Andy's with them. We walk her to school together, fix dinner and eat as a family. I love tucking her in bed and reading her stories. And then Andy and I either settle in and watch a movie or we go to bed and snuggle. I love this life we have. It just feels so right, you know?"

"That's awesome!" Madeline said. "I'm happy for you Kenzie. I know it started out with bad stuff, oh there's a saying I can't remember, something about going through the bad to be rewarded with the good or something. I'll find it and text you it later."

I chuckled at her. I knew our time together was coming to an end. I'd made it through though, got myself here, sat alone out in the open on the outside patio, had a great visit with a girlfriend, and told her about it all. I felt empowered and strong. And now I was going to go home to Andy, to his place where I now lived, and make some more wedding plans. I was having Margot over for lunch if she didn't catch a case that would interfere, and I would tell her about the pregnancy too. I would also ask her to be my Maid of Honor. I knew I had turned a corner in recovering from it, from the attack.

Madeline and I hugged each other goodbye as the server came back to our table to clear it. Madeline began flirting, and he was clearly flirting with her. I left, sneaking a few glances back. I was pretty sure I saw them both tapping on their phones, adding each other's numbers no doubt.

***

Margot came up the back stairs as she was now accustomed to doing. I saw her through the open screen door and waved her in. "Hey woman," I said hugging her. "I'm so glad you could make it for lunch."

"Yeah, me too. Things are quiet for once."

I placed the plates on the table and got us each a bottle of water. I had made one of her favorite salads for us, a strawberry chicken salad over mixed greens with a light vinaigrette that Madeline had given me the recipe for years ago. I kept my left hand on my lap again.

"So, I have a date you need to put in for vacation," I told her.

"You do?" She asked as she forked another bite into her mouth.

I reached out with my left hand and took hers as I told her the date, one month out. "Please do me the honor of being my Maid of Honor."

Her face showed how shocked she was. "Married? You and Stevens are getting married in a month?"

I nodded with a smile. I'm sure it made me look like a crazy woman. "I'm pregnant, Margot, so you are going to need another vacation day after he or she is born for the Christening. The God Mother has to be there."

"Oh, Kenzie," she said and then tears fell out of her eyes. I'd only seen Margot cry once before. She tried to always be tough.

I knew she was finally okay with Andy. Her tone had quickly changed after the shooting. She had even been nice to Logan. "Logan will be best man. It'll be just a small ceremony in Andy's mom's back yard. I'll have Maddie and my sister be bride's maids and of course Trina will be our flower girl."

"You're sure about this? Just because you're pregnant you don't have to get married."

I laughed. "I love him, Margot. More than I ever thought it was possible to love a man." I got up and led her out the back door. I pointed to the house. "We're buying that brick house, the one with the green flag. Wait till you see the inside of it!" I was happy to tell her.

We went back in and finished eating. Margot was amazingly supportive. Whatever I needed help with, she pledged her assistance. When Andy came in towards the end of our lunch, she hugged him and congratulated him. I was so happy they had come to a peace. I couldn't imagine how this would work if they were still at each other's throats. Margot was my best friend. I wanted her to remain in our lives.

Later, after she left, I called my sister. This wasn't optimal, having this conversation over the phone, but I couldn't fly out to Oceanside too. I swore her to secrecy then told her all of it, in reverse order, starting with the proposal and the pregnancy, and going back in chronological order from there, hitting only the important points. I surely did not tell her all of what occurred, just the gist of the threat and the high points of my relationship with Andy, including how it began.

She promised not to tell Mom or Dad, promised she would be at and in my wedding. But she made me promise to text her pictures of Andy and Trina as soon as we got off the phone. I did, and she immediately texted back shocked at how cute Andy was. She too said that Trina looked like she could be my daughter. I loved it when people said that because I knew Trina didn't want to tell anyone I was not her real mom. Andy had hugged her and told her I was better than that because I was choosing to be her mom because I loved them both so much. We agreed that no one had to know if she grew in my tummy or not. That was our business. That satisfied her, that and calling me her Kenzie-Mommy. It was so cute! I smiled every time she said it.

I felt so proud of myself for telling three people about it today. Doc Tony had been right. It would come naturally to confide in those I was close with. I wasn't reliving it by telling anyone. I had been through it and survived and what I relayed were just words. The fear and emotions had been dealt with and put in their proper places. I knew I was stronger and had learned the proper coping skills. I was due to see him that afternoon, just to touch bases on how it had gone today. I planned to drive myself there again alone. It felt good to be in charge of my life again and not feel ruled by fear.

CHAPTER 19

Kenzie

After landing, getting our luggage, and rental car, we stopped by the store to pick up some groceries that I knew my parents wouldn't have but were staples in our lives. Our lives, Andy, Trina and me. We had a routine, a normal, a life. We were a family. I loved what we had. But I was nervous to tell my parents about it, about everything.

We pulled into the driveway and saw my dad in the garage through the large open doorway. He was at his workbench. He called into the house no doubt to tell my mom we had arrived. Andy squeezed my hand knowing how anxious I was. I got out of the car as my dad approached and my mom hurried out of the house.

"Hi Dad," I greeted giving him a big hug. "Dad, this is Andy Stevens. Andy, this is my Dad, Gunnery Sergeant Mike Collins, and my mom, Maggie."

Dad and Andy shook hands. I could see that my dad was sizing him up. "Nice to meet you, Andy."

"Gunny, Kenzie has told me a lot about you. It's nice to meet you."

Mom embraced me. Then she greeted and hugged Andy. Trina had fallen asleep in the car. Andy pulled her out of her booster seat. She stayed asleep. I went to get the grocery bags. "I'll come back out for them, babe," he said.

"I've got them. I'll leave the suitcases for you, though," I teased him.

We all went into the house. I directed Andy to lay Trina on the couch in the family room, which the kitchen opened into. She came awake as he laid her down on it. Mom was watching them carefully. She was sizing Andy up as a father, no doubt. I set the grocery bags on the counter and then went to the couch.

"We're here, sweetie," I said to Trina as I sat beside her. She hugged me, acting uncharacteristically shy.

"I'll help you bring in the bags," Dad said to Andy. They stepped out together.

My mom sat near us on the couch. "Trina, this is my mommy."

"Hello Trina," Mom said with a big smile focused on Trina. "It is nice to meet you."

Trina clung to my neck. "It's nice to meet you, Kenzie's mommy."

I was so proud of her. She was tired but still remembered her manors. Andy had done so well raising her. I was glad he was the father of my baby too.

Mom beamed a smile at me. "She's so sweet," Mom said quietly.

I nodded and smiled as Dad and Andy came through the door. They took all the bags into the back hall to the two guest rooms. This would be interesting. Would Dad get into which bags belonged to whom and would go into which room?

"We sat all the bags in the blue room," Dad said. "You can figure out where they should go later."

"Thanks, Dad," I said. "Trina, this is my Daddy. Dad, this is Trina, Andy's daughter."

"Hello, Trina," Dad said. He took her little hand in his and shook it.

"Hello Kenzie's daddy," her little voice said.

Mom had gone back into the kitchen. She was unpacking our grocery bags. I joined her, amused by the look on her face as she examined the items we had bought. "I could have picked this up for you sweetie," she said, holding up a bunch of kale.

"It's okay, Mom. It was no trouble for us to swing by the grocery store on our way here. And we couldn't expect you to buy for three more people. It's all good," I said.

"I did pick up a few special things, for his daughter. I hope it's okay." She held up a package of fresh baked cookies.

"That was very nice of you," Andy said when he saw what she held. "Of course, it's okay." He lifted Trina from the couch.

"I hope you brought bathing suits," Mom said. "The pool is the perfect temperature."

"Yes, we did," I said. "We thought we would just hang out here today, swim, and visit with you."

Andy

We got Trina settled at the shallow end of the pool and made sure she knew she could only go as far as the rope. It was one of those zero depth pools that mimicked wading in at the beach. Kenzie asked that her parents sit with their backs to Trina so that she and I could watch her from our seats while we talked. I wanted their backs to Trina because I didn't want her to see any angry faces and I was sure Gunny would become angry.

"So, we're having an adult conversation, are we?" Kenzie's dad said as I sat. He had his Gunnery Sargent face on. I didn't know the guy, but even I could see the stern look that settled over his face when Kenzie had said we wanted to talk without Trina near.

Maggie Collins patted his arm. "Mike, don't be like this." There was a warning in her voice.

I took Kenzie's hand. I looked her dad right in the eye. "I love your daughter and I asked her to marry me last week."

"Oh, my," Maggie exclaimed. She beamed a wide, surprised smile at Kenzie. Her dad was silent.

"I expected a reply of yes or no, or maybe it's too soon to talk about that," I told her parents. Then I smiled at Kenzie. "The answer I got was I'm pregnant and I quit my job today."

Maggie Collins sucked in a breath, her face taking on a horrified expression. Gunnery Sargent Michael Collins' face turned red and his hands fisted on the table's surface.

"Surprise, you're going to be grandparents again," Kenzie said only half-jokingly after a few quiet seconds.

"Kenzie, this is just such a surprise," her mom said.

"Yeah, tell me about it," Kenzie said. "So, we're getting married in a month and I need you to be there." Her eyes shifted to her dad. "I want you to give me away, Dad."

"Seems to me you already gave it away," he said harshly.

"Michael Collins, don't you be like this!" Her mom paused, and her expression took on a softer expression as her eyes shifted to Kenzie. "A baby? You ready for this, sweetie?"

Kenzie laughed nervously. "Doesn't matter if I am or not."

"We've got this," I said confidently.

"He's been solely responsible for Trina since she was born. *He's* got this," Kenzie said, a smile gracing her beautiful face.

"My mom and dad helped a lot early on, well, my mom still does," I said.

"What about Trina's mother?" Maggie asked.

"It's a very long story. I will tell you later because there are more important things Kenz and I need to tell you now, but Trina's biologic mother was out of our lives since the day she was born," I said very quietly. Maggie got that pitying look on her face. Gunny just looked angrier.

"Dad, Mom," Kenzie said with a tight voice. "I didn't want to worry you, so I didn't tell you anything over the phone, but something happened I need to tell you now. You have to hear us out." Her eyes pinned her dad in place. "No leaving this table until we're done."

"You've known each other two months and you're pregnant. What more do you have to say? I'm disappointed Kenz. I thought you were smarter than this," her father blurted out.

"Michael!" Her mother admonished. "I'm sorry Kenzie, Andy, continue. We'll both stay at this table till we're through." She gripped the Gunnery Sergeant's bicep, holding him in place.

"Thanks, Mom." Kenzie reached across the table and squeezed her mother's hand.

I knew Kenzie was nervous about this part, even more nervous than the news of her pregnancy. "So, I met Kenzie in a bar one night. She was leaving as I got there. It was only around eight o'clock," I said. "We had a couple of beers and talked, and I couldn't believe how open and honest she was. She was unlike any woman I've ever known. Not only is she beautiful, but she is one of the nicest people I've ever met. If you believe that two people can fall in love that fast that's exactly what it was for me. I normally wouldn't bring a woman home I met like that, but Trina was at my mom's overnight, so I did." Gunny's fists were turning red he was squeezing them so tightly.

"It was that Friday night everyone from work went out after we found out five were losing their jobs," Kenzie said. Her mother nodded, forcing a sympathetic expression. "The thing is, I didn't drink that much. As everyone was leaving, after I said goodnight to all my coworkers, I went to the bathroom. As I left the bathroom, I suddenly felt really drunk, way too drunk. And that was all I remembered when I woke up in Andy's bed the next morning."

Kenzie breathed out extremely hard. I squeezed her hand. I don't think her mom was breathing, the shocked expression was frozen on her face. Her dad's eyes stared through me. If he could get away with killing me, I'm sure he would. His jaw was twitching, and I think I saw a vein popping out of his temple.

"I called Margot on my way home that morning and she met me at my place. She had a lab-tech friend of hers come to my house to take blood, which later came back positive for a specific street drug. I suspected I had been roofied and Margot was pretty sure of it before the blood test, but I never thought Andy did it."

"Oh, my God!" Her mom gasped. Her dad took her hand into his.

"You took her home drugged," her father growled. He was trying to figure out where he would hide my body, I was sure.

"It wasn't a traditional date-rape drug," Kenzie defended me. "I functioned just fine. Andy had no way of knowing. Margot said it makes people lose their inhibitions and do things they normally wouldn't, but nothing they absolutely didn't want to. For instance, no one could be talked into committing murder. In higher doses, it causes memory loss, so he gave me way too much because that night is a blank slate."

I leaned over and pressed a kiss to the side of her face. "We went out to dinner the next night, that Saturday night, a real date, and when I brought her home, someone had broken into her place, was still in her kitchen. He went out the back door and I didn't go after him because I didn't know if anyone else was inside, and I didn't want to leave Kenzie alone in there," I added.

"The only thing he touched was my vitamins. Margot took them to be analyzed, and they too had that drug in it," Kenzie continued. Both of her parent's faces had worried expressions.

"Oh, my God, Kenzie. Why didn't you call your father and me?"

"Mom, I didn't want to worry you or make you fly to Lexington. You were leaving on a cruise that week. I didn't want you to have to cancel." She squeezed her mother's hand again. Her dad still sat stone-faced, but at least his fists were no longer clenched. "Andy had a friend install a security system at my house the next day."

"First smart thing I'm hearing," her dad hissed. He was staring daggers through me. "You should have called me Kenz."

"There were a few other incidents over the course of a few weeks. Kenzie was followed one night but was smart enough to go straight to a police station. Her security alarm went off a couple of times, but no one breached her house," I told them, ignoring her father's statement.

"Kenzie, you should have told us," her mother said. "You shouldn't have had to go through all that alone."

"I wasn't alone. Andy was with me through all of it," Kenzie said beaming a smile at me that melted my heart. "He kept me safe."

"Until three weeks ago," I said. Kenzie squeezed her eyes tightly shut. "Breathe babe," I said quietly. She nodded. "The security cameras my friend installed at her house, I had him put a feed to my phone, so I could see for myself she was safe. After Kenzie had gone to bed, I saw a figure go into her bedroom from the hallway camera. I called the police, then Margot, and had a friend stay with Trina. I broke every speed record to get over there."

"Margot got there first. She had the code, and she unlocked the front door, so she could come in quietly. He had a gun, and he threatened me with it, wouldn't drop it when Margot told him to, and Margot had to shoot him," Kenzie said. Her voice was strong and confident. I was so proud of her.

"Oh, my God!" Her mother exclaimed. She rose and rushed around the table to embrace her daughter. "Oh, Mackenzie!"

"I'm fine Mom. Andy was there with me through all of it."

My eyes went to Gunny. He was seething. "So, who was this asshole? And is he pleading guilty or are you going to have to go through a trial?"

"It was a guy from work, Marcus Holland," Kenzie answered.

"Marcus? You brought him to dinner when you were in Orlando one time," Maggie said, shocked.

Kenzie nodded.

"No trial. Margot's a good shot." I motioned to my forehead, my fingers forming a gun.

"Thank God for that," Gunny said.

"What dead? Margot killed him?" Maggie asked.

"Yeah, right on Kenzie's bed. She stayed at my apartment for a while after, while Margot and I cleaned her place up." Kenzie didn't want them to know about the PTSD she suffered from after, so I didn't mention that part.

"I guess during that month I didn't take all of my birth control pills as I should have. I know I doubled up on them more than a few days."

"Oh, honey, of course. It's not your fault." Maggie Collins' eyes stared a stern warning at her husband.

"I love Kenzie and I want to marry her. I asked her before I knew she was pregnant."

"You've already made one mistake, don't make another," Gunny said. "Don't rush into marriage. It's not something anyone should enter into lightly."

"I'm trying to do the right thing, Sir," I said to him.

"Had you wanted to do the right thing, you never would have taken my daughter to your bed the first night you met her."

"Dad!" Kenzie scolded him.

I waved her off. "Sir, with all due respect," I began, but Gunny cut me off mid-sentence.

He raised a shaking finger to me. "Let me stop you right there, son. If you had respect, respect for my daughter, respect for yourself, my daughter wouldn't be pregnant." His voice was firm, a quiet, menacing growl. "Actions have consequences."

I pointed to Trina. "You don't think I'm aware of that? Let me tell you, Sir, I don't normally do that, pick up women in bars or anywhere else." My voice was a whisper. I was trying to keep my anger in check. The last thing I wanted was for Trina to see or hear any of this. "I have only had a couple of relationships since Trina was born and had been in a self-imposed celibacy for a really long time until that night I met Kenzie."

"Stop, both of you," Kenzie whispered. "Everyone sit back down and chill." She reached into her pocket and pulled the engagement ring out and slid it back on her finger. Gunny's eyes were angry slits that gazed at the ring.

"It's beautiful," her mom said. Kenzie reached her hand across the table, so her mom could get a good look at the ring.

The smile on Kenzie's face was stunning. Her happiness assured me we were doing the right thing. "I love Andy, and we are getting married."

"I am asking for your blessing, Sir, but I believe I should be married to the mother of my child before he or she is born."

"The fact is Dad after I went back to my own place after staying with Andy and Trina, after it happened, I missed being with them. I don't want to go to sleep without Andy holding me ever again."

I could see anger flare in the Gunnery Sergeant's eyes at her declaration of sleeping together. "I love your daughter, and where I come from, you marry the woman you love. Living together for any period of time is not acceptable. And I don't believe that's the right example to set for Trina."

Her dad remained silent.

"Is Margot okay?" Her mother asked. "Killing another human being couldn't have been easy for her."

Gunny's eyes were on mine. I could see his thoughts regarding his wife's statement. He'd been in combat, had killed. His face was stone, much the same I'm sure mine was. One Vet who saw action could always identify another. It was a brotherhood none of us wanted, a place that changed a man.

"The force has great counselors for when that happens," Kenzie answered.

"And she knew she had no choice. That scumbag wasn't going to let it end any other way," I added. I nodded to Kenzie. "Why don't you and your mom go play with Trina."

She nodded and prodded her confused mom to her feet. I waited to speak until they were at the edge of the pool with Trina. Gunny figured some conversation was coming that was not suitable for his wife. I think I saw the first hint of his anger calming.

"Kenzie doesn't want to know yet how unhinged that son-of-a-bitch was," I said quietly. "But Margot let me see just how fixated that bastard was on Kenzie. His bedroom was a freaking deranged-stalker haven, pictures of Kenzie all over it. He'd been stalking her for quite a while by the looks of it. He had a diary where he ranted on about how much he loved her and how he would take her away to be with him if she didn't realize her love for him right away. He had notes about everyday interactions that he interpreted as her love for him. He even mentioned being invited here for dinner while they were at an on-site in Orlando. He believed you would welcome him as your son-in-law," I told Gunny. He was seething. "He had restraints on his bed, intending to keep Kenzie there," I growled. I think my clenched jaw matched her father's.

"Why did he act when he did?" His voice was strained.

"It looks like he planned it for that night, not sure if he or Kenzie would be among those losing their jobs, unable to fathom not seeing her at work every day. He had it set to go, so he decided to go ahead with his plan, even though neither of them lost their jobs. He was waiting in the parking lot for her and watched her leave with me hours later. If I hadn't taken her home, that bastard would have gotten her," I finished with a shudder. "God was looking out for her, Gunny. I love her, and I promise you, I will never hurt her, ever. I'm a father, I understand. You aren't happy about this, I get that. But I love her, and I will never let anything happen to her. You have my word."

Gunny silently nodded and rose from the table. He went into the kitchen and I heard him opening and closing doors. Then I heard the door to the garage close. He didn't return. Kenzie had said he had a habit of stepping away when he needed to rein in his anger and think before he spoke or acted. I assumed that's what this was.

CHAPTER 20

Kenzie

"Kenzie's mommy," Trina said to Mom. "I like your pool."

Mom smiled wide. "You can call me grandma if you'd like, sweetie," Mom said.

"Now I have two grandmas," Trina said with a wide smile. "Do you think I can call Kenzie's daddy grandpa? I had a grandpa, but he died so I don't have one anymore."

"Now you do, sweetie," Mom said. "Yes, I think it would be just fine. The other kids call him Grandpa Gunny. I'm sure he would like it if you called him that too."

I smiled. I knew Mom would treat Trina just as she did Katie's kids right away. I knew Dad would come around too after the shock wore off. I glanced back and saw his empty chair. Andy sat alone at the table, his eyes on us. I was sure Dad just needed to cool off and think things through. He was probably out in the garage tinkering with something mechanical, maybe cleaning a gun.

Andy glanced back into the house and then at me. He rose from his seat. "Leave him, Andy. He needs a few minutes."

Andy nodded and joined us at the edge of the pool. He took his shirt off and went into the water, pulling Trina in deeper with him, his arms keeping her safe. Mom's eyes went wide at the sight of his muscled body. Then they met mine. I smiled. Yeah, he had a great body! I was proud to be with him. I couldn't wait to see Katie's reaction when she saw him in person.

Once Andy had moved far enough away, Mom scooted a little closer and locked her eyes on mine. She took hold of my hand. "Are you really okay, sweetie?"

"I am," I told her honestly. "I really do love him, Mom, and would want to marry him even if I wasn't pregnant."

"He seems like a good man. Your dad will come around," she said. "You're going to be taking on a whole lot of responsibility really quick. You ready for this?"

I squeezed her hand. Trina giggled playing with her dad. They splashed around, the water forming crystal droplets that sparkled against the sunny, blue sky. "Trina's great and deserves a great mom. I'm going to do everything I can to be that mom for her. I'll grow into the role before this baby comes and Andy will be there with me. He's an amazing dad. I couldn't pick a better guy to have a baby with."

Mom hugged me. "You'll be a wonderful mom, sweetie. I know you will. You let me know if you would like me to come and stay with you for a week when the baby comes. I can help with Trina, the cooking, housework, anything you need."

"Thanks, Mom! I'd like that and I'm sure Andy would appreciate it too."

"Will you be living at your house?"

"No, we're buying a house a block from Andy's gym. It's in a great family neighborhood. Wait till you see the kitchen!" I knew I was grinning like a fool. "It's got four bedrooms, so there will be a guest room for you and Dad whenever you come to visit."

We sat silently and watched Andy play with Trina in the water, the sound of their laughter and the splashing water filling the void. She completely trusted him, just as I did. She was such a lucky little girl to have him as her dad. Tears came to my eyes. I felt so blessed that he was the father of my baby too. I circled my feet in the water concentrating on reining in my emotions. Must be the pregnancy hormones causing me to feel so emotional.

"Why'd you quit your job, honey?"

My eyes met Moms. "My boss was kind of shitty about the time I took off after Marcus was shot and the whole situation, really. And he was worried that I'd find a reason to bring a lawsuit against them because we both worked there. I just knew I couldn't stay. And I have been thinking of getting back into Marketing. I did up a campaign for Andy's gym and it reminded me of what I really wanted to do."

"So, will you look for another full-time job in Marketing? Sweetie, you may not have the energy to do that right now and you'll be adjusting to a new life and new responsibilities," she said nodding to Andy and Trina.

"I really don't know what I'm going to do yet. I may just get the wedding together, get settled in the house and be a mom for a little while. Andy could always use help at the gym too, so I'll probably do that. He said we could set me up my own Marketing office inside the building the gym is in, if I wanted, but I'm not sure."

Mom looked concerned. "But what about medical benefits Kenz? Having a baby is expensive."

I chuckled a little. "I negotiated one year of medical benefits, fully paid by ATS when I left. It was in the package they gave those who got let go so I knew they could give it to me. The baby will be covered by Andy's plan. We're covered, Mom. I didn't go off half-cocked and just quit."

"I'm sorry sweetie; I didn't mean to say you did." She saw the tears in my eyes and looked very concerned.

"I'm okay, Mom, just feeling emotional, the pregnancy hormones I guess." I think it was just the after effects of finally telling them everything.

"You've been through a lot in a short period of time, honey. Maybe you need to talk with someone."

"I have been. I wouldn't leave Andy's apartment for a few days after it all happened." I still couldn't bring myself to say the words to my mom of what it was. "Andy brought up one of the gym members, a trauma counselor. He and Andy were the only reasons I was able to go back to my house and function. I plan to continue seeing him for a while, just to be sure I've moved past it."

Mom hugged me again. "I am so proud of you. Anything you need, you let me know."

I hugged her back. I loved my parents so much. It was such a relief to have told them everything. "Thanks, Mom."

"Let's talk about something happy. Tell me about your wedding plans." She had a supportive smile on her face.

I grinned. "It's just going to be small, maybe fifty people in Andy's mom's back yard. His mom is a total sweetie, the best mother-in-law I could ask for. You'll like her when you meet her. Maddie's going to cater it and it will be pretty simple." I giggled. "Kind of has to be putting it all together in a month."

"Why are you rushing it?" There was no judgment in her question.

"We want to be married before we close on the house. And I want to do it before I'm showing too much." My hand found its way to my somewhat flat stomach that wouldn't be that way for much longer.

"We need to go shopping for your dress, while you're here. I want to buy it for you," Mom said.

Just then Dad appeared in the lanai. He had a bouquet of flowers in his hands and a bottle of champagne. I rose as he came over to Mom and me and he hugged me. It felt so good. I started to cry.

"I love you, Mackenzie," Dad said. "And no matter what the circumstance, you're getting married and having a baby. That calls for champagne."

We all went to the table on the lanai as Dad opened and poured the champagne. Dad even made sure Trina joined us. He produced a bottle of carbonated white grape juice. He made a big deal about pouring it into a matching plastic champagne flute for Trina. He handed a glass to each of us.

Dad raised his glass into the air. "Andy, Trina," he said, his eyes sweeping between the two, "welcome to the family." Then his eyes settled on me. "Mackenzie, God was looking out for you by sending Andy to be there when I was not, to protect you. You will be a wonderful mother. I love you and I am very proud of you."

Seeing the tears in his eyes brought tears to mine. I hugged him again.

CHAPTER 21

Andy

I motioned for Gunny to follow me back into the hallway. I cracked open the bedroom door and I couldn't contain the smile that spread across my face as I saw Kenzie holding Trina. It was early. They both still slept. My daughter had a mom now, and the sight was humbling. He gazed in at my two black-haired beauties. I saw a smile come to his lips. I soundlessly closed the door, and we crept back into the kitchen.

"Those are my girls in there, Gunny. I love them and will always protect them with whatever it takes. Nothing and no one will ever hurt my girls."

Gunny's eyes invaded mine. "So, how'd Margot take credit for the kill when we both know you shot that scumbag, son?" I stared him down. That wasn't anything I would admit to. "I know of your unit and I did some checking into you. I still have connections. You're a sharpshooter. Expert with every caliber you can get a ribbon for. Margot was never that good, wouldn't have been able to make that shot. And she wouldn't have the stones to take it with Kenzie that close."

"That was a million years ago, during a different life," I said flatly. "We going to go for that run, or what? The sun will be up soon."

"You're not taking your daughter to Disney today?"

"No, we'll go tomorrow."

"Then we'll go to the range this afternoon." It wasn't an invitation. He left no room for me to decline.

"The girls can go shopping. Maggie wants to buy Mackenzie's wedding dress."

He still had not moved towards the door. He was staring me down. "That's very nice of her. You have no idea how anxious Kenzie was to tell you about everything. An afternoon shopping with her mom is just what the doctor ordered."

"I'm not pleased I wasn't called as it was occurring, and I'm even less pleased my daughter is pregnant this way."

I glanced back towards the hallway to the bedrooms. "I'm a father, I get it."

"But if she had to get knocked-up by anyone this way, I'm glad it was by someone with honor, who I know will always protect her," he said, much to my surprise.

"I will. You can bank on it."

"If she is ever in any danger again, I want to be called." His voice was firm. I nodded. He then nodded towards the door to the garage. "Try to keep up, Army boy. I'll show you what a run is to a Marine," he said. I followed him out.

***

When Gunny and I got back from our run, Kenzie and Trina were awake, much to my surprise. Trina was watching cartoons in the family room off the kitchen and Kenzie sat on the adjacent lanai with her mom, sipping coffee. I kissed Trina's face and greeted her a good morning, then I went to the lanai. I was dripping wet and couldn't wait to get into the shower, but I wanted to give Kenzie a good morning kiss.

"Good morning, Maggie," I said as I came up next to Kenzie. I placed a kiss on her forehead. "Morning, babe." I dropped my voice down low, my lips beside her ear. "I think your father tried to kill me, run me into the ground."

A smile spread over Kenzie's beautiful face. "He thinks he's still twenty-five."

Maggie laughed. "Well, did you keep up?"

"Yes, ma'am."

"Then you're in like Flynn," she said with a smile.

"Maggie," Gunny said coming into the room. "Army-boy and I are going to the range today. Why don't you take Kenzie and Trina shopping for their dresses for the wedding while we're gone?"

Kenzie's surprised gaze went between her dad and me. "There's not going to be an accident at the range, is there Dad?"

Gunny laughed a full belly laugh. "Andy and I have come to an agreement, haven't we son?"

"Yes, Sir," I agreed. "I should have gone into the Marine Corps." Kenzie and her mother laughed. Evidently, there was a deep significance to it that I didn't understand.

Kenzie

The second dress I tried on was perfect. Mom and I both knew right away that it was the one. It was white with a tank style top to it. It was airy, slightly loose fitting, and hung down to just above my knee. Along the bottom few inches were tiny flowers in shades of blue. It wasn't from the wedding department, just a summer dress, which was what I wanted to match the casual wedding we had planned. Andy and his groomsmen would wear blue dress pants with a white button downed shirt, sleeves rolled up, no tie. Margot, Madeline, and Katie were told they could wear any style dress they wanted to in any shade of blue they would like. Margot didn't wear dresses often, but I knew she had a dark blue tank dress that she liked.

In the little girl's department, we found an adorable dress for Trina that had many of the same elements as mine. On hers though, the little flowers dotted the entire dress which made Trina smile. She was thrilled we would match. Mom suggested a ring of flowers with ribbons for her hair the day of the ceremony. Trina's eyes grew wider than her smile at the suggestion. What little girl didn't want to wear a crown?

Then we sat outside a little ice cream shop and relaxed. It was a warm day, well into the eighties, but the humidity wasn't too bad. Trina devoured her ice cream cone, Mom sipped a vanilla shake, and I enjoyed a chocolate and peanut butter sundae. I had been craving peanut butter and chocolate all day. Was it too early in my pregnancy for cravings? We returned to their house, arriving home before the guys. I went into the pool with Trina so she could swim for a few hours before an afternoon rain was due.

Andy

When Gunny and I got to the shooting range, he introduced me to Jerome, the owner who stood behind the counter and said that I was going to be his son-in-law. I smiled proudly. Gunny had accepted me.

"He knocked-up my youngest," Gunny added. "But he's a good guy, even if he went Army instead of Marines, would have made a hell of a Marine, though."

Jerome reached his hand over to me. "That's a hell of a statement on Gunny's part," Jerome said shaking my hand. "Not many men would make great Marines in Gunny's book."

"It's nice to meet you, too," I said, relieved to know that after Gunny's knocked-up statement.

"You do any tours overseas?" He asked.

I could tell right away he was a fellow Vet. Probably Marine Corps. "Yeah, several, spent nine years in the sandbox," I replied.

"I thought so," he said. "I think the sand changes us. I can always tell."

I nodded. It wasn't the sand that changed us. I knew that for sure. We talked a few more minutes while Gunny checked us in. He wouldn't let me pay for my range time or any ammo, which I appreciated. I'd return the favor when he was visiting Lexington. Jerome and I discovered we had been in the same area at the same time on numerous occasions. I didn't know of his unit, but he knew of mine.

"We're going out to the far end, if that's okay with you, Jerome," Gunny said.

Jerome nodded it was. "Yeah, I'm not worried about either of you."

We carried the bags to the far end of the range. It was a nice outdoor range, with large separate firing stalls and range masters patrolling the firing line. The majority of shooters were clustered in the middle section where the range masters were. We walked past them, Gunny greeting them by name, and went to lanes one and two. Gunny opened the two rifle cases.

"Oh, now this is a beauty," I said as I pulled the weapon out. It was in pristine condition, the wood unscratched and still had a nice luster to it. I examined it closely, all nine pounds of it. An M-14. I'd never fired one. Gunny was unpacking the other rifle. He pulled it from its case. "Whoa, a Bullpup?" I asked.

Gunny laughed. "My two favorite toys."

Gunny watched me closely as I fired. He used a spotting scope to see my hits downrange at the 200 yard mark, which were in the kill zone every time. The sights on both rifles were perfectly adjusted. He took great care of his toys. Then we switched to pistols.

"What caliber was my daughter's attacker taken out with?" He asked me as he unzipped three pistol cases.

"A nine," I replied eyeing him. He handed me a pistol and pointed to the target he was running out. "What distance?"

"Fifteen feet."

I checked the weapon out, dropped the magazine and then replaced it, pulled the slide back and aimed it down range at the target now three yards away. I squeezed off six rounds into the figures chest, all bulls-eyes, perfect sights on this gun too, and then I popped off one, striking the figure in the forehead, dead center. My eyes met Gunny's. That was what he needed to see. He'd let it go now, I was sure.

Kenzie

The remainder of the visit with my parents was wonderful. Dad seemed to accept Andy after that first day. I wasn't sure what Andy had said to him after Mom and I went over to the pool with Trina, but that was what had softened my dad. Dad had acted as I expected initially, hard-nosed, worried, and pissed off. They seemed to have really bonded at the range though. Katie's husband Alex had never served. He didn't like guns either, so I wasn't sure what he and Dad had in common besides Katie and the kids. I could already see a tighter bond between my dad and Andy than Dad had with Alex as our short visit came to an end.

We brought Trina to Disney on Saturday and Monday. We had a great time. Sunday, we hung around my parent's house and let Trina swim. We barbequed steaks and stayed up playing cards after Trina was in bed. We made plans for the wedding week. Mom and Dad would drive up to Lexington a few days before the wedding and stay at my old house. Dad wasn't afraid of staying where a man had been killed. Katie, Alex and their kids would stay there as well. The wedding was on a Saturday. Katie and her family would only be in town from Friday through Sunday. She couldn't take off more than the one day from work because she took so many days off for her children. I understood, but I missed her. I hadn't seen her in well over a year and I wished she could stay longer.

I drew back from the hug and smiled at my dad. "Thanks for everything. We'll see you in less than a month." Then I hugged my mom. "I'll miss you," I whispered to her. Our five-day visit had passed so quickly.

"Son," Dad said with a head nod, his right hand extended to Andy.

I saw the smile on Andy's face as he shook hands with my dad. "Gunny."

Happiness warmed me everywhere. My mom hugged Andy and said her goodbyes. She embraced Trina and then my Dad scooped Trina up and gave her a big hug too. He deposited her in her booster seat. I was still smiling as we backed out of their driveway.

"Thank you," I said to Andy. "We needed that, all of us." I appreciated he had suggested this trip and understood the need to tell my parents everything in person.

Andy smiled and nodded.

CHAPTER 22

Andy

It had been a busy few days with relatives coming to town for the wedding, which was in exactly thirty-two hours. Even though Kenzie had been with me every day since I had proposed, the thought of making it official brought me more happiness than I would have imagined.

Her parents had gotten into town yesterday and had stayed the night at the apartment with us. Kenzie and her dad had just left to go to the airport to pick up her sister and her family who were flying in from California. They would all stay at Kenzie's house the next few nights. Gunny and Maggie had driven up in their big Caddie, so they took it to the airport. Maggie stayed at my place with Trina to keep her out of our hair while we set things up here. Trina was about to meet her new cousins. She was thrilled with the idea. Katie's oldest, her son Owen, was eight. Her daughter, Kayla, was five. Kenzie was sure that Kayla and Trina would get along well.

We had just told Trina about the baby, as well, as we were sure it would be talked about at the wedding, and I didn't want Trina blindsided that way. Plus, I'd always given her information the way I wanted it delivered. This was no exception. She was so excited. I knew that she would tell everyone about her new baby brother or sister! Our secret would be out fast.

I was at my mom's house with Logan, Butch, and Brian. We were doing some prep work for the wedding in the backyard, setting up chairs and tables. We'd put the tent up tomorrow morning. I'd go straight from here to pick up my brother, Sam. His flight was due in, in a couple hours. It had come down to the wire if he would be granted leave to be here and I would be lying if I said I wouldn't have been disappointed if he couldn't attend. He was three years into his enlistment, stationed at Ft. Hood, Texas. I was thankful he had never seen combat. I didn't want him to go through what Logan and I had.

My youngest sister, Nikki, and her roommate were driving in from Cincinnati where she had just wrapped up her sophomore year of college. They had just moved off campus and into an apartment. Nikki had a job and had informed Mom during her Christmas break that she wasn't moving home for the summer. I know my mom had taken it pretty hard, the last of her flock to leave the nest. I was happy she had had Trina to focus on. We had been careful to still have my mom actively involved with taking care of Trina. I didn't want her to feel replaced by Kenzie, and Kenzie was sensitive to it as well. It had only been a little over a year since my Dad had died and I knew my mom missed him terribly. She needed to be needed. After our baby came, she surely would be!

I had two other sisters who lived in the area. Melanie, two years younger than me, lived in Louisville and worked long hours teaching and coaching every sport imaginable at the junior high where she had worked since her college graduation. Teresa lived with her boyfriend, Seth, on the other side of Lexington. None of us were sure if we liked him or not. They hadn't spent much time with the family since getting together and they had moved in together a bit too quickly for us all to process.

I chuckled to myself with that thought. Wasn't that the pot calling the kettle black? Kenzie and I had surely moved faster than they had, and I was still not giving them a break when it came to how I thought about them and their fast-progressing relationship. And Teresa wasn't even pregnant like Kenzie was! I seriously needed to adjust my thinking. I'd make peace with Seth tonight. They'd be at Madeline's restaurant for a prewedding party, the equivalent of a rehearsal dinner with no rehearsal.

Madeline insisted she throw this party for us in her restaurant, The Toad and the Hoot Owl. It was for family and wedding party members only. I knew Butch couldn't make it tonight. He was on at the firehouse. His twenty-four-hour shift started at 2:00 this afternoon. The wedding was at 4:00 tomorrow, no problem. Kenzie was hoping Margot could make it tonight, but she doubted it. Margot was off tomorrow for the wedding, but was on today working a case, so I invited Brian and his girlfriend, Tiffany to the dinner tonight. They'd both be at the wedding. Brian had agreed to be a stand-in groomsman for me if my brother hadn't made it, so he was kind of part of the wedding party.

Kenzie

"Maddie, thank you for this. You didn't have to do all this for us," I said giving Madeline a hug. Andy and I had arrived early. He was in the men's room. She had our party set up in the same back corner of the restaurant where Andy and I had dinner that night, our first real date. She remembered that detail. What a great friend!

"I wanted to," she insisted. She waved her hand dismissively. "It's a small party of what, twenty? No big deal."

"And you're catering the wedding tomorrow," I reminded her. That was a big deal.

"My staff and I have all day tomorrow to prepare the food. I'd never thought about catering out of my restaurant too, maybe this will lead me in a whole new direction, and that's thanks to you!" She smiled excitedly. "Besides, you're paying for the wedding. This is my gift to you," she said with a smile. "Just say thank you, because you're not winning this one." She laughed.

"Thank you." She and I had gone around and round about this dinner being on her.

Maddie's eyes left me. I followed her gaze to the doorway. I giggled aloud. Logan stood there, looking around the room. He smiled at Maddie and me before his attention became focused behind him where Andy and my entire family were approaching the room.

"Whoa, who is that stud-muffin?" Madeline whispered her eyes on Logan. "And is he single?"

"That's Andy's best friend Logan, our Best Man," I answered as quietly. "And trust me, you don't want to go there. Logan is a great guy, but when it comes to women, he's a one night only guy, if you know what I mean."

"Play-er? Yeah, he's gotten it written all over him. Even so, with that body, I bet it would be one incredible night," she said with a giggle.

Madeline rushed over to great my parents, Katie and her family, and then Andy introduced her to Logan. He shook her hand, his gaze wandering all over her curvy body and then Madeline pulled him into a hug. She shot me a lusty grin as she embraced him. I had to laugh. I wished Butch would have been able to make it. He was the one I wanted to introduce Madeline to. He was a nice guy and I could see the two of them together. I could always start a fire, I thought with a laugh to myself. That'd get him here. No. Tomorrow, they'd meet tomorrow.

Andy's family arrived soon after, all of them except for his sister Teresa and her boyfriend Seth. I felt like I already knew his siblings as both Andy and his mom had told me so much about them and I'd seen all the family pictures both at Andy's and his mom's house. He introduced each one to me, and they each greeted me warmly, welcoming me to the family.

His youngest sister Nikki was even cuter in person than in the pictures, oh to be twenty-one again! Sam was a younger version of Andy; one look and you knew they were brothers. He didn't have quite the muscle mass that Andy had though. His sister Melanie fit the stereotype of the junior high gym teacher. I was a little surprised. Andy had never mentioned she was gay. Just then his sister Teresa and her boyfriend Seth entered. I recognized her face from the pictures, but not her belly. She was clearly pregnant, something else Andy had never mentioned.

"Holy shit," Melanie exclaimed at the sight of her.

Andy and his mom rushed over to her. The other siblings followed. This was not going to be good, I could tell already from their shocked facial expressions. She lived in Lexington. How long had it been since they had seen her to not know she was pregnant?

"Surprise," Teresa said sarcastically. "And you thought Andy was the only one in our family giving you grandbabies," Teresa said to her mom, Sheri.

I had to hand it to Andy. He quickly diffused the situation. "This explains why you were throwing up at Easter. Congrats, Tere," he said giving her a hug. He offered his hand to Seth. "Congrats, man."

Seth acted surprised and cautiously shook Andy's hand, probably expecting it to be a trap, a friendly greeting followed by a beat down for knocking-up his little sister. "And congrats to you on your wedding tomorrow and your girlfriend's pregnancy too."

Andy's other siblings followed his lead and greeted Teresa and Seth warmly. His mother though pulled Teresa close, and I heard her say, "we will talk about this after tomorrow. I am very disappointed you kept this from me." Then she moved away and returned to the conversation she was in the middle of with my parents when Teresa and Seth had come in.

After the family cluster disbursed Andy summoned me over, just as Sam wandered back over to Teresa. "Real classy, Sis, letting this news out here on Andy and Kenzie's day," Sam said quietly.

"Tomorrow's their day," I heard Teresa reply.

"Hi Tere, it's nice to meet you," I said. "Seth, it's nice to meet you too."

"Welcome to the family, Kenzie," Teresa said. "I'm so glad you're pregnant too, otherwise I'm sure my big brother here," she said motioning to Andy, "would have been all over Seth's ass."

"I'm excited these cousins will be so close in age," I said. "Congratulations. When are you due?"

"Beginning of December," she answered.

"Seth, it's an open bar so order whatever you'd like when the waiter comes back through," Andy said.

"Excuse me?" Teresa demanded, "just for Seth? I can have a glass of wine if I want one," she corrected her brother.

"Yes, I was just about to have my one glass of cabernet. We will definitely all want a beverage as we sit down to eat. My girlfriend Madeline, who owns this restaurant and is throwing this party for us said she has a special toast," I said to diffuse this situation. I had been told that Teresa was the black sheep of the family and I could see how defensive she was, which I was told was pretty much her personality.

She smiled at me, appreciating I had stuck up for her. I smiled at Andy. He knew what I was doing. And then Andy flagged down the waiter. Brian Porter and his girlfriend Tiffany had come in at some point. I saw them in the corner with Logan and Ashley. I had not met her yet. Tiffany was a knock-out! Tall, thin, blond, a complete opposite of Brian in every way, not that Brian was fat, he wasn't, he was muscular and solid. They made a cute couple. They didn't have drinks either. I sent the waiter that way after he had taken our order.

Andy

I had to purposely keep my eyes off Tere and Seth as we all took our seats at the table. I was really ticked with them for not telling my mom about the baby. I wasn't mad at them because she was pregnant, couldn't be, pot-black and all that. It's not like I was the poster child for abstinence, but they should have told Mom. That was really shitty.

"Everyone, thank you for being here for this rehearsal dinner for the wedding with no rehearsal," Madeline said with a smile, lifting her wineglass into the air. She looked around to be sure everyone had a drink. She'd even had the bartender make Kiddie Cocktails for the kids. The three of them sat at the far end of the table together. "Dinner will be out soon, served family style. First though, I get to make a toast. To Kenzie and Andy," she said, raising her glass higher. "Sometimes you find the right person at the wrong time. Sometimes it's the wrong person at the right time. But when you find the right person at the right time in the right situation, it's because you're meant to be together. Fate has grabbed both your hands. Don't let go. I wish you many happy years together!"

I raised my beer glass, clanked it against those around me and drank. Madeline took a seat next to Kenzie. Conversations instantly sprung up around the table. Kenzie's brother-in-law, Alex, sat next to me. I hadn't had a chance to meet the guy yet, so I welcomed the opportunity to talk with him and get to know him.

Alex Monroe was a decent guy, worked as an accountant, loved his family, tolerated Gunny but didn't really have much in common with him. Those were the few things I learned about him before the meal came in a dozen large serving dishes set around the table by the servers. Madeline was treating us to quite a spread.

Mom asked us to all join hands. She wanted to say the grace over the meal. "Dear, God, bless this meal and all who helped to prepare it as well as those of us who gather round to enjoy it. We are blessed with our expanding family to include so many others, Kenzie and her family, Seth, and the two babies that will arrive within the next year. Someone once said that the greatest things in life are unexpected surprises. This has always shown itself to be true to me. And so, I offer this prayer of thanksgiving for the surprises in our lives, those we hold dear, and those we have lost. Amen."

Murmurs of Amen answered Mom's conclusion of the grace. Immediately after, the clank of serving spoons in dishes filled the void, followed by conversations increasing in volume.

Katie sat across from me. "Andy, how would you feel about not staying at your apartment this evening?" She asked.

Huh? I had talked with Kenzie's sister on the phone a few times over the past month, but had just met her. "Why would I do that?" I asked her.

"There's really nothing traditional about this wedding, but, I'd like Kenzie and you not to see each other tomorrow until she walks down the aisle. And I'd like tonight alone with my little sister. I know she'll be more comfortable at your place, than hers. Besides," she nodded to the kids at that end of the table, "Kayla and Trina would like to have a sleep over too. I figured it could be just us girls at your apartment tonight."

Before I could answer, Melanie who sat next to Katie spoke up. "I agree. You should be at Mom's house with her and Sam. He's only in for the weekend. It'll be fun, like old times."

"It seems the decision has been made," I said. Kenzie sat on the other side of me, but she had not been paying attention. She was engaged in conversation with my mom, Madeline, and her parents. "Babe," I said, tapping her arm. She gazed at me with her gorgeous brown eyes. They sparkled. She was happy. "Katie wants to spend the night at the apartment with you, Trina and Kayla. I'm going to stay at my mom's. You okay with that?"

Kenzie's eyes went to her sister. "Katie, I told you I don't believe it's bad luck for the bride and groom to see each other the day of the wedding."

"Come on, do this one thing for me. My family and I did fly all the way out here, and you can't blame me for being selfish wanting tonight alone with you."

Kenzie laughed and caved to her sister's guilt tactics. "You don't mind, do you, Andy? It will be nice to have this time with my sister and the girls."

I pressed a kiss to her temple and whispered in her ear. "No wild bachelorette party."

Kenzie laughed freely. I was still amazed how far she had come since the attack. "Yeah, right, with Kayla and Trina with us."

Kenzie

"I, Mackenzie Collins, take you, Andrew Stevens, to be my husband, and these things I promise you," I repeated after Pastor Tom recited the phrase. Happy tears were in my eyes. My eyes hadn't left Andy since I walked down the short isle on my dad's arm under the tent here in his mom's backyard. His eyes sparkled, the brilliant green holding my attention like I'd never gazed into them before in my life. "I will be faithful to you and honest with you," I repeated, my hands held by his as we faced each other here in front of our families and best friends. "I will respect, trust, help, and care for you," I promised. "I will share my life with you; I will forgive you as we have been forgiven," I said when prompted, admiring the smile on his attractive face. "And I will try with you to better understand ourselves, the world, and God; through the best and worst of what is to come, and as long as we live," I said as I slid the ring onto his finger.

Andy repeated the vows next, each phrase spoken with love and confidence. I hung on each word as though it was a riveting story I had never heard before. "As long as we shall live," he ended the vows, smiled, slid the ring onto my finger and then said, "whew!"

Everyone laughed.

The pastor said a quick prayer, about a union blessed by God and then he pronounced us husband and wife. It happened so fast. "You may kiss your bride, Andy," he said with a smile.

"Don't mind if I do," Andy whispered as his lips neared mine.

"Ladies and Gentlemen, Mr. and Mrs. Andrew Stevens," the pastor said.

Hoots and clapping rose up around us from our fifty guests. For a small group, they sure were loud. We ended our kiss and turned to face our family and close friends. I couldn't recall a moment when I had been happier. Cell phones were snapping pictures, and everyone was all smiles.

Andy

Logan, who of course stood next to me congratulated me first. Ironic as the man didn't believe in marriage. He didn't believe in monogamy, for that matter. My brother, Sam, next to him embraced me in a fierce hug. Brian Porter, beside Sam congratulated me next. I was still disappointed that Butch didn't make it. It must have been a hell of a fire that delayed him. I hoped he would at least make it later for the party portion.

Kenzie had scooped Trina up. I hugged them both. I was glad that I had not seen Kenzie all day. That moment she came out of the house and walked down the aisle, my heart leapt into my throat and my eyes were riveted on my beautiful bride. That moment wouldn't have been the same if I had woken up beside her and spent all day with her.

We were swarmed with family and friends, hugs, congratulations and the sound of popping corks filled my ears. Logan, Madeline, Brian, and Sam were getting the champagne ready for the toasts, which would be followed by the food Madeline had prepared. She and Kenzie had decided on a meal of many appetizer-sized portions, gourmet flatbreads, large spoons, kabobs, and picks with a single serving of meat and seafood specialties. They figured these could be eaten easily.

Kenzie

Everyone had a champagne flute in their hands, waiting, eyes on Logan. Even the children had plastic replicas with carbonated grape juice. Logan donned his cowboy hat. "That's better," he said. "As best man I have the honor of giving Andy and Kenzie the first toast. I promise I'll try not to fuck it up," he began.

"Logan!" We all admonished, some playfully others in disbelief.

"Oh, shit! I mean, shoot, sorry, told myself I wouldn't cuss," he said.

"Good luck," a few said laughing.

Everyone who knew Logan laughed. My parents exchanged surprised glances.

Trina was laughing hysterically. "Uncle Logan cusses a lot," she told Kayla. They had been inseparable since they met the day before. Our sleepover the previous evening was a blast.

"Sorry," he said, his eyes sweeping the crowd. "I've known Andy for a really long time. He's the best friend I've ever had, that anyone could have. He's the best father," he smiled at Trina, "the best son," he said with a nod to my mom, "the best brother," he said his eyes going to each of Andy's siblings, "the best soldier, the best trainer, the best boss, the best all-around guy. Kenzie, I'm sure he will be the best husband too. He's a man who does nothing without purpose, who is trustworthy, and has more common sense than anyone I've ever known. So, when he told me he knew you were it, not even forty-eight hours after he met you I wondered if he had lost his freaking mind!" Everyone laughed. "But as I got to know you, saw Andy with you, and saw how Andy was when you were not there, I came to understand what a soul mate is. Kenzie, Andy never realized he had been lonely until you came into his life and became his friend and his lover," Logan paused hearing the reaction to his proclaiming Kenzie Andy's lover. "Come on folks, seriously? She's pregnant for God's sake!" Logan said. "I could not be happier for the two of you. I've seen the love you have for each other and have watched you become a tight family, all three of you," he said with a smile beaming at Trina. "Congratulations on the marriage, the new home, and on the baby. He or she is coming into one hell of a family, with the best mom, best dad, and best big sister anyone could hope to get!" He raised his glass higher. "To Kenzie and Andy," he said.

"To Kenzie and Andy," everyone repeated raising their glasses high before drinking to the toast.

"I guess I'm next, as Maid of Honor," Margot said. She smiled at me. I knew making public speeches was not her thing. "Not many Maids of Honor get to thoroughly investigate their best friend's significant other," she said with a small laugh. Andy, Logan, and I all laughed too. A few others chuckled. "But I did and let me tell you what I found," she said.

"There are children present, Margot, keep it PG," Logan teased her. Everyone laughed.

Margot laughed too. "I'm reporting on Stevens, not you, Logan," she replied playfully. She waited for the laughter to die down before she continued. "I didn't have to look too deeply to find out that Andrew Stevens was an honest man with honor, who puts everyone else and their needs ahead of his own, who would do anything for anyone he cared about, and he was, is someone who is perfect for my friend Mackenzie, who deserved only the very best. Because you see, Kenzie is the best friend anyone would be blessed with having in their lives. She's the kindest soul that brings light into the world just by being in it. Kenzie is open and honest and doesn't judge anyone. In Kenzie's world, we are all accepted for who we are, we are loved without question, and trusted like family. That was something I forgot when she and Stevens first got together. Like Logan, I thought Kenzie had lost it when she had so much faith and trust in this man she had just met. But as always, her instincts were point-on and that faith she had in Andy was not misplaced. I'm used to Kenzie bringing out the very best in everyone around her. But somehow, with Andy in her life, that Kenzie-light burns brighter, the acceptance is sweeter, and the love stronger. I guess that's what happens when you find your true love, even the perfect person is enhanced. Congrats guys. I wish you many years of happiness together and lots of babies as you sure figured that one out fast!" She raised her glass in the air. "To Kenzie, Andy, Trina, and the baby! Congrats!"

Applause rose up all around. We sipped our champagne and we kissed. The level of happiness I felt was off the charts and the love I had for Andy was stronger than anything I thought possible.

"Folks, I have been asked to bless the meal," Pastor Tom said. "Trina will help me at the end though." Trina came beside him and took his hand. He bowed his head. "Dear Lord, bless this union of Andrew and Mackenzie and shine your love upon them for all of their lives. Bless everyone present as we all have a special role in their new life together. Provide safe passage home to those who travelled to be here with us today, and may you each feel God's love in your lives. Bless this meal we are about to enjoy in celebration of this marriage," he said. He then recited the Lord's Prayer, and we all joined in saying it with him.

Before we got to the Amen, part, Trina piped up. "And God, thank you for bringing Kenzie to my Daddy and me." She paused, her eyes going to Andy. "Can I say it now Daddy?"

Andy nodded. "Yes, you can say it now, sweetie," he replied, a proud smile on his face.

Her eyes smiled as much as her lips did when her gaze returned to mine. "My Daddy said God would bring my Mommy to us and I knew you when I saw you, Kenzie. Amen."

I don't think there was a dry eye under the tent after Trina spoke. I dropped to my knees in front of her and brought her in for a close hug. "That's what you were going to say that day at lunch, when I met your grandma, isn't it sweetie?" I asked Trina when I could speak. I was so choked up.

Trina nodded. "I knew you would be my mommy when I met you, and not just because we both have black hair."

I cried harder, so touched by Trina's words. Out of the mouths of babes! And Andy had known she felt this way back then. I stood and embraced my husband. My husband, Andy was now my husband. "You knew," I whispered in his ear.

His sparkling emerald eyes gazed into mine. "I knew that first night I met you and wasn't surprised Trina felt the same way when she first met you too."

I wished I could remember that night. "How?" I asked.

Andy smiled. "I know you don't remember, but when we first locked eyes in that bar you said to me, wow, you have got to be the most beautiful man I've ever seen. I'd sure like to get to know you and see if you're as great inside as you are out. As we talked, you openly told me you wanted to get married and have children and then later you invited me to be your happy ever after. That was the only reason I took you home with me that night, otherwise, I wouldn't have done that either, just like you I wouldn't have. It didn't hurt that the sex was phenomenal on top of all that. I knew that night you were it." Andy winked, and I knew he was telling me the truth.

Logan was our DJ, and he started the music immediately. We didn't do any traditional first dances, we invited everyone to join in that first dance. Logan and Madeline made sure everyone danced with us. Margot even danced with Logan. And then, everyone just had a good time for the rest of the night, eating Madeline's delicious food and drinking from the self-serve bar. We danced, laughed, and enjoyed everyone's company late into the night under the twinkling lights that were strung all under the tent.

The next morning, Andy and I left for our honeymoon in Aruba. My fairytale ending, no, it was my happily ever after and it was just beginning.

Not the End

Look for the other books in the Stevens Street Gym Series:
Book 2: Scorched at Stevens Street – Madeline & Butch's story
Book 3: Seduced at Stevens Street – Gia & Logan's story
Book 4: Seized at Stevens Street – Ashley & Blake's story
Book 5: Surrender at Stevens Street – Faith & Cosimo's story
All books are stand-alone stories and while the story does continue from one book to the next, they do not need to be read in order.

ACKNOWLEDGEMENTS

I truly say thank you, to you, the reader, for choosing this book. If you enjoyed it, would you please leave a review, so others might find this book to enjoy, as well? I would greatly appreciate it.

Thank you to my sisters, RK Cary and Margaret Kay, who are also writing their own series of Erotic Romance. RK is just finishing up her Destined & Redeemed series and has several other Science Fiction/Fantasy stories in the works, and Margaret is working on a collection of Military Romance stories in the Shepherd Security Series. Both have been wonderful friends with the honesty that only a sister can give. Thank you to Margaret's husband for advising me on any parts of this story requiring knowledge of the military or weapons.

Thank you to my mother who shared with me her love of books. As a child, the wonderful example my mother set for me as an avid reader led my sisters and me to write our stories. She has encouraged me to publish and I thank her for her support.

My friend, photographer, and graphic artist, Harry R., shot all of the covers for this series. Thank you, Harry!

The model for this cover, Craig Kastning is a Personal Trainer, Yoga Instructor, Fitness Model, Coach, Entrepreneur. Connect with him on Instagram@CKFit45, Twitter@Kastning45, or on Facebook: Facebook.com@theCraigKastning Thank you Craig!

ABOUT THE AUTHOR

Hello, I am Charlie Roberts. I live on a 40-acre farm with my husband, horses, and three barn cats. In addition to writing romance I enjoy reading many different genres, quilting, sewing, jewelry making, and just about every other craft imaginable. I am also fitness-minded and work out at least four days a week. I believe as we age, exercise is a component needed to maintain good health. A healthy diet alone can't do it! The release of endorphins breaks my writers block whenever the creativity has slowed to a trickle and of course gives me energy for whatever I'm doing. This series came to be while spending countless hours at the gym and enjoying the well-built men who were around me.

Visit our website: www.sistersromance.com
Email me at: CharlieRoberts@sistersromance.com
I'd love to hear from you.

Made in United States
Orlando, FL
24 June 2022

19112287R00117